False Alarm

Alex Golder-Wood

Dedicated as always to the best person I know, Emma, my little Daisy, and baby Billy Nacho.

© 2025 Alex Golder-Wood. All rights reserved.

No part of this publication may be reproduced, distributed, or transmitted in any form or by any means, including photocopying, recording, or other electronic or mechanical methods, without the prior written permission of the publisher, except in the case of brief quotations embodied in critical reviews and certain other non commercial uses permitted by copyright law.

Disclaimer

This is a work of fiction. Names, characters, businesses, places, events, locales, and incidents are either the products of the author's imagination or used in a fictitious manner. Any resemblance to actual persons, living or dead, or actual events is purely coincidental.

First Edition: June 2025

CHAPTER 1

James

The fire alarm's screech cuts through the quiet of the office like a knife. I freeze mid email, fingers hovering over my keyboard, wondering if it's just another test or false alarm. We've had three this week I hear people moaning, but I've missed them whilst on annual leave. The length of the siren suggests another false alarm rather than test, and soon enough, people start moving. I sigh, grab my coat from the back of my chair, and join the slow shuffle towards the exit.

Stepping into the stairway, the hum of voices and the shuffle of shoes echo against the concrete walls. I gorm about towards the back, hoping to avoid any awkward small talk. Five years since Sarah passed away, and I still haven't figured out how to handle these forced social interactions. Most people know my situation, but I can't be arsed with their pity.

I make my way down the steps, lost in thought. I never imagined being here, living this life, raising Lily alone, but life has a way of taking everything you know and flipping it on its head.

On the third floor landing, an unfamiliar voice brings me out of my head. 'James, right?'

I look up and see her. I think I've seen her around the building, like in the lobby or passing in the corridor. I think she works a few floors above me, and we've exchanged polite smiles a handful of times. She's the kind of person you notice: blonde hair, warm smile, bright, hazel eyes. Someone who seems to have their shit together.

'Yeah,' I reply, trying to sound casual. 'Sorry, what's your name again?' I add, pretending I knew already.

'I'm Melissa,' she says with a half smile. 'Any idea if this is another drill, or should we actually be worried?'

'I'm hoping for a drill,' I say, looking around at the unimpressed faces in the stairs. 'I'd rather not add "fire evacuation" to my to do list today.'

She laughs, and surprisingly, it doesn't irritate me the way most small talk does. 'Yeah, I had a pretty important meeting scheduled, but I guess that's out the window now.'

We walk down a few more flights in silence before the crowd bottlenecks at the exit, forcing us to wait our turn to get outside. I look over at her, wondering if I should say something to keep the conversation going. It's been years since I've been in this sort of situation, and part of me feels out of my depth. Play it cool James. Say something about not being able to use the lift because of the alarm. Or something about the weather, I mean, it's pretty cold. No, wait, think of something funny…

'You work on the fifth floor, right?' she asks, tearing me away from my incredible potential conversation topics.

'Yeah. IT support.' I pause, trying to think of something more interesting to add. Nothing, you loser. 'You?'

'Marketing,' she says. 'It's… well, it's marketing.' She smiles again, and, for some reason, I find myself smiling too.

Once outside, the sea of employees scatters across the car park, and we end up standing together near the curb. The cold hits me, but I ignore it, hoping to look tough in front of Melissa. She folds her arms across her chest, looking up at the building. 'You think they'll let us back in soon?'

'Knowing this place?' I shrug. 'Could be a while. I heard there's been a couple of accidental activations this week, but I've been off because it's the school holidays'.

She blows out a breath, her hair fluttering in the breeze. 'Oh of course! Do you have many children? You look like a dad.'

'No, just the one, a little girl who's 5. I'm her only parent, so I have most of the holidays working from home or on annual leave. It's hard, but I make it work.' I realise what she just said, and add playfully 'Wait, what do you mean I look like a dad?'

She turns to look at me, her smile getting wider. 'You just seem the type. Like I imagine you building a playhouse or giving a kid a piggyback ride.'

I'm enjoying the mild banter between us. I give a small chuckle. OK, time to say something funny... 'Are you enjoying the weather?' *Shit*. 'I like it this time of year' I add on, 'the weather isn't the best but there's Bonfire night, and the run up to Christmas... also Halloween too! Are you a Halloween girl?' *Oh god. What does that even mean*?

'I love Halloween!' she replies to my ramble. 'I used to have a party every year, but since I've been single I haven't bothered'.

She's single. Thank god! Now I don't feel bad for using my incredible charm. 'That's a shame, maybe we should throw a Halloween party together one day?' Smooth. You've still got it.

She laughs at my suggestion and replies 'Sure, maybe one day.'

I can't help but smile. Ok, calm down James. What will interest her?

'I went to a halloween party when I was a teenager and someone did a shit in the closet'

Wow. Just wow. What was that? But, to my surprise, she laughs!

'You're so funny! Where did that come from?' She says, giggling.

'Oh god, sorry! I'm going to be honest, I'm not massively used to interacting with people. Between working full time and having my daughter, I don't really have time to socialise. You think its a muscle that needs to be trained? And if you don't, you lose it?'

'Erm...' she ponders the question like I'm not an idiot. 'I do think there's something to that. Although in your case, I think you're just strange.' She winks as she says this.

'With all due respect, you're the one who laughed at my anecdote about someone shitting in a closet?'

She laughs again. 'Well I can't argue with that, James, but as they say, all the best people are a little strange. I'm glad to be part of the gang.'

'Funny, isn't it? How life gets so busy, you forget to have fun?' I blurt out, almost killing our playful back and forth.

'Yeah, I guess you're right. Sometimes I think we need these forced moments to stop and breathe, you know? Otherwise, we'd just keep running.' She replies.

'Maybe that Halloween party isn't such a crazy idea after all?' I am half joking, monitoring her reaction for signs of positivity.

'Maybe not. Who knows? Could be a night to remember.'

We stand there in the chilly October air, watching the crowd around us, neither of us saying anything for a moment. Normally, I'd feel anxious when conversations hit a lull, but this time it doesn't feel uncomfortable. It feels... easy. Before I can second guess myself, I blurt out, 'Want to grab a coffee sometime?'

Her eyebrows raise slightly, and for a second, I regret saying anything at all. But then she smiles! Actually smiles! 'Yeah. I'd like that.'

We exchange numbers as the crowd starts to move again, the fire alarm finally silencing. I walk back inside with Melissa beside me, feeling lighter than I have in years. I never thought I'd date ever again, and although everyone says that, I have not flirted, or spoken to a girl really, for over 5 years.

I drive home with every scenario conceivable playing out in my head. What if she realises how dull I am? What if she hates my daughter? What if this is all a trap and she's setting me up to murder me? And, the craziest, scariest scenario of all: what if she *likes* me?

That night, after I put Lily to bed, I sit on the sofa, phone in hand, staring at the new contact in my phone. I haven't properly dated since Sarah. I haven't even thought about it. I buried myself in raising Lily, in work, in just getting through each day. There was one person I talked to for a little while, but she ended up being pretty nasty. I don't get them vibes from Melissa, something about her makes me think it might be time to at least try. To let myself live a little, even if it's terrifying.

    As I turn off the lights and head to bed, I feel something I haven't felt in a long time. *Hope*. Maybe this fire alarm was more than just a drill after all.

CHAPTER 2

Rachel

'You're a twat.'

I say it with a smile, but I mean it. James stands in my kitchen, leaning against the counter with that stupid grin on his face, the one I haven't seen in years. The one Sarah used to tease him about. He's just finished telling me about some woman he met during a fire alarm at work, and he looks like a teenager with his first crush.

'Thanks for the support,' he says, rolling his eyes as he reaches for the mug of tea I've just made him. 'You're supposed to be encouraging me.'

'I am encouraging you. I'm encouraging you to recognise when you're being a twat.' I hop up onto the kitchen counter, swinging my legs slightly. My home office setup is visible through the doorway; spreadsheets abandoned mid calculation when James text saying he was coming over.

'What's twattish about meeting someone?' James asks, eyebrows raised in mock offense.

'Nothing. It's the way you're overthinking it. "Do you think she's interested? What should I text her? Is it too soon to ask her out properly?"' I mimic his voice, making it higher and more panicked than it actually is. 'You're forty, not fourteen.'

'Thirty eight,' he corrects automatically.

'Whatever. The point is, she gave you her number. Just text her.'

He sighs, staring into his tea like it might contain the answers to the universe. 'I haven't done this in so long, Rach. What if I mess it up?'

This is the James I know, the overthinker, the worrier, the man who planned each of Lily's birthday parties six months in advance with colour coded spreadsheets. Sarah always balanced him out, pulled him out of his head when he got stuck there. Since she's been gone, that job has somehow fallen to me.

'Then you mess it up,' I say with a shrug. 'The world continues turning.'

'Easy for you to say. You're always dating.'

'Occasionally,' *cheeky twat.* 'Very occasionally.'

My phone buzzes on the counter next to me. I glance at it: a text from Greg. 'Landed in Singapore. All good. Call tomorrow?'

I put the phone face down without replying. Greg's my boyfriend of eight months. He works for an engineering firm and spends more time abroad than in England. It suits me more than I'd like to admit.

'That Greg?' James asks, nodding toward my phone.

'Yeah. Another business trip.'

'Where to this time?'

'Singapore. For two weeks.'

James takes a sip of his tea. 'Don't know how you do it, Rach. The long distance thing.'

I almost laugh. How I do it is by spending most of my free time with James and Lily, filling my life with enough of them that I barely notice Greg's absence. But I can't say that.

'It works for us,' I lie. 'We're both independent.'

What I don't tell him is that my last three proper relationships ended specifically because I just can't seem to find the right person. Maybe my standards are unrealistic. Greg is different only because he's never around enough for the small annoyances to become bothersome.

'I think about Sarah,' he says quietly. 'About what she'd

think.'

A familiar ache blooms in my chest. 'She'd think it's about bloody time.'

'Yeah?'

'Yeah. You know what she told me, right before Lily was born?' I wait until he looks up at me. 'She made me promise that if anything happened to her, I'd make sure you didn't become a hermit.'

His eyes widen slightly. 'She did not.'

'She absolutely did. "James will bury himself in work and fatherhood and forget he's allowed to have a life too." Her exact words.'

James smiles sadly. 'That sounds like her.'

'So,' I say, jumping down from the counter. 'This Melissa woman. Tell me what she's like.'

He brightens immediately. 'She's funny. Confident. Works in marketing. She didn't get weird when I mentioned Lily.'

'The bare minimum, but okay.'

'And she's pretty,' he adds, then looks embarrassed for saying it.

'Is she now?' I keep my tone light, teasing. 'What does that mean, exactly?'

'I don't know. Blonde. Nice smile.'

'Fascinating description. Shakespeare's quaking.'

He rolls his eyes again. 'You know I'm rubbish at this sort of thing.'

'I do know.' I take a sip of my own tea, using the mug to hide whatever my face might be showing. 'So when are you seeing her?'

'Tomorrow. Coffee after work.' He looks nervous just saying it.

'Well, look at you, moving at lightning speed.'

'Is it too soon?' There's genuine concern in his voice.

I put my mug down and look at him properly. 'James. It's coffee, not a proposal. And it's been five years.'

'I know, I know.' He runs a hand through his hair and I

can almost see him thinking. 'I just... I never thought I'd be here again, you know? Dating. Starting over.'

'Life's weird like that,' I say softly.

The sound of small feet pattering down the hallway saves me from saying anything more. Lily appears in the doorway, rubbing her eyes sleepily. She'd been napping in my spare room; the one I've gradually filled with toys and books over the years for her frequent visits.

'Daddy!' she squeals, running to James, who scoops her up effortlessly.

'Hey, pumpkin. Good nap?'

She nods against his shoulder, then turns to me with a smile that's pure Sarah. 'Rachel, can we finish our painting now?'

Earlier, before she got tired, we'd been working on watercolours at my dining table. I've kept every masterpiece she's created here, tucked away in a folder I'm saving for when she's older.

'Of course we can, love. Why don't you go set it up while I finish talking to your dad?'

She wriggles out of James's arms but doesn't leave immediately. Instead, she comes over and wraps her arms around my legs in a tight hug. I bend down to her level, tucking a strand of hair behind her ear, something I've done a thousand times... the same way I used to do with Sarah when we were at uni together.

'Can we have spaghetti for dinner?' she asks, her voice a cheeky whisper, as if James can't hear her from three feet away.

'If your dad says you're staying, then absolutely.'

She jumps with delight and runs off down the hall, the prospect of pasta apparently energising her completely. James watches her go with such love on his face that it makes my throat tight.

'You're so good with her,' he says. 'I don't know what we'd do without you.'

'Well, you'd have to pay for childcare, for starters.'

He laughs. 'True. But it's more than that. You keep Sarah

alive for her.' His voice catches slightly. 'You tell her stories about her mum that I've forgotten or never knew.'

I swallow hard. 'She was my best friend for twenty years. I've got the stories to prove it.'

'Remember when she was about two,' James says, 'and she went through that phase of calling you "Mama"?'

My heart clenches at the memory. 'God, yes. You nearly had a heart attack the first time.'

'She was so confused,' James says, shaking his head with a sad smile. 'She saw you more than any other woman in her life. It made sense to her little brain.'

What I don't tell him is how much I loved it. How for those brief weeks, before James gently corrected her, I'd allowed myself to pretend. It sounds a little crazy, but I just loved it.

'She knows who her mum is now,' I say instead. 'You've done an amazing job keeping Sarah real for her.'

'We both have.' He takes a step toward me and gives me a hug. 'Thank you. For everything.'

'It's nothing,' I lie. 'Now go have your crisis about what to wear tomorrow. I've got a budding Picasso waiting for me.'

His face changes, that same stupid grin from earlier. 'You really think it's okay? To move on?'

'I think,' I say carefully, 'that happiness doesn't come around often enough to ignore it when it does.'

He nods, seeming to take this in. 'Are you and Greg happy?'

The question catches me off guard. 'We're... comfortable.'

'That doesn't sound very romantic.'

I laugh, perhaps a bit too sharply. 'Not everyone gets the epic love story, James. Some of us settle for good enough.'

His look changes slightly. 'You deserve more than good enough, Rach.'

'Go home. Think about what shirt brings out your eyes or whatever it is you're going to obsess over. Text me after and tell me how it went.'

After he leaves, I sit with Lily at the dining table, watching her splash colours across the page with abandon. So different from her father, who calculates every move. Just like her mother, who lived boldly.

'What are you painting?' I ask her.

'A family,' she says simply. 'Me and Daddy and you.'

I look down at the three wobbly figures holding hands. I find it so genuinely cute. 'That's lovely, sweetheart.'

'And a dog,' she adds, dabbing brown paint in a rough circle beside the figures. 'We should get a dog.'

I laugh. 'Tell your dad that, not me.'

'But you'd help us walk it when Daddy's at work,' she says with absolute certainty. 'You'd come over even more!'

'Would I now?'

'Yep.' She dips her brush into the red paint, swirling it with a focus that reminds me so much of Sarah it hurts. 'Daddy says you're family.'

I blink back the sudden sting in my eyes. 'Does he?'

'Mmm hmm. When Adam at school said I don't have a mummy, I told him I have you instead, and Daddy said that was right, that you're our family even if you don't live with us.'

I don't know what to say to that, so I just stroke her hair and watch her paint, this child who has my heart so completely it sometimes frightens me.

'Rachel?' she asks after a while, not looking up from her artwork.

'Yes, love?'

'Why don't you have babies? Don't you like them?'

The question hits me like a punch to the stomach. 'I... I love babies. Especially you. You were the best baby ever.'

'So why don't you have your own?'

I consider how to answer, how much is appropriate to tell a five year old. 'Well, sometimes people's bodies don't work quite the way they're supposed to. The doctors told me my body probably can't make babies.'

It had been devastating news, delivered in a doctor's office three years ago after months of tests. Diminished ovarian reserve, they called it. Early menopause likely by my late thirties.

The irony wasn't lost on me; Sarah, who never particularly wanted children until she met James, had Lily with apparent ease. And here I was, the one who'd always dreamed of a house full of kids, facing the likelihood I'd never have my own.

Lily looks up at me, her expression serious. 'That's sad.'

'It is a bit sad,' I agree. 'But you know what makes it better?'

'What?'

'Having you in my life.' I tap her nose gently. 'I get to be part of watching you grow up, and that's pretty special.'

She considers this, then nods sagely. 'And when I'm bigger, I'll have babies and you can be their grandma.'

I laugh despite the lump in my throat. 'I think I'd be more like an aunt, sweetheart.'

'No,' she says with the absolute certainty only a five year old can muster. 'A grandma. Because you're like my mummy sometimes, so you'd be my babies' grandma.'

I don't correct her logic. Instead, I just drop a kiss on the top of her head and suggest we start dinner.

As we make spaghetti together, with Lily standing on a chair to 'help' stir the sauce (which means getting more of it on the counter than in the pot), I find myself thinking about James meeting this Melissa woman tomorrow. About him smiling at her the way he smiled in my kitchen. About the possibility of him finally moving on, finding happiness again. I should be happy for him. I am happy for him. It won't affect how much I see Lily. It can't, she'd be crushed.

As Lily chatters away, telling me about her day at school and how her friend Zoe has a loose tooth, my phone buzzes on the counter. Another text from Greg: 'Missing you already x'

I look at it, then at Lily, who's now got spaghetti sauce smeared across her cheek as she enthusiastically tastes her creation. At the kitchen I know as well as my own, at the child I love as if she were mine. At the life I've built on the periphery of the one I actually want. I text back a quick 'Miss you too' that feels hollow even as I type it.

After dinner, bath time, and two bedtime stories (because

Lily always manages to negotiate a second one), I tuck her into the bed in my spare room. This happens often enough that it doesn't feel strange anymore. James heading out for an evening, Lily staying with me. We have a good routine. He's at the gym tonight. He once asked if I'd go with him but I used babysitting as an excuse because I find exercise abhorrent.

'Rachel?' Lily asks sleepily as I'm about to turn off the light.

'Yes, love?'

'Is Daddy going to marry someone like he did Mummy?'

The question catches me off guard. 'I don't know, sweetheart. Maybe someday. Would that be okay with you?'

She thinks about it seriously, her little face lighting up. 'Only if she's nice. And only if she lets me still see you all the time.'

I sit on the edge of her bed, smoothing her hair back from her forehead. 'No matter what happens, you and I will always be family. Nothing will ever change that.'

She nods, satisfied, and snuggles deeper under the covers. 'I love you, Rachel.'

'I love you too, Lily bean. More than all the stars in the sky.'

'And all the fish in the sea,' she adds, our familiar bedtime exchange.

'And all the sand on the beach,' I finish, switching off the lamp and leaving just the small night light glowing.

Later, once she's asleep, I curl up on my sofa with a glass of wine, staring at the painting Lily made earlier. The three wobbly figures holding hands. The dog she's trying to convince James they need. The sun shining above them all.

I take a deep breath and focus on the colours bleeding together at the edges, creating something new. Something unexpected.

My phone buzzes with a text from James: 'She asleep?'

'Out like a light. Fed, bathed, storied. You're off duty till morning.'

'You're the best. I don't deserve you.'

I stare at those words for a long time, trying to ignore

the ache in my chest. 'No, you don't,' I finally text back with a laughing emoji to make it seem like a joke.

James finally dating has made me consider my own life. Maybe it's time I gave Greg a real chance, stopped keeping him at arm's length. Maybe I do deserve the whole love story thing. I throw on a murder documentary, down the rest of my wine and decide to think about this another time.

CHAPTER 3

James

I stare at my phone, fingers hovering over the keyboard. Delete, type, delete again. God, I'm terrible at this. The cursor blinks mockingly at me, a digital reminder of how painfully out of practice I am at the whole dating thing.

Melissa's last message sits at the top of our conversation: 'Looking forward to seeing you tomorrow! x'

That 'x' has been throwing me for the past ten minutes. Is it friendly? Flirty? Am I overthinking a single letter? (Yes, definitely yes.)

I type out: 'Me too! Any preferences on where we go?'

Too eager? Too open ended? I delete it and try again.

'Me too! I was thinking coffee at that place near work?'

No no no, too boring. Delete.

'Me too! I know a great little Italian place if you like pasta?'

Ugh, now I sound like I'm trying too hard. Delete.

I throw my phone onto the sofa and rub my hands over my face. This shouldn't be this difficult. It's just a text message to arrange a date. A date. With a woman who isn't Sarah.

Lily's stopping at Rach's tonight, which is nice because I don't have to worry about her waking in the night, but it still feels weird every time. My house feels quiet in a way it usually doesn't. Like it's holding its breath, waiting to see what I'll do next.

I've got it! I pick up my phone again and, before I can second guess myself for the fiftieth time, I type:

'Me too! I was thinking maybe that 50s style milkshake diner on Bridge Street? They do amazing burgers too. Unless you'd prefer something fancier?'

I hit send before I can delete it, then immediately regret my choice. A milkshake diner? What am I, sixteen? I only know the place because of taking Lily. Shit! Melissa seems sophisticated, the type who probably expects proper restaurants with wine lists and tablecloths. I hold my head in my hands.

My phone buzzes almost immediately, and I nearly drop it in my haste to check her response.

'A milkshake diner?? That's so random!' She replies, laughing emoji included. Oh, fantastic. Now she's laughing at me. I can feel my face burning even though there's no one here to see it. I'm about to type a hasty retraction when another message comes through.

'Actually, that sounds fun! I haven't been on a milkshake date since uni. What time?'

I stare at the screen, mouth agape. She's... into it? The feeling in my chest eases slightly. I can breathe again Maybe this won't be a complete disaster after all.

'Great! How about 7? I can pick you up if you'd like?'

The reply comes quickly again. 'Perfect. I live at 27 Elmwood Gardens. See you at 7! x'

Another 'x'. I still don't know what to make of it, but at least I have a plan now. A date. At a milkshake diner. I'm thirty eight years old.

I navigate to my contacts and call Rachel, needing her particular brand of blunt reassurance.

'Let me guess,' she answers without preamble. 'You're having a crisis about tomorrow.'

'How did you know?'

'Because I know you, you muppet. What's the problem?'

I sigh. 'I suggested a milkshake diner for our date.'

There's a pause, then Rachel bursts out laughing. The sound is so genuine and familiar that I can't help smiling despite my embarrassment.

'A milkshake diner?' she manages between chuckles. 'What are you, twelve?'

'That's exactly what I thought right after I sent it! But she seems... oddly okay with it?'

'Well, that's... something. Maybe she appreciates originality.' Rachel's voice has that warm, slightly teasing tone she always uses when she thinks I'm being ridiculous but isn't going to be too harsh about it.

'Or maybe she's just being polite and secretly thinks I'm an idiot.'

'James.'

'What?'

'Stop overthinking. If she agreed to go, she's interested. Just be yourself.'

'Being myself is what got me into this milkshake situation,' I grumble.

Rachel sighs. 'Look, it's actually kind of sweet. Different from the usual "let's go to an overpriced restaurant and make awkward conversation" first date. It shows personality.'

'Really?'

'Really. And if she doesn't appreciate your particular brand of awkward charm, then she's not the right person anyway.'

I lean back, closing my eyes. 'When did you get so wise about dating?'

'I've always been wise. You've just never needed my wisdom before. Now, stop panicking and get some sleep. You need to be well rested for your teenage dream date.'

I laugh. 'Goodnight, Rach.'

'Night, James.'

I hang up feeling marginally better. Rachel always has that effect on me, grounding me when my thoughts start spiralling. I don't know what I'd do without her steady presence in my life.

With one last glance at my phone (still no further messages

from Melissa), I head upstairs and go into Lily's room.

'Wish me luck tomorrow, pumpkin,' I whisper to nobody. 'Daddy's a bit rusty at this whole dating thing.'

I wonder, not for the first time, what Sarah would think of all this. Would she be happy I'm finally moving on? Amused at my awkward attempts at dating? I like to think she'd be both.

I stroll out of Lily's room and head to my own, already mentally sorting through my wardrobe for something appropriate to wear to a milkshake diner. Do I go casual? Smart casual? Is there a dress code for drinking milkshakes as an adult? God, I'm out of my depth here.

***

The next day passes in a blur of IT support tickets and clock watching. By five, I'm a bundle of nerves, and by six, when Rachel arrives with 'Daddy Bunny', Lily's favourite teddy named after me that she'd left behind, I'm practically vibrating with anxiety.

'You look like you're about to defuse a bomb, not go on a date,' she says, handing me the well loved teddy bear. She's still in her work clothes, a smart blazer over a simple blouse and trousers, but has her hair down, which always makes her look softer somehow.

'I feel like it,' I admit, ushering her in. 'I've changed my shirt three times.'

'And yet you've settled on the blue one. Again.' She shakes her head, a small smile playing at her lips. 'Predictable.'

'What's wrong with blue? Blue is safe. Professional.'

'Nothing's wrong with it. Blue suits you.' She steps past me into the living room where Lily is watching her favourite cartoon. 'Hey, trouble. Look what I rescued from my sofa cushions.'

Lily's face lights up. 'Daddy Bunny!' She leaps up and grabs the teddy, hugging it fiercely. 'Thank you, Rachel!'

'You're welcome, love.' Rachel ruffles her hair

affectionately. 'Now, your dad tells me you've got a very important job tonight. What was it again?'

Lily stands up straight, clearly taking this responsibility very seriously. 'I'm going to be good for Mrs. Wilson next door and go to bed on time and not ask for extra stories.'

'That's right,' I nod. 'Mrs. Wilson is eighty three. She doesn't need you running circles around her.'

'I'm always good,' Lily protests.

Rachel laughs. 'You're always charming, which isn't the same thing.'

'Like mother, like daughter,' I say without thinking, then feel the familiar pang that always comes with casual references to Sarah. It's less sharp than it used to be, but still there.

Rachel's eyes meet mine for a moment, something unreadable in them, before she turns back to Lily. 'So, what are we watching?'

While they settle on the sofa, I head upstairs for one final wardrobe check. The blue button down shirt stays (Rachel's right, it does suit me), paired with dark jeans that I hope strike the right balance between casual and making an effort.

I check my phone. No new messages from Melissa, but she knows the plan. Twenty seven Elmwood Gardens at seven o'clock. I've already googled the address, it's in one of the nicer areas of town, all well maintained semi detached houses with neat front gardens. It's about a fifteen minute drive from here.

Back downstairs, Lily and Rachel are engrossed in the cartoon, their heads close together as they laugh at something on screen. The sight of them makes my chest tighten with a strange mix of emotions. Gratitude, certainly. A touch of sadness. And something else I can't quite define.

'Right,' I say, checking my watch. 'I'd better head off. Mrs. Wilson should be over any minute.'

Lily jumps up and runs to hug me. 'Good luck, Daddy. Don't drink too many milkshakes or you'll get a tummy ache.'

I laugh, crouching down to her level. 'I'll be careful. Be good, okay? I won't be too late.'

'Kay.' She kisses my cheek. 'Will you tell me about your date tomorrow?'

'Every boring detail,' I promise.

Rachel stands, smoothing down her trousers. 'I should get going too. Good luck tonight, James. Try not to overthink it.'

'That's like telling water not to be wet.'

'Is water wet or are the things it touches wet?'

'Great. I'll be overthinking that crazy scenario now.'

She smiles. 'It might relax you. Just... have fun, okay? You deserve it.'

'Thanks, Rach.' I hesitate, then add, 'For everything. Not just the teddy bear rescue.'

'Don't get sappy on me, James. It doesn't suit you.' But her smile softens the words.

The doorbell rings, Mrs. Wilson with her impeccable timing, and soon both Rachel and I are heading out to our respective cars. As I'm about to get into mine, Rachel calls out.

'Hey, James?'

'Yeah?'

'If the milkshake thing is a disaster, at least it'll make a funny story.'

With that reassurance ringing in my ears, mixed with a wild debate about what 'wet' means, I drive to Elmwood Gardens.

**

Melissa's house is exactly what I expected; a nice little house with a neat front garden and stylish exterior lighting. I park outside, taking a moment to check my reflection in the rearview mirror (hair still reasonably in place, no obvious signs of panic) before walking up to her door. My hand shakes slightly as I press the doorbell. This is ridiculous. I'm a grown man with a child and a mortgage. I shouldn't be nervous about a date, yet my heart is hammering in my chest like I'm about to face a firing squad instead of dinner with an attractive woman.

The door opens, and for a second, I forget how to speak. Melissa looks stunning. Her blonde hair falls in soft waves around her face, and she's wearing a simple but elegant dress that makes my casual smart outfit feel decidedly under dressed. She smiles, and I realise I'm staring.

'Hi,' I manage, my voice only slightly strained. 'You look... wow.'

Great start, James. Really eloquent.

She laughs, the sound light and musical. 'Thank you. You don't look so bad yourself. Blue suits you.'

'That's what my friend said,' I reply without thinking.

'Your friend has good taste.' She grabs a small handbag from a console table by the door. 'Shall we? I'm actually really looking forward to these famous milkshakes.'

The tension in my shoulders eases slightly as we walk to my car. At least she's not visibly disappointed by the diner plan. I open the passenger door for her, an automatic gesture that feels simultaneously old fashioned and natural.

'Such a gentleman,' she laughs as she slides into the seat.

'My mum would have my head if I didn't open doors,' I say with a small smile. 'Some things stick with you.'

Once I'm in the driver's seat, a brief silence falls. I rack my brain for something interesting to say, something that doesn't involve IT support problems or children's TV shows.

'So,' I begin as I start the car, 'marketing. That must be interesting.'

Brilliant conversation starter, James. Really riveting stuff.

But Melissa seems happy enough to talk about her work, and by the time we reach the diner, I've learned that she specialises in digital marketing for luxury brands, that she moved to our building six months ago from a firm in London, and that she finds most of her colleagues 'perfectly nice but a bit dull.'

'Except you, of course,' she adds with a smile as we park. 'You seemed interesting right away.'

I raise an eyebrow. 'I did? How? I'm pretty sure I was just

standing in a stairway looking confused.'

She laughs, but there's something evasive in her expression. 'Just a feeling I had. I'm usually good at reading people.'

The diner is exactly as I remembered it; all chrome fixtures, red vinyl booths, and retro memorabilia on the walls. A waitress in a 1950s style uniform shows us to a booth by the window, handing us menus shaped like vinyl records.

'This place is adorable,' Melissa says, looking around. 'I can't believe I've never been here before.'

'I used to bring Lily here for special treats,' I say. 'They do these chocolate milkshakes with about five different kinds of chocolate in them. She loves them, but they make her bounce off the walls for hours afterwards.'

As soon as I mention Lily, Melissa's expression changes, becoming more focused, more interested. 'Your daughter sounds adorable. How old did you say she was?'

'Five. Going on fifteen, sometimes.'

'That's such a wonderful age,' she says, leaning forward slightly. 'They're so curious about everything, so full of personality. I'd love to meet her sometime.'

Something about her keenness makes me pause. We've known each other for exactly two days, and she's already angling to meet Lily? It seems a bit quick. But then again, what do I know about dating etiquette? Maybe showing interest in a date's child is just being polite. Maybe she wants to make herself seem into the idea of becoming a stepmum…

'Maybe,' I say noncommittally. 'So, what milkshake are you going for?'

She accepts the change of subject gracefully, and we spend a few minutes debating the merits of various flavour combinations. I end up ordering a classic vanilla malt (boring but reliable, as Rachel would no doubt point out), while Melissa goes for a strawberry cheesecake concoction that sounds tooth achingly sweet.

Once the waitress leaves with our orders, including

burgers and fries, Melissa folds her hands on the table and fixes me with a smile that's probably meant to be encouraging but feels slightly rehearsed.

'So, tell me more about yourself, James. How long have you been at the company?'

'About eight years now. I started in basic tech support and worked my way up to IT management. Not the most exciting career trajectory, but it's stable.'

'Stability is underrated,' she says. 'Especially when you're raising a child alone.'

There's that focus on Lily again. I shift in my seat, oddly uncomfortable.

'What about you?' I ask. 'Have you always been in marketing?'

She nods, launching into a story about her first job out of university. I try to focus, to be engaged, but my mind keeps catching on small details. The way she keeps steering the conversation back towards Lily. The slight rehearsed quality to some of her responses. The fact that, despite talking a lot, she doesn't seem to be revealing much about herself.

Our milkshakes arrive, momentarily distracting me. Melissa takes a sip of hers and makes an appreciative noise that's just slightly too enthusiastic.

'Oh my god, this is amazing,' she gushes. 'You have to try it.'

Before I can respond, she's pushing her glass towards me, her fingers brushing mine in a way that can't be accidental. I take an awkward sip, the sweetness feeling like it will put me in a diabetic coma.

'Good, right?' she says.

'Very sweet,' I cough out. 'But nice.'

She smiles, satisfied, and takes her glass back. 'So, your daughter... Lily, right? Does she look like you or her mother?'

There it is again. 'A bit of both, I suppose. She has Sarah's hair and my eyes.'

'And her mother... she passed away during childbirth?' Her voice drops to a sympathetic murmur.

I feel my shoulders tense. How does she know that? Did I mention it during the fire alarm? I don't remember going into details about Sarah's death.

'Yes,' I say carefully. 'There were complications.'

Melissa reaches across the table to touch my hand, her expression the perfect blend of sympathy and admiration. 'You're amazing, raising her on your own. It must be so hard.'

'I have help,' I say, thinking of Rachel. 'I'm not completely on my own.'

'Still,' she insists, 'it's impressive. And Lily must be such a special little girl.'

The waitress returns with our food, giving me a moment to gather my thoughts. Maybe I'm just out of practice. Maybe this is normal dating conversation, and I've been out of the game for so long I've forgotten the rules. I take a bite of my burger, using the food as an excuse to shift the conversation.

'This is great,' I say, pointing down to the burger. 'How's yours?'

Melissa looks momentarily confused by the abrupt change of topic, but recovers quickly. 'Delicious. So, do you have any help with Lily? Family nearby?'

'Not family, no. My parents are both gone, and Sarah's live up north. But my friend Rachel helps a lot. She was Sarah's best friend, actually. She's been a godsend.'

'Rachel?' Melissa repeats. 'The one who said blue suits you?'

I nod, not sure why I feel like I've stepped into dangerous territory.

'And she helps with Lily? Like a babysitter?'

'More than that,' I say, feeling slightly defensive. 'She's like family to us. Has been since before Lily was born.'

Melissa takes a sip of her milkshake, her face looking thoughtful. 'That must be... convenient.'

There's something in her tone I can't quite place, but the conversation moves on, and soon we're discussing films we've seen recently, books we've enjoyed. Safer topics that don't involve my daughter or my relationship with Rachel.

By the time we finish our meal, I've relaxed somewhat. Melissa is funny, well read, and seems genuinely interested in what I have to say. She's really good company.

'Excuse me for a moment,' she says after declining a dessert. 'Just need to freshen up.'

As soon as she disappears towards the restrooms, I pull out my phone and text Rachel.

'Date in progress. At diner. She keeps asking about Lily. Normal or weird?'

The reply comes almost immediately, suggesting Rachel was already looking at her phone.

'How keeps? Like polite interest or third degree?'

I think for a moment. 'Somewhere in between. She already knows Sarah died in childbirth but I don't remember telling her that.'

The three dots appear, disappear, then appear again.

'Red flag, James. How would she know unless you told her? Maybe you did mention it and forgot?'

'Maybe.' But I don't think I did. The fire alarm conversation had been light, focusing on work and general small talk.

'Trust your gut. If something feels off, it probably is.'

I stare at the message, feeling conflicted. Does something feel off? Or am I just so out of practice with dating that normal interest seems excessive? Melissa is attractive, successful, and seems to like me. Maybe I'm looking for problems where there aren't any.

'She's really nice,' I text back. 'I'm probably overthinking it.'

'You? Overthinking? Surely not. Anyway, stop using me to avoid your date.'

I smile at Rachel's response, imagining her curled up on her sofa with a glass of wine, rolling her eyes at my message.

'Yes, boss.'

I slip my phone back into my pocket just as Melissa returns, her makeup refreshed and her smile bright.

'Everything okay?' she asks, noticing my expression.

'Fine, just checking in on Lily.'

Her face softens immediately. 'You're such a good dad. It's one of the things I noticed about you right away. Don't worry, I've asked for the bill.'

'My treat,' I insist when it arrives. 'My bizarre milkshake idea, my treat.'

She doesn't argue too hard, which I appreciate. 'Next time, I'll choose. Maybe somewhere we could take Lily too?'

I smile at her noncommittally as I pay. 'Maybe.'

The drive back to her house is pleasant enough, filled with easy conversation about the neighbourhood we're passing through, the unusually mild weather for October, other restaurants we might like to try.

When I pull up outside her house, there's the inevitable awkward moment of wondering what happens next. Do I kiss her? Shake her hand? Just say goodnight and drive off? She solves the dilemma by leaning over and pressing a quick, soft kiss to my cheek.

'I had a lovely time, James. Thank you for the milkshakes.'

'Me too. It was nice.'

She pauses, her hand on the door handle. 'I'd like to see you again. Maybe this weekend? If you're free?'

'I have Lily this weekend,' I say automatically.

'I don't mind. Like I said, I'd love to meet her. Maybe a park? The zoo? Whatever she'd enjoy.'

'Let me check what we've got on. I'll text you.'

She seems satisfied with this, giving me another quick kiss, this time closer to the corner of my mouth, before getting out of the car. I wait until she's safely inside her house before pulling away, my thoughts a jumble of mixed signals and confused emotions.

Back at home, Mrs. Wilson greets me at the door and says goodbye. The house is quiet, peacefully undisturbed from how I left it. I check on Lily; fast asleep, Daddy Bunny clutched tightly in her arms, before heading to my bedroom and collapsing onto the bed fully clothed.

I feel elated. A successful date with an attractive,

intelligent woman who seems interested in me. How is this possible? I pull out my phone and, without really thinking about it, call Rachel.

'How was the teenagers date?' she answers, her voice warm with amusement.

'Good,' I admit. 'Or maybe a little weird. I can't tell anymore.'

'Elaborate.'

I sigh, kicking off my shoes and laying back on the bed. 'She was nice. Beautiful, funny, smart. But... I don't know. Something felt off.'

'The Lily thing?'

'Partly. She kept bringing her up, wanting to meet her. Even suggested our next date should include Lily.'

Rachel is quiet for a moment. 'That's... interesting.'

'Is it? I wasn't sure if I'm just overthinking. Maybe it's totally normal to want to meet your date's kid early on. How would I know? The dating rulebook has probably been rewritten ten times since I was last single.'

'James.' Rachel's voice is gentle but firm. 'It's a bit soon, don't you think? You hardly know this woman.'

'She seemed to know things about me, though. Like about Sarah dying during childbirth. I swear I didn't mention that during the fire alarm.'

'Maybe you did and you've forgotten? You were pretty nervous.'

'Maybe.' But I don't think so. 'Or maybe someone at work told her. Office gossip and all that.'

'Maybe,' Rachel echoes, not sounding convinced. 'Did you agree to the weekend thing?'

'I said I'd check what we had on and text her.'

'Good. Keep some distance. See how she responds to that.'

I rub my eyes, suddenly exhausted. 'Am I making a mess of this?'

'Of what, exactly?'

'Dating. Moving on. All of it.'

Rachel is quiet for so long I wonder if the call has ended. When she finally speaks, her voice is softer than before. 'You're doing fine, James. There's no right way to do this. No timeline you have to follow.'

'I just... I want to get it right. For Lily's sake as much as mine.'

'I know you do. That's why you should trust your instincts. If something feels wrong, listen to that feeling.' I sigh, staring up at the ceiling.

'When did life get so complicated?'

'Around the time you became a single dad trying to date again,' she replies, a smile in her voice despite the serious subject.

I laugh despite myself. 'Fair point. Thanks, Rach. For talking me down from the ceiling.'

'Anytime. That's what I'm here for.'

We say our goodnights, and I hang up feeling slightly better. Rachel has that effect on me; like a compass pointing north when I'm lost in my own thoughts. I change into pyjamas and brush my teeth, mulling over the evening. Maybe I'm reading too much into Melissa's interest in Lily. Maybe it's just her way of showing she's okay with the package deal that is dating a single parent. Maybe I should give her another chance before jumping to conclusions.

I send her a quick text: 'Thanks for a lovely evening. Will check our weekend plans and let you know.'

Her reply comes almost immediately: 'Amazing! I was thinking the zoo on Saturday? Little girls love animals! x'

I stare at the message, feeling flattered by her enthusiasm. Does she know Lily loves animals? Then again, it's not exactly an amazing guess. All kids love the zoo. I put my phone on charge and get into bed, my mind still whirring with uncertainties. Dating as a single parent is clearly a minefield I'm absolutely not equipped to navigate. Every instinct I have when it comes to Lily is protective, suspicious of newcomers in her life. But I can't keep her or myself in isolation forever.

As I drift off to sleep, my thoughts turn, as they often do, to Sarah. What would she think of Melissa? Would she approve? Or would she share Rachel's slight hesitations? I dream of fire alarms and milkshakes, of blonde hair and friendly smiles. And somewhere in the dream, Sarah and Rachel stand side by side, their expressions impossible to read as they watch me navigate this new, strange territory alone.

CHAPTER 4

Rachel

Mondays are bad enough without having your brain hijacked by overthinking. I stare at my laptop screen, the spreadsheet I've been trying to make sense of for the past hour blurring before my eyes. The figures refuse to add up, or maybe I'm just not giving them the attention they deserve.

I take a sip of my now cold coffee. I've been off all morning, in fact since last night, when James called me about his date with Melissa. About how it went 'really well', how she was 'funny and smart', but also how she seemed weirdly eager to meet Lily. I advised caution, of course. But James, despite his own overthinking tendencies, clearly has a blindspot when it comes to women showing interest in him.

My phone buzzes on my desk, and I practically lunge for it, hoping it's Greg finally responding to the message I sent last night. But no. It's James again.

'She's asking about the zoo this weekend again. I tried to say we're busy but she suggested next weekend instead. She's very keen to meet Lily.'

I stare at the message, a knot forming in my stomach. I type back: 'Don't you think that's a bit quick? You've had one date.'

The typing bubble appears immediately. 'That's what I

thought. But maybe it's different when you date as a single parent? Maybe it's normal to want to check if you get on with the kid early?'

Oh, James. Sweet, naive James. 'No. It's not normal. Trust me.'

'She keeps saying how much she knows Lily will love her. Seems confident.'

My stomach tightens even more. There's something off about this woman. I've dated single fathers before. I've never pushed to meet their children until we'd been seeing each other for at least a few months, sometimes longer. It's about boundaries. About protection. Children aren't accessories to be paraded in front of potential partners.

'James, listen to me. This is a red flag. A big one.'

The typing bubble appears and disappears several times before his response finally comes through. 'You're probably right. But she's also really lovely. Maybe she's just enthusiastic?'

I resist the urge to throw my phone across the room. Instead, I take a deep breath and type, 'Maybe. Just... take it slow, okay? Protect Lily. And yourself.'

'Always. Thanks, Rach. You're the best. Off to a meeting x'

I put my phone down and try to refocus on my spreadsheet, but it's useless. My mind is stuck on Melissa and her odd behaviour. I can't help but be overprotective of Lily. She's the closest thing I'll ever have to a daughter. I better look into her, just in case.

Before I can talk myself out of it, I open up Facebook on my phone. I type 'Melissa' into the search bar, but realise I don't know her surname. James never mentioned it. I check Instagram instead, looking at James's recent followers. There she is: Melissa Chambers. Private account, but her profile picture shows her smiling on a beach somewhere, looking every bit the carefree, attractive woman James described.

I click on her profile, knowing I won't be able to see much without following her, which I'm certainly not going to do. But even the limited view gives me some information. Account created: December last year. Only 14 posts. 127 followers. Not much of a digital footprint for a woman in her thirties who supposedly works in digital marketing.

I switch back to Facebook and search for Melissa Chambers. Several profiles pop up, but I recognise her immediately in one of them. This profile is also locked down, but there are a few public photos. I click through them, feeling like a stalker but unable to stop myself. Most are standard social media fare: Melissa at a restaurant, Melissa with a cocktail, Melissa on holiday. Nothing suspicious, but nothing particularly revealing either.

I'm about to give up when I notice something in her 'About' section that's publicly visible. Under 'Work', it lists 'Bennett & Holloway Marketing, 2020 present'. That's James's company. She really does work there.

Curiosity piqued, I go a step further and check James's Facebook profile. He rarely posts anything these days, but there's a photo from last Christmas, the company party that I attended as his plus one. It's a group shot, everyone wearing silly hats and pulling crackers. James has his arm around me, and we're both laughing at something Lily had just said off camera. I remember that night clearly: Lily in her cute little dress, falling asleep under a table after too much cake, me carrying her to the car while James gathered her colouring books and new toys from the Santa visit.

I look at the likes on the photo. Seventeen in total. And there, among them: Melissa Chambers. The Christmas party was *ten months* ago. Long before the supposedly chance meeting during the fire alarm. *Weird...* I think to myself, leaning closer to the screen. Could it be a coincidence? Maybe she just went through his profile after they met and liked some old photos? But a nagging feeling makes me check his other recent posts. A photo of Lily on her first day back at school in September: liked by Melissa Chambers. A post about a charity fun run he did in July: liked by Melissa Chambers. A photo from May, Lily blowing out candles on her birthday cake, me beside her helping to steady the knife: liked by Melissa Chambers. This is more than a coincidence. Melissa has been following James's social media for months, well before their 'first meeting'.

I sit back in my chair, unsure what to do with this information. It's creepy, certainly, but is it dangerous? Should I tell James? He's clearly smitten with her; would he even believe me, or would he think I'm interfering?

My desk phone rings, startling me out of my thoughts. I look at the caller ID: *Lily's school*? My heart immediately picks up speed.

'Rachel Whittaker speaking,' I answer, trying to keep my voice steady.

'Miss Whittaker, this is Maggie from the office at St Catherine's. I'm trying to reach Mr Porter, but he's not answering his mobile or work number.'

'Is Lily okay?' I ask, already reaching for my car keys. I'm listed as her emergency contact, have been since she started school last year.

'Lily's fine,' Maggie assures me. 'But we've had a… situation. A woman came to the school about an hour ago, claiming to be a family friend. She asked to see Lily's classroom and wanted information about her schedule. Said something about planning a surprise.'

'What woman? Did she give a name?'

'Lizzie something. She wasn't on our approved list, so we didn't let her in or give her any information, of course. But she was very persistent. Almost upset when we refused.'

'Lizzie,' I repeat, knowing full well it was Melissa. No prizes for originality in that pseudonym. 'Blonde? About my height? Well dressed?'

'Yes, that's her. She said she was Mr Porter's girlfriend and was planning a special day for Lily. When we explained our policy, she became quite… intense. Insisted that Mr Porter would want her to have access. That's when we tried to call him.'

I'm already grabbing my bag, shutting down my computer. 'I'll be there in twenty minutes. Please make sure Lily stays inside until I get there.'

'Ms Whittaker, there's no immediate...'

'Twenty minutes,' I repeat, ending the call.

I hurry out of my office, stopping briefly at my boss's door to explain that there's a family emergency. He waves me off with concern; he knows about my relationship with James and Lily, has been understanding in the past when I've needed to leave unexpectedly.

The drive to St Catherine's feels endless, even though traffic is light. My mind races with possibilities, each more alarming than the last. Melissa, turning up at Lily's school after one date with James. Melissa, who's been stalking his social media for months. Melissa, trying to get access to his daughter without his knowledge.

By the time I pull into the school car park, I feel anxiety I wasn't expecting, but, Lily is fine. The school didn't let Melissa in. Everything is okay. I just need to see Lily, talk to the school, and figure out what's going on.

Maggie, the school secretary, greets me at the reception desk with a reassuring smile. 'Ms Whittaker, thank you for coming so quickly. As I said on the phone, there's no immediate concern.'

'Has Mr Porter called back?' I ask, trying to sound calm and professional despite the situation.

'Yes, about ten minutes ago. He was in a meeting. I explained the situation, and he's on his way as well.'

I nod. 'Where's Lily now?'

'In her classroom. It's reading time. Would you like me to get her?'

'No, that's okay. I don't want to disrupt her if she's settled. Can you tell me more about what happened with this woman... Lizzie?'

Maggie's expression grows more serious. 'She arrived just after lunch, said she was a close friend of the family. Wanted to see Lily's classroom to plan some sort of surprise for her. When I explained our policy about only allowing listed individuals access, she became quite... insistent. Said she was Mr Porter's partner and that he'd want her to be involved in Lily's school life.'

'Did she seem angry? Threatening?'

'Not threatening, no. More... disappointed. Almost hurt. Like she genuinely expected to be allowed in. When I suggested she have Mr Porter call to add her to the approved list, she said something about wanting it to be a surprise for him too. That's when I became concerned.'

'You did the right thing,' I assure her. 'Did she leave contact details? Or say anything about where she was going?'

Maggie shakes her head. 'No, she just left. Seemed upset, but not aggressive.'

The front door of the school opens, and James rushes in, his face pale with worry. When he sees me, relief floods his features.

'Rach,' he says, coming to stand beside me. 'What's happening? Is Lily okay?'

'She's fine,' I tell him, keeping my voice low and calm. 'She doesn't even know anything's going on. But James...' I glance at Maggie, not wanting to discuss my suspicions in front of her. 'Can we talk privately for a minute?'

Maggie seems to understand. 'I'll go and check on Lily, let her teacher know you're both here.'

Once she's gone, I turn to James, not bothering to hide my concern. 'It was Melissa, James. She came to Lily's school, trying to get access to her classroom, asking questions about her schedule.'

His brow furrows in confusion. 'Melissa? Are you sure?'

'Blonde woman, claimed to be your girlfriend, said she was planning a surprise? Yes, I'm sure.'

'But... why would she do that?'

'That's what I'd like to know.' I take a deep breath, trying to organise my thoughts. 'James, I found something else. Melissa has been following your social media for months. Liking your posts, including ones with Lily. Going back to at least last Christmas.'

He stares at me, disbelief written across his face. 'What? How do you know?'

'I looked her up after you texted me this morning. I was worried about how pushy she was being about meeting Lily. It didn't feel right.'

'So you stalked her online?' There's an edge to his voice that I wasn't expecting.

'I checked her public profiles,' I clarify, feeling defensive. 'And I'm glad I did. James, this isn't normal behaviour. She's showing an obsessive interest in Lily after one date with you. She's been monitoring your social media for months before "accidentally" meeting you during the fire alarm. And now she's turning up at Lily's school? None of this concerns you?'

He runs a hand through his hair, a move I know means he's stressed and conflicted. 'Maybe there's an explanation. Maybe she...'

'Maybe she what?' I interrupt, struggling to keep my voice down. 'Maybe she just happened to work at the same company as you for months without introducing herself? Maybe she just happened to be in the stairwell during that fire alarm? Maybe she's just really, really enthusiastic about meeting the daughter of a man she's been on one date with? Come on, James. You're smarter than this.'

He pauses, and then takes out his phone. I see him open Facebook and check the pictures 'Likes'. Nothing. Melissa has unliked them. Bizarre...

'See? She hasn't been watching me on Facebook. I know you're trying to help, but you're making it sound like she's some kind of stalker. She's a nice woman who might be moving a bit fast, that's all.'

Before I can respond, Maggie returns with Lily in tow. At the sight of us, Lily's face lights up with surprise and joy.

'Daddy! Rachel!' she exclaims, running towards us. 'Why are you both here? Is school over early?'

James crouches down to her level, his face softening into a smile that doesn't quite reach his eyes. 'No, pumpkin. We just decided to come and say hello. How was your day?'

As Lily launches into an excited recounting of her morning

activities, I watch James's face. I can see the conflict there, the worry beginning to seep in despite his defence of Melissa. He might not want to believe it, but he knows something isn't right.

After a brief discussion with Lily's teacher, James decides to take her home early. It's already past two, and the disruption to her routine has been minimal. As we walk to the car park together, Lily skipping between us, I can feel the tension radiating from James.

'I need to get back to work,' I tell him as we reach our cars. 'But call me later? Please?'

He nods, his expression unreadable. 'Yeah. Thanks for coming, Rach.'

'Rachel, are you coming for dinner?' Lily asks, tugging on my hand. 'Daddy's making spaghetti!'

I look at James, not wanting to impose if he needs space. He gives me a small, tired smile. 'You're welcome to join us. Around six?'

'I'd like that,' I say, relieved that he's not shutting me out. 'I'll bring garlic bread.'

As I drive back to the office, my mind is a whirl of theories and suspicions. There's more to Melissa than meets the eye, I'm sure of it. And I'm going to find out what.

***

By five o'clock, I've accomplished very little actual work, but I've dug deeply into Melissa Chambers' online presence. Or rather, the lack thereof. For someone who supposedly works in digital marketing, she has a remarkably small digital footprint. Her LinkedIn profile was created just six months ago and lists her current position at Bennett & Holloway Marketing, but with virtually no connections or activity. Her Instagram goes back only to January, as does her Facebook. It's as if Melissa Chambers didn't exist before this year. Or at least, not online…

I check my phone, hoping for some response from Greg to my increasingly worried messages. Still nothing. Our last proper conversation was three days ago, and even that was brief and distracted on his end. I tell myself it's the time difference, the busy schedule of his Singapore meetings, but a small, insecure part of me wonders if he's pulling away. If he's found someone else who doesn't spend all her free time with another man and his daughter.

I push these thoughts aside. Greg's emotional unavailability is a problem for another day. Right now, I need to focus on the potential threat to Lily. A quick search of the company directory confirms that Melissa does indeed work for Bennett & Holloway, but not in marketing. She's listed under *Human Resources*, specifically in the division that runs the company's on site childcare facility. The facility Lily occasionally attends when James's childcare arrangements fall through...

Bingo. I *knew* it. My heart rate picks up. This changes everything. Melissa doesn't work on the floor above James; she works in the company childcare centre. Where she would have had ample opportunity to observe Lily. To learn about her routine, her preferences, her relationship with James.

I grab my phone and call James, but it goes straight to voicemail. He's probably busy with Lily, getting dinner started. I send a text instead.

'Need to talk before dinner. Important. Call when you can.'

I shut down my computer and gather my things, my mind racing. Should I go straight to James's house? Wait for him to call? Go to the supermarket for garlic bread as planned and pretend everything's normal until I can talk to him privately?

As I'm debating, my phone rings. Not James, but Greg. Finally.

'Hey,' I answer, trying to keep the irritation out of my voice. 'Nice of you to check in.'

'Sorry, babe,' he says, sounding genuinely apologetic. 'The meetings here have been non stop, and the time difference makes it hard to catch you when you're not at work or asleep.'

'It's fine,' I lie, because now isn't the time to get into our relationship issues. 'How's Singapore?'

'Hot. Humid. Beautiful. You'd love it.' There's a pause, then, 'I miss you.'

The words should warm me, but they just make me feel guilty. Because while Greg has been gone, I haven't missed him as much as I should. I've been too preoccupied with James and Lily. With being the family I sort of pretend we are.

'I miss you too,' I say, because it's what he expects to hear.

'Listen, there's been a change of plans. They want me to extend the trip, head to Malaysia for another project. It would mean another two weeks away.'

I should feel disappointed. Instead, I feel something close to relief. 'Oh. Well, if it's important for your career...'

'It is. This could mean a promotion when I get back.' His voice is eager, excited. 'You don't mind?'

'Of course not,' I assure him, already mentally moving on to the more pressing issue of Melissa. 'We'll catch up properly when you're back.'

We chat for a little longer before ending the call with promises to speak soon. I sit in my car, phone in hand, feeling a strange mix of emotions. Guilt about Greg. Fear for Lily. Frustration with James for not seeing what's right in front of him.

My phone buzzes with a text from James: 'Just got your message. What's up?'

I type quickly: 'Melissa doesn't work in marketing. She works in the company childcare centre. The one Lily goes to sometimes.'

Three dots appear immediately, then disappear. Then appear again. Finally, his response comes through: 'Are you sure?'

'Positive. Just checked the company directory. She's in HR, childcare division. She lied to you, James. She's been watching Lily for months.'

The three dots appear and disappear several times, as if he's typing and deleting multiple responses. Eventually: 'Come over now if you can. Need to talk about this.'

I start my car, a sense of urgency propelling me forward. The pieces are starting to fall into place, and the picture they're forming is deeply concerning. Melissa isn't just moving too fast; she's been calculating and manipulating from the start. Setting up a meeting that wasn't chance at all. Lying about her job. Showing an unhealthy interest in a child she has no connection to.

The drive to James's house takes twenty minutes in evening traffic. When I arrive, I find him pacing in the living room while Lily sits at the kitchen table, happily coloring and oblivious to her father's distress.

'Rachel!' she calls when I enter, waving a crayon in greeting. 'I'm drawing our family for school!'

I force a smile, walking over to see her artwork. 'That looks beautiful, love. Is that a dog?'

'Yep! The one we're going to get. And that's you, and Daddy, and me.' She points to three stick figures standing beside the dog.

'Gorgeous,' I say, dropping a kiss on top of her head. 'Keep working on it while I talk to your dad, okay?'

James leads me to the living room, far enough away that Lily won't overhear but where we can still keep an eye on her. His face is calmer than I expect.

'I checked after I got your text. You're right. She is listed in childcare, not marketing. I thought she'd lied to me, but I called her about it. Apparently it's just an error on the company directory, nothing to worry about.'

'James, I'm sorry, but this is bullshit. She's been watching Lily, learning about her. That's why she knew so much about her on your date. The fire alarm, the "chance" meeting... none of it was random.'

'Rachel... I get it. You're worried that Melissa will take over and replace your relationship with Lily. But I promise, that will not happen. Alright? Lily loves you so much. I'd never take you away from her.'

I stand there, stunned. Is he for real? All the evidence, all the weird stuff, and he's believing her over *me*?

'Well what about her coming to school today? What's her explanation for that?'

'Rach, she was at work. It was probably a mistake. I'm worried it was...' he pauses, and thinks to choose his words carefully. 'Remember the last girl I was talking to? The one who turned out to be nasty?'

'Anna? How can it be Anna? She has dark hair.'

'When I last saw her, it was lighter. Maybe she was doing it to get back at me for ghosting her?'

Ghosting her was the right decision. Even for a man almost 40. She was awful. I sigh. Ugh. He's giving this woman the benefit of the doubt and it's annoying me. I'm about to reply when Lily comes running in.

'When's tea ready big Daddy?' She says

We all laugh. The things kids say.

'Spaghetti, coming right up, pumpkin,' James says, his voice deliberately light as he fills a pot with water. 'Why don't you show Rachel what you learned at school today while I cook?'

Lily launches into an enthusiastic demonstration of her new knowledge about dinosaurs, complete with roaring and stomping around the kitchen. I watch her, laughing at her antics, but my mind is elsewhere. On Melissa, and what her obsession with this child might mean. On the lengths she's already gone to, and what she might do next. And James' obliviousness.

Dinner is a strained affair, at least for the adults. Lily, blissfully unaware of the tension, chatters happily about her day, her upcoming school trip, her friend Zoe's loose tooth that finally came out during lunch. James and I respond appropriately, ask the right questions, laugh at the right moments, but our eyes meet frequently over Lily's head, silent communications passing between us.

After dinner, once Lily is bathed and in bed, we reconvene in the living room. James brings out a bottle of wine and two glasses, pouring generously.

'Don't worry Rachel. I'm not going anywhere. Neither is Lily. If Melissa doesn't want you in our lives, then she's gone! Trust me. You mean so much to me... to us! You're the best.'

Ugh. Men are so annoying. We chat a little more about the plans for the weekend and I try to convince him that Lily meeting Melissa isn't a good idea. But I guess we will see. I can't be bothered to talk about Greg.

The drive home goes faster than I could imagine. I pull onto my drive and March straight in the house. James might be fooled, but not me.

I start with a fresh search, digging deeper than before. Melissa Chambers. HR professional. Childcare worker. Or at least, that's who she claims to be. But something tells me there's much more to this story. Much more that she's hiding.

I'm going to find it, whatever it takes.

CHAPTER 5

James

I stare at my phone, my thumb hovering over the screen. Melissa's latest message glows up at me: 'Please, James? Just a couple of hours at the weekend? I promise I won't try to replace you as Lily's favourite person x'

She's been persistent all week, messaging constantly about meeting Lily. Each text peppered with those little 'x' marks that I'm still trying to decipher. Are they friendly? Flirty? A habit? I've started adding them to my own messages just to mirror her, but it feels forced, like I'm speaking a language I barely understand.

Rachel's warnings echo in my head. The school incident. The childcare centre revelation. Melissa's apparent stalking of my social media. But Melissa had explanations for everything. The school visit wasn't her, clearly. She was at work. I didn't see her, but she rarely works in my building.

The company directory really did have her department wrong; she showed me her staff ID badge with 'Marketing' clearly printed on it. And as for the social media, well, she admitted she'd looked me up after we met in the stairwell, but insisted she hadn't been 'stalking' me for months.

My desk phone rings, jolting me from my thoughts. Another IT issue that needs my attention. I pocket my mobile and try to focus on work, but Melissa's request lingers in the back of my mind, mingling with Rachel's concerns and my own conflicted feelings.

By lunchtime, I've fixed three network problems, updated the security protocols on our server, and still haven't responded to Melissa's message. I hide in my office, unwrapping the sandwich I brought from home while I stare at my phone again.

The thing is, part of me wants to say yes. Not just because Melissa is attractive and interested in me; though there is that; but because there's a tiny, hopeful voice inside me that says maybe this could work. Maybe Melissa really is just eager to be part of my life, Lily included. Maybe Rachel is being overly protective, as she sometimes is with Lily.

I think about Sarah, about what she would do in this situation. She was always better at reading people than I am. She'd know if Melissa's interest was genuine or cause for concern.

My phone buzzes with another message, but it's not Melissa this time; it's Rachel.

'Have you given in to the child snatcher yet? x'

I smile despite myself. Rachel's dark humour has always been one of her most endearing qualities.

'Still deciding. She's very persistent.'

'So are mosquitoes, but you don't invite them in for dinner.'

'She explained the school thing. Said she was enquiring about volunteering.'

'And you believe that?'

I hesitate before responding. Do I? I'm not sure. But I also don't want to believe that someone could be as calculating as Rachel is suggesting. 'I don't know. Maybe.'

'James. Use your brain. Not the one in your pants. The one in your head.'

I laugh out loud at that. 'Very funny. But seriously, Rach, what if she's just really keen? What if I'm missing out on something good because I'm being paranoid?'

'Then you take it SLOW. Meet in a public place. Don't leave Lily alone with her. Watch how they interact.'

'Like a test?'

'Like a sensible precaution.'

I consider this. It seems reasonable. Meeting in public would be safer, and I'd be right there the whole time to see how Melissa is with Lily. If anything feels off, I can end it there and then.

'OK. You've convinced me. Public place it is.'

'Don't blame me when she tries to stuff Lily in a sack and run off with her.'

'Again with the child snatcher theme. You've been watching too many crime documentaries.'

'Just looking out for my favourite people x'

I put my phone down, my decision made. I'll agree to let Melissa meet Lily, but on my terms. Somewhere public, somewhere with an easy escape route if needed. Somewhere Lily would enjoy, regardless of how the meeting with Melissa goes.

I pick up my phone again and text Melissa. 'OK, we can meet this weekend. But not the zoo. How about Willow Farm Park? It has animals, a playground, and a nice café. Saturday around 11?'

The response is immediate, as if she's been waiting with her phone in hand. 'That's perfect!! I love that place! Can't wait to meet your little princess! She's going to love me, I know it! xxx'

Three kisses this time. Her enthusiasm practically radiates from the screen. I feel a mixture of emotions: excitement at the prospect of moving forward with this relationship, nervousness about introducing someone new into Lily's life, and a lingering unease that I can't quite place.

I send a quick text to Rachel before returning to work. 'Farm park on Saturday. Will keep you posted.'

'I'll have my rescue team on standby.'

The rest of the workday passes in a blur of IT emergencies and meetings. By the time I get home, pick Lily up from her after school club, and start dinner, I've almost managed to push thoughts of Saturday from my mind. Almost.

'Daddy, can we have pasta tomorrow?' Lily asks, carefully colouring in a picture at the kitchen table while I chop vegetables.

'Not tomorrow, pumpkin. Remember? We're going to the farm park.'

She looks up, eyes bright with excitement. 'With the baby lambs?'

'It might be too late in the year for lambs, but there'll be other animals. And the playground.'

'Is Rachel coming?'

My hands pause on the chopping board. 'Not this time. We're going to meet a... friend of mine. Her name is Melissa.'

Lily considers this, her head tilted to one side in that way that reminds me so much of Sarah. 'Is she nice?'

'I think so. She's excited to meet you.'

'Does she like animals?'

'She says she does.'

'OK,' Lily says, decision made with the easy acceptance of a five year old. 'Can I show her my new wellies?'

'Of course.'

'And can we have pasta for dinner tomorrow instead?'

I smile. 'Yes, we can have pasta for dinner tomorrow.'

'With cheese?'

'Definitely with cheese.'

Satisfied, she returns to her colouring. I watch her for a moment, her small face scrunched in concentration as she carefully stays within the lines. My heart swells with love for her, this amazing little person who somehow survived when Sarah didn't.

I finish making dinner, and we eat together while Lily tells me about her day at school. She's learning about space, and her excited chatter about planets and stars makes me smile. After dinner, bath, and two bedtime stories, I tuck her in with a kiss on her forehead.

'Goodnight, pumpkin. Love you more than all the stars in the sky.'

'Love you more than all the stripes on the zebras,' she responds, our familiar exchange warming my heart.

I close her door partially, leaving it open a crack the way she likes, and head downstairs. The house feels quiet, as it always does after Lily goes to bed. I pour myself a glass of wine and sink onto the sofa, my phone in hand.

There are three messages from Melissa, sent while I was putting Lily to bed.

'So excited for tomorrow! What time shall I meet you there?'

'Does Lily have any allergies I should know about? I wanted to bring her a little gift x'

'Also, what's her favourite colour? And animal? Just so I know what to talk to her about! x'

The questions seem innocent enough, the sort of things you might ask before meeting a child for the first time of course. I imagine Rachel would find an issue with it though.

'11am at the main entrance,' I reply. 'No allergies, but please don't bring gifts. It's too soon and I don't want her to expect presents from everyone she meets.'

There's a slight pause before her response comes through. 'Of course, I understand. Just excited! See you tomorrow! xxx'

I sit with my wine, the television playing in the background though I'm not really watching it. Tomorrow feels like a test, not just of Melissa and how she is with Lily, but of my judgment.

I think Rachel is wrong. I think Melissa is genuinely just an enthusiastic woman who happens to be interested in a single dad and his daughter... I don't want paranoia and overprotectiveness to hold me back from potential happiness. I finish my wine and head to bed, setting out clothes for tomorrow before I turn in. It's a small ritual that helps keep the morning chaos manageable. Lily's red wellies by the door, her favourite jumper and jeans laid out on her dresser. My own jeans and a casual shirt that Melissa once commented looked good on me. Prepared, but not too prepared. Casual, but not sloppy.

I go to sleep thinking of what Sarah would think of Melissa. I am sure she would have wanted me to move on at some point...

***

Saturday morning dawns bright and crisp, a great October day for a trip to the farm park. Lily is up early, bouncing with excitement as she pulls on her wellies and chatters about the animals we might see.

'Do you think they'll have pigs, Daddy? I want to see the pigs!'

'I'm sure they will,' I assure her, helping her with her coat. 'And sheep, and cows, and maybe even horses.'

'And I can show Melissa my wellies?'

'Yes, you can show Melissa your wellies.'

She nods, satisfied, and runs to get her backpack; a small unicorn bag that she insists on bringing everywhere these days. I check that I have everything we need: tissues, hand sanitiser, snacks, water bottles, sun cream (optimistic, perhaps, for October; but the weather forecast is good), and my phone, fully charged.

'Ready!' Lily announces, backpack on and a determined expression on her small face.

The drive to Willow Farm Park takes about twenty minutes. Lily sings along to her favourite songs in the back seat, occasionally interrupting herself to ask if Melissa likes animals, or music, or unicorns.

'I don't know, pumpkin,' I answer truthfully. 'You'll have to ask her yourself.'

The car park is already filling up when we arrive. Perfect, I think. Lots of people around. I help Lily out of her car seat and take her hand as we walk towards the entrance. She skips alongside me, wellies making satisfying clomping sounds on the gravel path.

Melissa is already waiting by the ticket booth, a vision in a casual outfit that somehow still manages to look put together. Her blonde hair is tied back in a ponytail, and she's wearing jeans, a warm looking jumper, and wellies of her own. I hate myself for noticing how good she looks in those jeans.

'There she is,' I tell Lily, pointing. 'That's Melissa.'

Lily observes her with the unflinching scrutiny only children can get away with. 'She's pretty,' she decides after a second.

'Yes, she is,' I agree, feeling my face go warmer.

Melissa spots us and waves, her face lighting up with a smile that seems genuine in its enthusiasm. She waits for us to approach rather than rushing over, which I appreciate. No overwhelming Lily straight off the bat.

'Hi,' she says, giving me a hug before crouching down to Lily's level. 'You must be Lily. I'm Melissa. Your dad has told me so much about you.'

Lily looks at her cautiously for a moment before announcing: 'I've got new wellies.'

Melissa takes this conversational offering seriously, examining the red boots with appropriate admiration. 'They're fantastic for puddle jumping!'

'That's what I said!' Lily agrees, looking pleased. She turns to me. 'Daddy, Melissa knows about puddle jumping.'

'Everyone should know about puddle jumping,' I say with a smile. 'It's an essential life skill.'

Melissa straightens up, her eyes meeting mine. 'It's really good to see you again, James. Thanks for inviting me today.'

There's a warmth in her voice that makes my heart beat a little faster. Despite my reservations, despite Rachel's warnings, I find myself genuinely glad to see her.

'Shall we go in?' I suggest, gesturing towards the entrance.

I pay for our tickets, waving away Melissa's offer to contribute. 'My idea, my treat,' I insist, though she protests until I relent and let her buy the map guide.

Lily impatiently tugs at my hand. 'Can we see the pigs first?'

'Of course we can,' Melissa says before I can respond. She looks at the map and points. 'They're just over there, past the shop!'

Lily beams at her, apparently won over by this knowledge

of pig locations. She lets go of my hand and, to my surprise, reaches for Melissa's. 'Let's go!'

Melissa glances at me, as if seeking permission. I smile, and she takes Lily's small hand in hers. 'Lead the way, Captain Lily.'

The morning unfolds better than I dared hope. Melissa is wonderful with Lily, answering her endless questions with patience, helping her spot animals, and showing genuine interest in her excited observations. She never talks down to her, never uses that artificial voice some adults adopt with children. Instead, she speaks to Lily like she's a person, which, of course, she is.

We visit the pig enclosure, where Melissa impresses Lily by knowing the difference between a Gloucester Old Spot and a Berkshire pig. We feed pellets to eager goats, Lily shrieking with laughter when one particularly bold goat tries to eat the sleeve of her coat. We watch the horses walk around, Melissa lifting Lily onto her shoulders so she can see better over the fence.

'Higher, higher!' Lily demands, and Melissa tries her best to comply, holding Lily's legs securely as she raises her up.

'Careful,' I caution, hovering nearby in case Lily falls.

'She's fine,' Melissa assures me. 'I've got her. Trust me.'

And strangely, I do. In that moment, seeing Melissa's careful handling of my daughter, her attentiveness to Lily's safety while still allowing her the thrill of adventure, I do trust her.

After the animal viewing, we stop at the café for lunch. Lily devours her chicken nuggets and chips, chattering between bites about the animals we've seen and which ones are her favourites.

'I liked the pigs best,' she declares. 'But the horses were good too. And the goats.'

'So basically all of them,' I tease.

'Not the cows,' she says decisively. 'They were boring.'

Melissa laughs. 'You're right. The cows were a bit boring today. Maybe they were tired.'

'Or maybe cows are just boring,' Lily suggests, reaching for her apple juice.

'Hmm, I don't know about that,' Melissa says. 'I grew up on a farm, and our cows could be quite interesting sometimes. One of them, Daisy, used to escape all the time. She'd find the weakest spot in the fence and squeeze through.'

Lily's eyes widen. 'Did she run away?'

'No, she just wanted to explore. We'd find her in the neighbour's garden, eating their flowers.' Melissa smiles at the memory. 'My dad used to say she was too curious for her own good.'

'Like me!' Lily says.

'Like you,' I agree, reaching over to ruffle her hair.

After lunch, we head to the playground. It's busy with children of all ages, screaming and laughing as they climb, swing, and slide. Lily immediately races for the climbing frame, her earlier hesitation around Melissa completely forgotten.

'She's amazing, James,' Melissa says as we watch Lily scramble up a rope ladder. 'So bright and confident.'

'She's the best thing in my life,' I say simply.

Melissa's hand finds mine, her fingers intertwining with my own. It feels nice. Right, somehow, despite the inner voice (which sounds suspiciously like Rachel) urging caution.

'I'm really glad you let me meet her,' Melissa says, her voice soft. 'It means a lot that you trust me that much.'

I watch Lily reach the top of the climbing frame, her face triumphant as she waves down at us. 'Daddy, Melissa, look at me!'

'We see you, pumpkin! Well done!'

'Be careful coming down!' Melissa calls, her voice carrying just the right note of caution without being overprotective.

Lily begins her descent, taking each step with careful consideration. Halfway down, she slips, catching herself but looking momentarily frightened. Before I can move, Melissa is there, positioning herself below Lily with arms outstretched, ready to catch her if needed.

'You're OK,' she says calmly. 'Take your time. One step at a time.'

Lily nods, her face serious with concentration, and continues down until she reaches the ground safely. She immediately looks to Melissa for approval.

'Brilliant climbing!' Melissa praises. 'That was a tricky bit, but you handled it perfectly.'

Lily beams, basking in the compliment. 'Can I go on the swings now?'

'Of course,' Melissa says, 'but remember to hold on tight with both hands.'

'I know that,' Lily says with the slightly exasperated tone of a child who thinks adults worry too much.

She races off towards the swings, leaving Melissa and me standing together, our hands still linked.

'You're good with her,' I say, surprising myself with how much I mean it.

Melissa shrugs, but looks pleased. 'Kids are just people. Smaller, more honest people, but still just people.'

We follow Lily to the swings, where she's struggling to climb onto one of the higher ones designed for older children.

'That one might be a bit big for you, Lily,' Melissa suggests. 'How about this one instead?' She points to a more appropriately sized swing.

'I want the big one,' Lily insists, still trying to haul herself up.

'Lily,' Melissa says, her voice firmer than I've heard it before. 'That swing is for bigger children. You could hurt yourself. Please use this one instead.'

I tense, waiting for Lily's reaction. She's at an age where being told 'no' sometimes results in tears or tantrums. To my surprise, she considers Melissa's words for a moment, then nods and moves to the smaller swing.

'Will you push me?' she asks Melissa.

'Of course I will,' Melissa says, her tone warm again. 'Hold on tight, now.'

As Melissa pushes Lily on the swing, I watch them together, trying to assess the situation objectively. Melissa is good with

Lily, there's no denying that. She's patient, engaging, and seems to genuinely enjoy Lily's company. The way she just handled the swing situation was impressive. Firm but kind, setting a boundary without creating conflict.

Rachel's suspicions gnaw at me still, even as I watch Melissa laugh with Lily, the two of them already developing inside jokes and shared experiences that feel alarmingly close to a bond forming.

I pull out my phone and, almost without thinking, text Rachel. 'Farm park going well. Melissa good with Lily. Firm but fair when Lily tried to use too big a swing. Not sure if that's good or concerning.'

Rachel's response is quick: 'Firm how? If she made Lily cry I'll smash her face in x'

I can't help but laugh at Rachel's overboard protectiveness. 'No tears! Just clear boundaries. Lily actually listened to her.'

'Well that's something I suppose. Still planning to stay all day?'

'Probably leave in an hour or so. Lily will be tired.'

'Text me when you're home safe.'

I put my phone in my pocket and rejoin Melissa and Lily at the swings. Lily is now trying to swing herself, throwing her legs around awkwardly, but with determination.

'Look, Daddy! I'm doing it by myself!'

'I can see that! You're getting so big, pumpkin.'

After the swings, Lily wants to try the slides. I take over supervision duty while Melissa goes to the toilet. Lily slides down the smallest one first, then works her way up to the tallest one, her confidence growing with each successful descent.

'Can I do the twisty one?' she asks, pointing to a spiral slide that looks a bit scary for her… or, rather, me.

'I don't know, Lily. That one's for bigger kids.'

'Melissa said I'm brave,' she argues.

I hesitate. 'OK, but I'm coming up with you.'

I follow her up the stairs to the top of the slide, watching as she positions herself at the entrance to the spiral. There's a moment of hesitation, a touch of fear in her eyes.

'You don't have to do it if you don't want to,' I reassure her. 'We can go back down the stairs.'

She shakes her head, determination setting in. 'I want to do it. I'm brave.'

'You're the bravest,' I agree. 'Ready?'

She nods, and I give her a gentle push to start her off. I watch her disappear into the spiral, hearing her shouts of excitement echo inside the tube. I rush back down the stairs to meet her at the bottom, arriving just as she shoots out of the exit, her face lit up with triumph.

'I did it, Daddy! I did the big slide!'

'You sure did, pumpkin! I'm so proud of you!'

Melissa returns from the restroom, and Lily immediately runs to her. 'Melissa! I went on the twisty slide! The big one!'

'Wow!' Melissa exclaims, looking genuinely impressed. 'That's amazing! Was it scary?'

'A little bit,' Lily admits. 'But I did it because I'm brave.'

'You are incredibly brave,' Melissa agrees. 'Probably the bravest girl in the whole park.'

Lily beams at this assessment, then suddenly yawns, the excitement of the day catching up with her.

'I think someone's getting tired,' I observe. 'Maybe time to head home soon?'

'Nooo,' Lily protests, but her eyelids are already looking heavy. 'I want to stay with Melissa more.'

'We can see Melissa another time,' I say carefully, glancing at Melissa to gauge her reaction.

Her smile is warm. 'Only if you and your dad want to. I've had a wonderful time today.'

'We do! Don't we, Daddy?'

I nod, finding that I mean it. 'We do, but for now, let's say goodbye and thank Melissa for spending the day with us.'

Lily surprises both Melissa and me by throwing her arms around Melissa's waist in a hug. 'Bye, Melissa. Thank you for showing me the pigs and pushing me on the swing and everything.'

Melissa looks a little stunned, then hugs Lily back, her expression so genuinely moved that it tugs at my heart. 'Thank you for letting me join you today, Lily. It was one of the funnest days I've had in a long time.'

We walk back to the car park together, Lily still chattering about the animals and the playground. At my car, there's an awkward moment as we say our goodbyes.

'I'd better get driving so she can nap,' I say, helping Lily into her car seat.

'Of course,' Melissa agrees. 'She's had a big day.' She walks closer and plants a quick kiss on my cheek. 'Thank you, James. Really.'

'I'll text you later?' I suggest.

'I'd like that.'

I watch her walk to her own car before getting into the driver's seat. Lily is already half asleep in the back, clutching the farm park map still.

'Did you have fun today, pumpkin?' I ask as I start the car.

'Mmm hmm,' she murmurs sleepily. 'I like Melissa. She knows about pigs and puddles.'

'Yes, she does,' I agree, pulling out of the car park.

Lily falls asleep within minutes, the excitement of the day finally overwhelming her. I drive with a podcast on, paying no attention, my thoughts going over everything that happened today. Melissa was great with Lily, better than I expected. She was patient, engaging, and seemed to genuinely enjoy spending time with her. The firm moment with the swing hadn't felt off to me. It felt like an appropriate boundary setting from an adult who cares about a child's safety.

When we get home, Lily is still asleep. I manage to pull her wellies off and carry her up to her bedroom without waking her, luckily. Bit of a danger nap, she will probably be up all night now… but oh well.

I text Rachel once I'm back downstairs. 'Home safe. Lily asleep. Day went really well actually. Melissa was great with her.'

The reply comes a few minutes later. 'Glad to hear it. Maybe I was wrong about her. Just be careful, OK?'

'Always am. Greg back yet?'

'Still in Singapore. Now going on to Malaysia for two more weeks.'

'That's rough. Want to come for dinner tomorrow? Lily's been asking for you.'

'Sure. The usual time?'

'Perfect. See you then x'

I put my phone down and make myself a cup of tea, enjoying the rare quiet of the house while Lily naps. The day has left me feeling cautiously optimistic. Maybe Melissa really is just a nice woman who's interested in me and, by extension, Lily. Maybe Rachel's concerns, while well intentioned, *were* overblown.

My phone buzzes with a message from Melissa. 'Had such a wonderful time today. Lily is amazing, James. So bright and full of life. Thank you for letting me meet her x'

I smile at the message, warmth spreading through me. 'Thank you for being so good with her. She's already asking when she can see you again.'

'Really? That makes me so happy! I'd love to see her (and you, of course) again soon x'

'Let's plan something for next weekend? Maybe something indoors in case the weather turns?'

'Sure. Let me know what works for you two x'

Lily sleeps longer than expected, not waking until nearly five in the evening. She comes downstairs rubbing her eyes, her hair sticking up in odd directions from her nap.

'Did I sleep too long, Daddy?'

'No, pumpkin. You were tired from all that playing and animal watching.'

'Is Melissa here?'

'No, she went home, remember? But she said to tell you she had a wonderful time today.'

Lily nods. 'Can we have pasta now? With cheese like you

promised?'

'Absolutely.'

I make her favourite pasta dish while she sits at the kitchen table, drawing pictures of the animals we saw today. She's focused on getting the spots on the pigs just right, tongue between her teeth in concentration.

'Is Melissa your girlfriend now?' she asks suddenly, not looking up from her drawing.

The question catches me off guard. She doesn't know what the concept of a girlfriend is. 'Um, not exactly. We're friends who are getting to know each other better.'

'Like you and Rachel?'

I think for a second. 'Not quite the same. Rachel and I have been friends for a very long time. I've only just met Melissa.'

'But you like her?'

'Yes, I do like her.'

'I like her too,' Lily declares, adding another large spot to her pig. 'She's nice and she knows about animals.'

'That she does.'

After we eat, we watch a film together, Lily curled up against my side on the sofa. She starts to fall asleep before the end, clearly still tired from our day out, despite her danger nap. I carry her upstairs, change her into pyjamas with the practiced ease of a single parent, and tuck her into bed.

'Goodnight, pumpkin,' I whisper, kissing her forehead. 'Love you more than all the stars in the sky.'

She murmurs something I don't understand in response, already deep in sleep.

Back downstairs, I pour myself a glass of wine and sit on the sofa, replaying the day in my mind. I pick up my phone and text Melissa. 'Lily's finally asleep. She had a great time today. Thank you again for being so wonderful with her.'

'It was my pleasure, truly. She's a special little girl, James. You must be so proud x'

'I am. Every day.'

There's a pause before her next message comes through.

'Would it be terribly forward of me to say I'm missing you already?'

My heart rate picks up. 'Not terribly forward. I'm missing you too.'

Another pause. 'I keep thinking about that goodbye kiss. Wish it could have been more than just a peck on the cheek x'

Heat rises to my face. We're moving into territory we haven't touched on yet. Despite our date and today's outing, we've only shared those brief, tame kisses.

'Maybe next time it can be,' I reply, feeling suddenly bold.

'Why wait for next time?'

I stare at the message, my pulse rises fast. 'What do you mean?'

'I mean... Lily's asleep. I'm all alone at home thinking about you. I wouldn't mind finishing off an amazing day by seeing you again tonight x'

The suggestion sends a bolt of both excitement and anxiety through me. 'Tonight? But Lily is here.'

'Lily is sound asleep, you said. I could come over... just for a little while. I'll be quiet. She'd never know x'

I hesitate, reason battling with desire. It's been so long since I've been with someone. Years of loneliness, of focusing solely on being a dad and nothing else. The thought of Melissa here, in my home, in my bed... it's intoxicating, and terrifying. Is it the right thing to do? We've only been on one proper date. I have only just introduced her to Lily. Isn't this moving too fast? I glance at Rachel's last message, still open on my phone. *Just be careful, OK?* But Melissa clearly isn't some predator targeting my daughter, as Rachel fears. She's a woman who's shown herself to be kind, patient, and genuinely interested in both me and Lily. A woman who I'm undeniably attracted to, who seems just as attracted to me.

'I'd like that,' I text back before I can overthink it anymore. 'If you're sure?'

'Very sure. Address? x'

I send her my address, then immediately panic about the

state of the house. It's not terrible because I've learned to keep things relatively tidy as a single parent, but it's certainly not prepared for a romantic guest. And my bedroom? When was the last time I changed the sheets? Shit! I dash around the house, picking up Lily's toys, straightening cushions, and giving all the surfaces a quick wipe. I run upstairs and change my bedsheets, thankful that I did the washing yesterday. I brush my teeth, consider and reject the idea of a quick shower, and change into a fresh shirt.

By the time Melissa texts to say she's outside, I've worked myself into a state of nervous anticipation. I check on Lily one more time. Still deeply asleep. I head downstairs to let Melissa in. She's standing on my doorstep, looking slightly nervous but also determined. She's changed since the farm park, now wearing a dress that hugs her figure in all the right places.

'Hi.' she says, voice soft.

'Hi,' is all I can reply. I step aside to let her in, then close the door behind her. We stand in my hallway for a second, the silence raising the tension.

'I don't normally do this,' I say finally. 'I mean, with Lily upstairs and...'

'We can just talk if you want,' she offers. 'Have a glass of wine. No pressure.'

But the way she looks at me, the way her hand comes to rest on my chest, makes it clear that talking isn't what either of us really wants.

'I've got wine,' I manage, leading her to the kitchen.

I pour us each a glass, hyper aware of her presence, of the way she looks around my home with curious eyes.

'Your house is lovely,' she says, accepting the wine. 'Very you.'

'Is that an insult?' I joke, but I am genuinely curious.

'No silly! Warm. Comfortable. A bit serious but with touches of fun... sorry. That sounded less cheesy in my head.'

I laugh, feeling some of the tension ease. 'No, I like it. Thank you.'

She takes a step closer to me, closing the distance between us. 'I had a really good time today, James. Not just with Lily, but with you.'

'Me too,' I admit.

Her free hand comes up to rest on my cheek. 'You're a good dad. The way you are with her... it's beautiful to watch.'

Something about the sincerity in her voice loosens a knot inside me that I didn't realise was there. The constant fear that I'm not doing enough, not being enough for Lily on my own.

'Thank you,' is all I can say. 'That means a lot.'

Melissa sets her wine glass down on the counter and takes mine from my hand, placing it beside hers. Then she steps closer, her eyes never leaving mine.

'You deserve to be happy too, James,' she whispers. 'Not just to be a dad, but to be a man. A man who's wanted.'

Her words hit something inside me, a feeling I've pushed down for years while focusing solely on being a father. When her lips meet mine, it feels like coming up for air after being underwater for too long. The kiss is gentle at first, then deepens as her arms slip around my neck. I pull her closer, my hands finding her waist, then the small of her back. It's been so long since I've held someone like this, since I've felt this rush of desire and connection. The loneliness of the past few years seems to melt away under her touch.

We break apart, both slightly breathless. Melissa's eyes are dark, her cheeks flushed.

'Maybe we should move somewhere more comfortable?' she suggests, her voice low.

I nod, taking her hand and leading her to the living room. A voice in the back of my mind, one that sounds suspiciously like Rachel's, urges caution, reminds me that Lily is asleep upstairs, that this is all moving very fast, but Melissa's hand in mine feels right, and the way she looks at me makes me feel good in a way I haven't in years.

We sit on the sofa, close enough that our thighs touch. Melissa tucks some of her hair behind her ear, suddenly looking almost shy.

'I don't want you to think I do this sort of thing all the time,' she says. 'Coming over late at night...'

'I don't,' I assure her. 'And for what it's worth, I definitely don't make a habit of this either.'

She smiles. 'Good. Because I really like you, James. This isn't just...' She gestures vaguely between us. 'It's not just this.'

'I like you too,' I admit. 'But I have to think about Lily. She has to come first in everything.'

'I understand that. I wouldn't want it any other way.' Melissa takes my hand, her fingers intertwining with mine. 'The way you love her, how protective you are; it's part of what makes you so special.'

Her words soothe something in me, a fear that wanting something for myself might somehow make me less of a father to Lily.

Melissa leans in and kisses me again, more insistently this time. I respond by pulling her closer until she's practically in my lap. Her hands slip beneath my shirt, cool against my skin, and I shiver at her touch.

'Is this okay?' she whispers against my lips.

'More than okay,' I manage.

We lose ourselves in each other, the world shrinking down to just the two of us on my sofa. Her dress rides up as she shifts to straddle me, her hair falling forward to frame her face. I've never seen anyone so beautiful.

A creak on the stairs freezes us both in place.

'Daddy?'

Lily's small voice sends a jolt of panic through me. Melissa jumps off my lap, hastily straightening her dress while I try to compose myself.

'In here, pumpkin,' I call, my voice unnaturally high. I clear my throat. 'What are you doing up?'

Lily appears in the doorway, clutching her stuffed elephant and looking confused. Her eyes widen when she spots Melissa.

'Melissa came back,' she says, stating the obvious in that

63

way children do.

'Yes, she... we were just having a chat after you went to bed,' I explain, feeling my face heat up. I've never been caught in a compromising position by my daughter before. It's a parenting milestone I wasn't prepared for.

'Why?' Lily asks, direct as always.

Melissa jumps in, her voice calm and natural despite the awkwardness of the situation. 'I forgot to give your dad something important at the farm park, so I stopped by to drop it off.'

'What thing?' Lily asks, immediately curious.

Melissa hesitates, caught in her improvised lie. I jump in to rescue her.

'Just some boring grown up papers. Why are you out of bed, Lily? Did you have a bad dream?'

Lily nods, her attention shifting back to her night time distress. 'The dinosaur was chasing me again.'

'Oh no, not the dinosaur,' I say sympathetically, opening my arms. She comes to me immediately, climbing into my lap where Melissa had been moments before. 'You know dinosaurs aren't around anymore, right? They can't hurt you.'

'But they were real once,' Lily points out, snuggling against my chest. 'And really big.'

'They were,' Melissa agrees, 'but they lived a very, very long time ago. Millions of years before there were any people.'

Lily considers this, then looks up at Melissa. 'Did you have bad dreams when you were little?'

The question seems to catch Melissa off guard. 'Yes, I did actually. I used to dream about wolves.'

'Real wolves?'

'Real in my dream, but not real in my room,' Melissa clarifies. 'My mum used to tell me to imagine I had a magic shield that no bad dreams could get through.'

Lily's eyes widen with interest. 'Did it work?'

'Sometimes. And when it didn't, I remembered that dreams can't really hurt you, even when they're scary.'

I watch this interaction with a mixture of emotions. There's embarrassment at being caught in a compromising position, for sure, but there's also something touching about seeing Melissa engage with Lily's concerns so naturally, even in this awkward moment.

'I think it's time to get you back to bed,' I say to Lily, standing up with her still in my arms. 'Say goodnight to Melissa.'

'Goodnight, Melissa,' Lily says obediently. Then, 'Are you going to be here in the morning?'

The innocent question hangs in the air. Melissa looks to me, clearly unsure how to respond.

'No, Melissa's going to go home to her own bed,' I say firmly. 'She just stopped by for a quick visit.'

Lily accepts this without question, resting her head on my shoulder with the easy trust of childhood. 'Can she come for breakfast another day?'

'Maybe sometime,' I hedge. 'Now, let's get you back to bed.'

I carry Lily upstairs, leaving Melissa sitting somewhat awkwardly on the sofa. I take my time settling Lily back in, making sure she feels safe and secure before eventually leaving her room, the door cracked open just the way she likes it.

When I return downstairs, Melissa is standing by the front door, her bag already over her shoulder.

'I should go,' she says quietly.

'You don't have to,' I begin, but she shakes her head.

'I think I should. This isn't... I mean, with Lily awake now, it doesn't feel right to stay.'

I nod, understanding her point even as the disappointment settles. 'I'm sorry about that. She doesn't usually wake up in the night anymore.'

'Don't apologise. She's a child having a bad dream. She needed her dad.' Melissa steps closer and places a gentle kiss on my cheek. 'That's one of the things I admire about you, James. You're a good father. Lily always comes first.'

Her understanding eases some of the awkwardness. 'Thank you for being so good with her. Even just now, with the dinosaur dreams.'

'She's easy to be good with,' Melissa says with a smile. 'Smart and funny and curious.'

'Like someone else was too curious for her own good?' I tease, recalling her story about the cow from earlier.

Melissa laughs softly. 'Maybe. Though I hope I've learned a bit more impulse control since then.'

We stand in the hallway, reluctant to say goodbye despite the interrupted evening. Finally, Melissa sighs.

'I really should go. It's getting late, and you have a little girl who might need you again tonight.'

'You're right.' I open the door for her. 'I'll call you tomorrow?'

'I'd like that.' She kisses me one more time, lingering just long enough to leave me wanting more. 'Goodnight, James.'

'Goodnight, Melissa.'

I watch her walk to her car and drive away before closing the door. Leaning against it, I let out a long breath. The evening hadn't gone as planned, but somehow I don't feel as disappointed as I might have expected. There's something comforting about how naturally Melissa handled the situation with Lily, how she understood that my daughter's needs had to come first. Rachel's warnings still echo in my mind, but they're growing fainter. Today, at both the farm park and here at home, I've seen a Melissa who seems genuinely caring, patient, and understanding; not at all the manipulative predator Rachel feared.

I tidy up our barely touched wine glasses and head upstairs to check on Lily one more time before going to bed myself. She's sleeping peacefully now, her teddy Daddy Bunny clutched tight against her chest. Whatever happens with Melissa, whether it develops into something serious or fizzles out, Lily will always be my priority, but for the first time in years, I allow myself to hope that maybe, just maybe, there's room in our lives for someone else too. Someone who understands what matters most to me, who fits into our world without trying to change it.

As I climb into my own bed, I find myself looking forward to tomorrow's call with Melissa, and to whatever might come next.

CHAPTER 6

Rachel

'And then Melissa got me a new dress! A pink one with sparkles!' Lily twirls around my kitchen, showing off yet another new outfit that definitely wasn't chosen by James. 'She says I look like a princess!'

I force a smile, placing a plate of dinosaur shaped chicken nuggets in front of her. 'That's nice. Is this dress number three or four this month?'

'Umm...' Lily counts on her fingers, face deep in concentration. 'I think five? There was the pink one, and the blue one with flowers, and the yellow one, and the purple one with the butterflies, and now this sparkly one!'

Five dresses in three weeks. That's excessive by anyone's standards, especially for a five year old who'll outgrow them in months. I glance at James, who's busy texting, undoubtedly Melissa, with that dumb smile that's become a permanent fixture on his face lately.

'That's a lot of dresses,' I say, keeping my tone as light as possible. 'Melissa must really like shopping.'

'She says every little girl deserves pretty things,' Lily announces, stabbing a nugget with her fork. 'And that I look extra special in pink.'

James finally looks up from his phone. 'Melissa's just being generous. It's sweet.'

'It's something,' I reply, turning back to the sink to hide my expression.

It's been three weeks since the farm park outing that apparently convinced James that Melissa was perfectly normal and not at all obsessed with his daughter. Three weeks of Melissa rapidly inserting herself into their lives with the precision of a surgeon and the determination of a bulldozer. Dinners, weekend outings, movie nights, and now, apparently, a wardrobe overhaul for Lily.

'Oh, before I forget,' James says, putting his phone down. 'Melissa was wondering if we could all have dinner together this weekend. She'd like to get to know you better.'

I nearly drop the plate I'm washing. 'Me? Why?'

'Because you're important to us,' James says, as if it's the most obvious thing in the world. 'You're Lily's... well, you're family. Melissa wants to make an effort.'

I turn to face him, drying my hands on a tea towel. 'How thoughtful of her.'

Either James doesn't notice the sarcasm in my voice or he chooses to ignore it. 'I thought we could go to that Italian place you like. Saturday night? Melissa's already offered to book it.'

'Of course she has,' I say, unable to keep the edge from my voice. 'Always so... helpful.'

James gives me a look that says he's hearing my tone but choosing not to address it. 'So, are you free?'

I glance at Lily, happily munching her nuggets, blissfully unaware of the undercurrents between the adults. The last thing I want is to spend an evening making small talk with Melissa, watching her play the potential stepmum role; but I also don't want to miss a chance to observe her up close. To gather more evidence that something isn't right.

'I suppose I could rearrange some things,' I say finally.

'Great!' James beams. 'Melissa will be thrilled.'

I bet she will, I think, turning back to the dishes. Thrilled to size up Lily's competition. That's what I am now, at least in

Melissa's eyes; competition. I've seen the way she looks at me when she thinks no one's watching, the calculation behind her smile. The way she's started mentioning how 'helpful' it must be for James to have a friend who can babysit so often, with just enough emphasis on the word 'friend' to make her meaning clear.

'Rachel, can we play Snap after dinner?' Lily asks, interrupting my thoughts.

'Of course we can, love.' I smile at her, my irritation momentarily forgotten. 'Finish your broccoli first, though.'

She pulls a face but obediently stabs a piece of broccoli. 'Melissa says green food makes you grow taller.'

Another Melissa pearl of wisdom. How convenient that she's always right about everything.

'Melissa says, Melissa thinks, Melissa bought me...' It's all I hear from both James and Lily these days. Melissa has somehow managed to become the centre of their universe in less than a month. It would be impressive if it weren't so unsettling. Annoyingly, I still haven't found much concrete evidence of her deception beyond the lies about her job and the weird school incident. Her social media remains sparse and heavily curated, offering little insight into her past or her motives. But my gut feeling remains unshaken; there's something off about Melissa Chambers, something that goes beyond simple jealousy on my part.

'Hey,' James says softly, coming to stand beside me at the sink. 'You okay? You seem a bit... tense.'

I shrug, keeping my voice low so Lily won't hear. 'I'm fine. Just tired. Work's been busy.'

'How's Greg?'

The question catches me off guard. Greg and his extended business trip have been the least of my concerns lately. 'Still in Malaysia. Probably coming back next week.'

'That's a long trip,' James observes. 'Must be tough.'

'We're managing,' I say vaguely, because the truth is I've barely noticed Greg's absence. Our nightly calls have dwindled to occasional texts, and I find I don't really mind. What does that say about our relationship? Too much to think about with Melissa.

'Well, it'll be good for you to have some adult company on Saturday,' James says, clearly trying to sell me on the dinner idea. 'And I really think you'll like Melissa once you get to know her properly.'

I seriously doubt that, but I force a smile. 'I'm sure it'll be lovely.'

Dinner finished, Lily and I settle into our usual game of Snap while James cleans up. There's something soothing about the simple card game, about Lily's delighted giggles when she wins a round, about the familiar rhythm of our time together. I cherish these moments, store them up like treasures I'm afraid might soon be taken away. That's what this feels like. Like Melissa is slowly, systematically edging me out of James and Lily's lives. Replacing their familiar routines with new ones that include her instead of me. Inserting herself into the spaces I've occupied for the past five years.

'Snap!' Lily shouts triumphantly, her small hand slapping down on the matching cards.

'You're too quick for me,' I laugh, surrendering the pile of cards.

'Melissa taught me a trick,' Lily says, gathering the cards. 'She says to watch the corners of the cards when they're being put down.'

UGH. Of *course* she did. Even my fucking card games with Lily aren't safe from Melissa's influence.

By the time James is ready to take Lily home, I've managed to regain my composure. I hug Lily goodbye, accepting her sloppy kiss on my cheek with a genuine smile.

'See you Saturday,' James reminds me as they leave. 'Seven o'clock.'

'Looking forward to it,' I lie, closing the door behind them.

***

Saturday evening arrives all too quickly. I stand in front of my wardrobe, trying to decide what to wear for this dinner from hell. Something casual enough to show I'm not trying too hard, but nice enough that Melissa can't make any subtle digs about my appearance. I settle on dark jeans and a simple blue blouse that James once said brought out my eyes. My phone buzzes as I'm applying mascara: Greg, finally video calling after days of silence.

'Hey,' I answer, propping the phone against my mirror. 'Where have you been?'

Greg's face appears on screen, tired but smiling. 'Sorry, babe. The signal here is terrible, and the schedule has been brutal. How are you?'

'Fine. Just getting ready to go out, actually.'

His eyebrows rise slightly. 'Oh? Where to?'

'Dinner with James and his new girlfriend.' I try to keep the distaste from my voice. 'She wants to "get to know me better."'

'Ah.' Greg's expression shifts subtly. 'James actually has a girlfriend now? That's... wow.'

There's something in his tone I can't quite place. 'Is that a problem?'

'No, no,' he says quickly. 'Just surprised. You've always said he's not the dating type.'

'He wasn't. Until Melissa appeared.'

Greg studies me through the screen. 'You don't sound thrilled about it.'

'I don't trust her,' I admit. 'There's something off about her.'

'Off how?'

'She's too interested in Lily. Too perfect. Too... everything.'

Greg is quiet for a moment. 'Are you sure this isn't about something else? Maybe you're just used to having Lily to yourself.'

'It's not like that,' I say, irritation flaring. 'I'm concerned about Lily.'

'If you say so,' Greg replies, clearly unconvinced. 'Look, I should go. Early start tomorrow. Have fun at dinner.'

'Thanks,' I say flatly. 'Call me tomorrow?'

'I'll try.' He blows a kiss at the screen. 'Miss you.'

The call ends, leaving me staring at my reflection. Is Greg right? Am I just jealous of her and Lily's relationship? No. This is about protecting Lily from whatever Melissa's game is.

I finish my makeup, grab my bag, and head out. The Italian restaurant is only a fifteen minute drive from my house, but I take my time, mentally preparing myself for the evening ahead. By the time I pull into the car park, I've adopted what I think of as my *professional* face; pleasant, engaged, but carefully guarded.

They're already at the table when I arrive. James, Lily, and Melissa, looking like a lovely little family. The sight sends an unexpected pain through my chest. Melissa is wearing a stylish dress that probably cost more than my entire outfit, her blonde hair falling in perfect waves around her shoulders. She's leaning towards Lily, helping her colour on the kids' menu, while James watches them with a soft expression I recognise all too well.

'Rachel!' Lily spots me first, her face lighting up. She jumps down from her chair and runs to hug me, a welcome that eases some of the tension in my shoulders. 'Look, I'm wearing my new dress!'

'I see that,' I say, admiring the pink, sparkly number I've heard so much about. 'You look beautiful.'

'Melissa says pink is definitely my colour,' Lily informs me importantly.

'Melissa's right about that,' I agree, glancing up to meet the woman's gaze across the restaurant. There's something calculated in her eyes, a subtle challenge disguised as warmth.

Melissa rises as I approach the table, her smile perfectly calibrated. Warm, but not too friendly. 'Rachel! I'm so glad you could make it. James has told me so much about you.'

I'm sure he has. 'All good things, I hope.'

'Of course.' She gestures to the empty seat across from her. 'Please, sit. We've only just ordered drinks.'

JAMES

Rachel looks great tonight. She's made an effort, which I appreciate. This dinner means a lot to me. Melissa has been so eager to get to know Rachel better, understanding how important she is to Lily and me. It's touching, really, how invested Melissa is in making sure all the important people in my life get along.

'Glad you made it,' I say, giving Rachel a quick hug. 'Traffic okay?'

'Fine,' Rachel replies, taking her seat. 'Sorry I'm a bit late.'

'Not at all,' Melissa says smoothly. 'It gave us time to settle Lily with her colouring.'

I smile gratefully at Melissa. She's so thoughtful that way, always making sure Lily is comfortable and entertained. The way she's taken to Lily, and Lily to her, has been one of the most wonderful surprises of our relationship.

The waiter arrives with our drinks. Wine for the adults, apple juice for Lily. He takes Rachel's order. As he leaves, there's a brief silence that feels slightly awkward, but that's to be expected. They're still getting to know each other.

'So,' I say, trying to get the conversation flowing, 'Melissa was just telling us about her family's farm. Apparently, they raised sheep as well as cows.'

RACHEL

'How interesting,' I say, taking a sip of my wine. 'Where was this farm?'

I watch her carefully. I've been looking into Melissa's background and found precisely fuck all about any farm.

'Devon,' Melissa answers promptly. 'Just outside Exeter. My parents sold it when I was twelve, but those early years really shaped me.'

No hesitation. No tells of lying. Either she's practiced this story thoroughly or it's true. I need to dig deeper.

'I'm sure they did,' I murmur. 'And what brought you to our little corner of the world?'

'Work, initially,' she says, her hand falling casually on James's forearm. A possessive gesture that sends a flare of irritation through me. 'But now I'm finding other reasons to stay.'

I resist the urge to roll my eyes. Instead, I turn my attention to Lily, who's busily colouring a cartoon dragon. 'That's looking fantastic, love. Is it for my fridge?'

'No, it's for Melissa's fridge,' Lily corrects me. 'I did one for you last week.'

The words hit harder than they should. I hide my hurt behind another sip of wine. 'So you did. Sorry, I forgot.'

Melissa smiles, a touch of triumph in her eyes. 'Lily's quite the artist. I've been thinking of signing her up for children's art classes at the community centre. They start next month.'

JAMES

Rachel seems interested in Melissa's background, which is a good sign. I want them to connect, to find common ground. Melissa's childhood on the farm is so different from our urban upbringings, but it explains her practical nature, her ease with Lily.

I notice Rachel looking at Lily's drawing. It's good of her to take an interest, even though I can tell she's a bit surprised when Lily says it's for Melissa's fridge. It's an adjustment for all of us, I suppose, having someone new in our lives.

'That sounds like a big commitment,' Rachel says, glancing my way. Is she concerned about the art classes? I can't quite read her expression.

'Oh, I don't mind,' Melissa says cheerfully. 'I think it's important to nurture children's talents early. Don't you?'

I'm about to agree when the waiter returns with bread and olives. Rachel seems to welcome the interruption.

'How's work, James?' she asks. 'Still having issues with the new server?'

I'm grateful for the familiar topic. 'God, yes. The migration's been a nightmare...'

I launch into an explanation of our IT issues, perhaps in more detail than anyone actually wants. Melissa listens attentively, asking questions at all the right moments. She's genuinely interested in my work, which still surprises me sometimes.

RACHEL

I watch Melissa as James rambles about his server problems. She's playing the role of attentive girlfriend perfectly, nodding at appropriate intervals, asking just the right questions to seem engaged without derailing his explanation. It's practiced, performative. I just need to catch her in a slip up.

'You must be so glad to have someone who understands computers so well, Lily,' she says when James finally finishes. 'Your daddy can fix anything, can't he?'

'Rachel can fix computers too,' Lily pipes up loyally. 'She fixed my tablet when it wouldn't turn on.'

I manage to stop a smile of satisfaction as Melissa's expression falters momentarily.

'Did she now?' Melissa's smile tightens. 'How useful.'

'Rachel's pretty useful all around,' James says, giving me a fond look. 'Don't know what we'd do without her.'

'I'm sure you'd manage,' Melissa says jokingly. 'After all, you have me now.'

They laugh, I manage to force out a fake one, but the implication still hangs in the air, so blatant I'm surprised James doesn't catch it. But he's already distracted by Lily tugging at his sleeve, asking for help reaching her juice.

JAMES

The dinner is going well, I think. Melissa and Rachel seem to be finding their rhythm, though there's a formality between them that I hope will ease with time. Melissa is making such an effort, asking Rachel about her work, her hobbies, even Greg. It's considerate of her to take an interest in Rachel's relationship too.

'It must be so hard, having a boyfriend who's never around,' Melissa says sympathetically. 'James was saying he's been gone for what, five weeks now?'

'Something like that,' Rachel replies, cutting into her lasagna with perhaps more force than necessary. Is she sensitive about Greg's absence? I should have warned Melissa that might be a sore point.

'His work takes him all over,' Rachel adds.

'I couldn't do it,' Melissa sighs, leaning slightly against my shoulder. 'I'm much too needy. I want my person right here, where I can see them.'

She gives my hand a gentle squeeze, and I feel a rush of warmth. After years of being alone, it's still novel and wonderful to be someone's 'person' again.

RACHEL

I nearly choke on my lasagne as Melissa delivers another carefully calculated barb. 'Some relationships thrive on a bit of distance,' I say, trying for a light tone.

'Maybe,' Melissa concedes with a smile that doesn't reach her eyes. 'But then, some people might wonder why you'd choose a relationship like that when there are... closer options.'

Is she really implying what I think she's implying? I look at James, but he's helping Lily cut her pizza and hasn't registered the exchange. Oblivious as ever when it comes to women's verbal sparring.

'I think people should choose relationships that make them happy,' I say carefully. 'Whatever form those take.'

'Absolutely,' Melissa agrees, all wide eyed innocence. 'As long as they're being honest with themselves about what, or *who*, truly makes them happy.'

Before I can formulate a response that won't start an outright war at the dinner table, Melissa excuses herself to visit the ladies' room. As soon as she's out of earshot, James turns to me with an expectant smile.

'So? What do you think? You two seem to be getting on great!'

JAMES

I've been watching Rachel and Melissa interact all evening, and I'm relieved to see they're making an effort with each other. There's been pleasant conversation, polite questions, even a few shared smiles. It means a lot to me that the two most important women in my life are getting along.

When Melissa steps away to the restroom, I take the opportunity to check in with Rachel directly.

'So? What do you think? You two seem to be getting on great!'

The look she gives me is perplexing. Disbelief, maybe? Or frustration?

'Great isn't the word I'd use,' she says carefully, looking at Lily who's absorbed in her drawing.

I frown, confused by her response. 'What do you mean? She's been lovely.'

'James...' Rachel leans forward, lowering her voice. 'She's been marking her territory all night. Surely you can see that?'

'What are you talking about?' This comes as a complete surprise. I thought they were getting along fine.

'The comments about how she's replaced me. The digs about Greg. The way she keeps touching you every time I speak.'

I replay the evening's conversation in my mind, but I don't see what Rachel's seeing. 'I think you're reading too much into things. She's just trying to fit in.'

RACHEL

'By pushing me out?' I can't keep the edge from my voice.

He sighs, that familiar 'Rachel is overreacting' sigh I've known for years. 'Rachel, I know this is an adjustment for everyone. But Melissa's important to me, and I really want you two to get along.'

'I'm trying,' I insist. 'But there's still something off about her. The constant gifts for Lily, the way she's rushing everything...'

'Being generous isn't a crime,' James says, a hint of defensiveness entering his voice. 'And she's not rushing anything. We're taking things at our own pace.'

'A pace that includes her planning Lily's activities for the next month? Buying her an entire new wardrobe? That doesn't strike you as moving a bit fast?'

He shakes his head. 'She's just enthusiastic. It's one of the things I like about her.'

'Look, James; '

I stop as Melissa returns, her smile fixed in place as she slides back into her seat. 'Did I miss anything exciting?'

'Not at all,' James says quickly. 'Just chatting.'

I watch her eyes dart between us, assessing. She knows exactly what we were discussing. I can see it in the slight tightening around her eyes, the way she positions herself just a fraction closer to James than before. The game is on, and she knows I'm playing.

JAMES

The rest of the meal passes pleasantly enough. Melissa shares stories about her work, Rachel talks about a book she's reading, and Lily keeps us all entertained with her school adventures. By dessert, I'm feeling good. There's still some reservations between Rachel and Melissa, but that's normal. It takes time to build a friendship.

I notice Rachel make a friendly remark toward Melissa.

'I like your dress, Melissa,' she says. 'The colour suits you.'

'Thank you,' Melissa replies, seeming genuinely pleased by the compliment. 'I thought the same about the dress I got for Lily. Pink is such a pretty colour on little girls.'

'It is,' Rachel agrees. 'She looks lovely in it.'

I smile, pleased to see them finding common ground, however small. This is exactly what I'd hoped for; the beginning of understanding between them.

'I'd have got the same one for my little girl, if I had one,' Melissa adds, her eyes momentarily distant. A flicker of the sadness I sometimes glimpse in her. 'It's exactly the style I'd choose.'

RACHEL

There it is. The slip I've been waiting for. Not just the wistfulness, which could be natural enough, but the specificity. 'It's quite a distinctive style,' I observe, watching her closely. 'Very... particular.'

Melissa smiles, the moment passing too quickly. 'I've always had clear ideas about what I like. Ask James. I know exactly what I want.'

She shoots him a creepy smile that makes my skin crawl. The bill arrives, and after a brief argument over who's paying (James wins), we make our way out of the restaurant. Lily is drooping with tiredness by now, rubbing her eyes and clutching her colouring book.

'Can Rachel put me to bed tonight?' she asks unexpectedly, reaching for my hand as we step outside.

I slyly watch Melissa's face carefully, noticing the flash of annoyance that crosses it before she realises and masks it. 'Actually, sweetie, I thought I could read you a story tonight? I brought that new book about the unicorn princess.'

Lily looks torn, her eyes switching between us. 'But Rachel does the best voices.'

'I'm sure Melissa does great voices too,' I say, not wanting to put Lily in the middle of adult tensions. 'Maybe another night, love?'

But I'm secretly pleased by Lily's preference. Some bonds can't be replaced by sparkly dresses and unicorn books.

JAMES

The evening ends on a slightly awkward note when Lily asks Rachel to put her to bed. I can see Melissa's disappointment, though she hides it well. She's been looking forward to sharing her new book with Lily, but there will be other nights.

'I think that's a bit much for one night, pumpkin. Rachel probably has her own plans,' I suggest, trying to smooth over the moment.

'Actually, I should be getting home,' Rachel says, giving Lily's hand a squeeze. 'But I'll see you soon, okay? Maybe tomorrow we could go to the park?'

'With the big slide?' Lily asks hopefully.

'The very biggest,' Rachel promises.

I appreciate Rachel being so understanding. She's been Lily's bedtime story reader for so long, it's natural they have their special routines. Melissa will find her own traditions with Lily, given time.

As we say our goodbyes in the car park, I feel optimistic. The dinner wasn't perfect, but it was a start. Melissa and Rachel may never be best friends, but they can certainly build a nice relationship for Lily's sake. And for mine.

CHAPTER 7

James

Melissa's laugh rings out across the living room as Lily spins in her new outfit, a twirling blur of pink and glitter. It's a sound I've come to appreciate over the past weeks; warm and genuine, softening the edges of my carefully structured life.

'You look absolutely gorgeous, my angel,' Melissa says, catching Lily mid spin to adjust the slightly crooked bow in her hair. 'Like a proper princess.'

'I'm going to show Daddy!' Lily announces, racing from the room in search of me, even though I'm already watching from the doorway.

She crashes into my legs with her usual enthusiasm, looking up at me with Sarah's dark eyes. 'Look at my new outfit, Daddy! Melissa says I can wear it for Zoe's birthday party!'

'Very fancy,' I say, even though, to my untrained eye, it looks similar to the several other outfits Melissa has bought her recently. 'You'll be the best dressed girl there.'

Melissa appears behind Lily, her expression tender as she smooths a hand over Lily's already smooth hair. 'She needs a proper haircut before the party, though. Those ends are getting a bit straggly.'

I look at Lily's hair, trying to see what Melissa means.

It looks fine to me, but then again, hair maintenance is one of many areas of parenting where I feel completely out of my depth. Rachel normally handles all of that. I tend to resort to simple ponytails, and to be honest, I'm pretty happy to just let it grow forever.

'Does it need cutting?' I ask uncertainly. 'I thought we just had it done a couple of months ago.'

'Well, they did a terrible job. Look at these split ends.' She lifts a section of Lily's hair, presenting it for my inspection as if I'll suddenly develop the ability to identify split ends.

'Oh, right,' I say, not seeing whatever it is I'm supposed to see. 'Well, I suppose we could book an appointment.'

'Actually,' Melissa says, her expression brightening, 'I've been meaning to suggest my hairdresser. Amelia does children's hair too, and she's amazing. Lily would love it; they have special chairs shaped like animals, and they give the kids little treats afterwards.'

'Treats?' Lily's ears perk up at the magic word. 'What kind of treats?'

'Chocolates and little hair clips and things,' Melissa tells her, then turns back to me. 'I could take her tomorrow, if you want? I'm free all day.'

Something about the suggestion makes me uneasy. Not because I don't trust Melissa with Lily; she's proven herself to be wonderful with her, patient and kind and genuinely interested in Lily's world. It's more that... well, it feels like a big step. Melissa taking Lily out, just the two of them, to do something as maternal as a haircut.

'I could come too,' I find myself saying. 'I've got that day off work anyway.'

I notice a smidgeon of something; disappointment, maybe, cross Melissa's face before she smiles. 'Of course. We can make a day of it. Maybe grab lunch after?'

'Can we go to the place with the teddy bear pancakes?' Lily asks, her face lit up with excitement.

'Absolutely,' Melissa agrees immediately, giving Lily a quick hug. 'Anything for my angel.'

She's been calling Lily that a lot lately, I realise. My angel. It's sweet, the affection she has for my daughter. I should be grateful that they've bonded so well, that Lily has accepted Melissa into our lives with such ease.

'So, tomorrow then?' Melissa prompts, her hand finding mine and giving it a gentle squeeze.

I nod happily. 'Tomorrow it is.'

Later, after Melissa has gone home and Lily is tucked up in bed, I find myself staring at the calendar on my phone. We've been dating for just over a month. Is that too soon for her to be buying Lily clothes, taking her for haircuts, planning outings? The modern dating rulebook is a mystery to me, especially when children are involved.

I'm tempted to call Rachel and ask her opinion, but I already know what she'll say. She's made her feelings about Melissa's 'overinvolvement' with Lily clear enough, and while I value Rachel's opinion more than almost anyone's, I don't need another lecture about moving too fast or letting Melissa get too close too soon. Besides, Rachel's been acting strange lately anyway. That dinner last weekend was awkward, with undercurrents I couldn't quite grasp flowing between the two women. Melissa insists it went well, that she and Rachel had 'reached an understanding,' but even Lily mentioned that Rachel seemed 'cranky' about something.

I'll just have to navigate this step of the relationship myself, I decide, setting an alarm for the morning. It's a haircut, not adoption papers. I'm overthinking this, as usual.

***

Melissa's hairdressers is nothing like the cheerful, chaotic children's hairdresser I usually take Lily to. This place is sleek and stylish, all exposed brick and minimalist furniture, with the kind of prices that make my eyes water when I sneak a look at the menu of services. The only concession to its younger clients is a small corner with two animal shaped chairs, a lion and a giraffe, and a shelf of children's books.

Lily, predictably, makes a beeline for the giraffe chair, clambering up and giggling as she pretends to feed it leaves from a nearby plant.

'Lily, don't touch that,' I begin, but Melissa is already there, gently redirecting Lily's attention to a picture book about hairstyles.

'Let's see if we can find something pretty for your hair today,' she suggests, flipping through the glossy pages. 'Something that'll make you look even more beautiful than you already are.'

The stylist, Amelia, greets Melissa with air kisses and nice compliments on her outfit before turning to Lily with a professional smile. 'And who's this little lady?'

'This is Lily,' Melissa says before I can introduce her. 'She's in desperate need of a proper style, aren't you, angel?'

Lily nods solemnly. 'My hair's all splitty at the ends.'

Amelia laughs. 'Well, we can certainly fix that. Do you know what kind of haircut you'd like?'

Lily looks to Melissa, who's already pointing to a photo in the style book. 'I was thinking something like this, but perhaps a bit shorter? To really frame her face.'

I crane my neck to see; it's a bob, shorter than Lily's ever worn her hair, with a fringe that would completely change the way she looks. 'That's quite different from her current style,' I say hesitantly.

'That's the whole point,' Melissa laughs. 'Time for something fresh and pretty, isn't it, angel?'

'Will it make me look like a princess?' Lily asks, eyeing the photo with interest.

'The prettiest princess in the whole kingdom,' Melissa assures her.

'I quite like her hair longer,' I say, feeling strangely defensive. 'It's just the ends that need tidying, right?'

Amelia switches looks between us, clearly sensing the

tension. 'We could do something in between? Keep the length but add some layers and maybe a side swept fringe instead of a full one?'

'That sounds more like it,' I agree quickly.

Melissa's mouth tightens and then forms into a smile. 'Of course, whatever you think best, James. I just thought something a bit more... styled would suit her. But it's your choice.'

There's a note in her voice, a hint of hurt that makes me immediately second guess myself. Am I being unreasonable? Is this really worth creating tension over?

'Actually,' I backtrack, 'let's see the shorter style. If Lily likes it, then why not try something new?'

Melissa beams at me, instantly sunny again. 'It'll look adorable on her, trust me. I had almost the exact same cut at her age, and it was so practical and sweet.'

This detail seems to satisfy something in me. Of course; Melissa's just suggesting a style she knows works well for little girls. Nothing strange about that. I'm being overprotective and ridiculous.

'Alright then, let's go with the bob,' I tell Amelia, who nods and begins preparing her station.

Lily is settled into the giraffe chair, a cape fastened around her shoulders. She looks so small and suddenly vulnerable, her blue eyes wide as she watches Amelia in the mirror. 'It's going to look so pretty,' she's saying. 'And it'll be much easier for Daddy to brush in the mornings. No more tangles to make you cry.'

I hover awkwardly nearby, feeling somewhat pointless to the proceedings. Melissa has everything well in hand, keeping Lily distracted with stories and questions as Amelia begins to cut. Long strands of hair fall to the floor, each snip of the scissors making my heart twist a little. Feels like Sarah's hair, falling away.

'She looks just like her mum with her hair that way,' I comment, almost to myself.

Melissa looks up, something flashing in her eyes too

quickly for me to identify. 'Does she? I thought she takes after you more.'

'She has my eyes, but Sarah's hair and smile,' I say, a familiar ache accompanying the words.

Melissa nods, her smile fixed in place. I watch in silence as Amelia continues to cut, shaping Lily's hair into the style from the book. It's strange how much a haircut can transform a face. With each snip, Lily looks less like the little girl I've known and more like... well, like a different child entirely.

'There we go!' Amelia announces finally, spinning the chair so Lily can see herself properly. 'What do you think, sweetheart?'

Lily stares at her reflection, wide eyed. Her hair, once falling past her shoulders, now stops at her chin in a neat bob, complete with a fringe that skims her eyebrows. It's undeniably cute, but it's also undeniably different.

'Do I look pretty?' Lily asks, her voice small.

'You look beautiful,' Melissa assures her instantly. 'Absolutely perfect. Don't you think so, James?'

'Very pretty,' I agree, because what else can I say now? 'It's a big change, but I like it.'

Lily breaks into a smile, apparently satisfied with our approval. 'I look like a big girl now!'

'You certainly do,' Amelia says, removing the cape and helping Lily down from the chair. 'And as promised, you get to choose a treat from the treasure chest.'

While Lily delightedly rummages through a box of clips and sweets, I pay the bill, wincing slightly at the cost. Melissa chatters with Amelia about their next appointments, the two of them falling into the easy rhythm of regular client and stylist.

'I'll need to touch up my highlights before the wedding,' Melissa is saying. 'Perhaps the Thursday before?'

'Wedding?' I ask, turning from the reception desk. 'What wedding?'

Melissa looks momentarily flustered. 'Oh, my cousin's. Did I not mention it? It's next month, in the Cotswolds.'

'You didn't,' I confirm, wondering why this feels significant somehow.

'Well, it's not a big deal,' she says with a dismissive wave. 'Just a family thing. Oh look, Lily's chosen her treat!'

Lily proudly displays a sparkly clip shaped like a crown. 'For my princess hair!'

'Great choice, angel,' Melissa says, bending to fasten it in Lily's newly shortened locks. 'Now you're ready for the royal ball.'

Lily beams, spinning to make her dress flare out. 'Can we get the teddy bear pancakes now?'

'Absolutely,' I say, glad for the change of subject. 'Let's go find a hungry teddy bear.'

The rest of the morning passes pleasantly enough. We have lunch at the café Lily loves, where they make pancakes decorated to look like animals. Melissa takes countless photos of Lily with her teddy bear pancake, exclaiming over how photogenic she is, how the new haircut frames her face perfectly.

'We should take her for proper portraits done,' she suggests as Lily attacks her pancake with more enthusiasm than precision. 'With that gorgeous face and her pretty new haircut, they'd be stunning.'

'Maybe for her next birthday,' I suggest, not wanting to commit to yet another expense, another activity, another step deeper into this rapidly evolving relationship.

Melissa's hand finds mine across the table, her touch warm and reassuring. 'Of course, whenever you think is best. I just get excited sometimes, with all these plans. It's been so long since I've had anything... anyone to plan for.'

The vulnerability in her expression melts my reservations. Melissa has been nothing but kind and generous with Lily, going above and beyond to make her feel special and loved. Is it fair of me to keep one foot out the door, to question her motives when she's given me no real reason to doubt her?

'The haircut does look cute,' I admit, squeezing her hand. 'You were right about that.'

She positively glows at the validation. 'I'm so glad you like it. I just want Lily to feel beautiful and confident. All little girls deserve that.'

'And teddy bear pancakes,' Lily adds through a mouthful of syrup soaked food.

'And teddy bear pancakes,' Melissa agrees with a laugh. 'Always those.'

By the time we drop Melissa off at her house that afternoon, my earlier misgivings have mostly faded. Lily is happy with her new haircut, proudly showing off her princess clip to anyone who'll look. Melissa has been nothing but patient and loving all day. And I... I'm slowly starting to believe that this could work, this ready made family that's forming around us.

'Can Melissa come over for dinner?' Lily asks as we pull away from Melissa's house. 'She promised to show me how to make friendship bracelets.'

'Not tonight, pumpkin. She's got things to do at her own house,' I explain. 'But she's coming over tomorrow night, remember?'

'And sleeping over?' Lily confirms, a fact that still makes my cheeks warm when I think about it.

'Yes,' I acknowledge, glancing at her in the rearview mirror. 'Is that okay with you?'

Lily considers this seriously. 'Yes. But she can't have my bed. She has to sleep in yours.'

I hold back a laugh. 'That's the plan.'

'Good. Because my bed is too small for big people.'

'Very true,' I agree, relieved that Lily's acceptance of Melissa extends to her increasingly regular 'sleepovers' at our house.

We've been careful, Melissa and I, to keep the physical aspects of our relationship private when Lily is around. Discrete kisses, hand holding, nothing that would confuse or upset her. But Lily seems to have taken Melissa's growing presence in our home completely in stride, accepting with a child's adaptability that Melissa is now part of our routine.

'Rachel is coming on Saturday, right?' Lily asks suddenly. 'For pancakes and the park?'

'That's right,' I confirm, making a mental note to text Rachel and confirm. 'And the really big slide you've been wanting to try.'

'I'm going to show her my new haircut,' Lily decides. 'And my princess clip. Do you think she'll say I'm pretty too?'

'Of course she will,' I assure her, though a small part of me wonders how Rachel will react to such a dramatic change. She's been uncharacteristically quiet about Melissa lately. After the slightly tense dinner last weekend, she's limited her comments to bland pleasantries whenever Melissa comes up in conversation. I'm grateful for the cease fire, but it also makes me wonder what she's really thinking. Saying that, it's a worry for another day. For now, I've got a happy daughter with a new haircut she loves, and a girlfriend who dotes on both of us. Things could certainly be worse.

***

'Are you sure you don't mind watching that documentary again?' Melissa asks later that night, settling onto my sofa with a glass of wine. 'We could find something else.'

Lily is finally asleep after a long bedtime routine involving three stories and a detailed explanation of how her new haircut makes her look like a Disney princess. Melissa has been at our house all evening, helping with dinner and bath time with a natural ease that still sometimes catches me off guard.

'I don't mind,' I assure her, though I've seen this particular documentary about deep sea creatures at least twice already. 'I know you like it.'

'I love how passionate you are about my interests,' she says, snuggling against my side. 'Not many men would sit through marine biology documentaries just to make their girlfriend happy.'

'I'm not most men,' I joke, wrapping an arm around her shoulders.

'No, you definitely aren't,' she agrees, her voice soft. 'You're special, James. You and Lily both.'

There's a vibe to her words that makes me look at her. 'Everything okay?'

She nods, but there's a slight sheen to her eyes that wasn't there before. 'Just... happy. I never thought I'd find this again. A family.'

The word hangs between us, significant and slightly terrifying. We haven't discussed the future in concrete terms; it's only been a month, after all. But 'family' implies real commitment, at least to me.

'Is that what we are?' I ask carefully. 'A family?'

Melissa looks up at me, looking vulnerable. 'I'd like us to be. Someday. If that's something you'd want too.'

The conversation has taken a serious turn I wasn't prepared for. 'It's... a big step.'

'I know,' she says quickly. 'And I'm not pushing, honestly. I just... I care about you both so much. More than I ever expected to.'

'We care about you too,' I say, because it's true. Whatever doubts I might have about the pace of our relationship, I can't deny that Melissa has carved out a place in both our hearts with remarkable speed.

She bites her lip, hesitating. 'I know I can be a bit... much sometimes. With Lily especially. Buying her things, planning activities, the haircut today. I don't want you to think I'm trying to take over or cross any boundaries.'

'I don't think that,' I assure her, though her acknowledgment of something I've been feeling but couldn't quite articulate takes me by surprise.

'It's just that...' She pauses, taking a deep breath. 'I've always wanted children. A little girl especially, and a few years ago, I thought I was going to have that.'

Something in her tone makes me sit up straighter. 'What happened?'

Melissa stares into her wine glass, her expression distant. 'I was pregnant. Everything was going fine, perfect really. We'd decorated the nursery, chosen a name. Olivia. My boyfriend at the time was so excited, already planning all the things he'd teach her. But, she was stillborn,' Melissa says, her voice barely above a whisper. 'At thirty six weeks. No warning, no explanation. One day she was kicking and healthy, the next... just gone.'

'I'm so sorry,' I say, the words painfully inadequate for the magnitude of her loss. 'That's... I can't imagine.'

'The worst part came after,' she continues, a tear slipping down her cheek. 'The depression. I couldn't get out of bed for weeks. Couldn't go back to work. Couldn't stop crying, and Mark, my boyfriend, he tried to be supportive, but eventually he couldn't cope with it anymore. With me. He left six months later.'

I pull her closer, at a loss for what to say. Losing Sarah was devastating, but at least I had Lily; a piece of her to hold onto, to pour my love into. To lose a child and then be abandoned by your partner... the cruelty of it is staggering.

'I'm so sorry,' I repeat, pressing a kiss to her forehead. 'I had no idea.'

'How could you?' she says with a watery smile. 'It's not exactly first date conversation. And I've worked hard to move past it, to build a new life. But sometimes, with Lily... I get carried away. All those maternal feelings I never got to express, they just come pouring out. I'm trying to be careful, to remember that she's your daughter, not mine. But it's hard sometimes.'

Her honesty disarms me completely. Suddenly, her enthusiasm for buying Lily clothes, planning activities, even the haircut... it all makes sense. She's not trying to insert herself inappropriately into our lives; she's healing from a wound so deep I can barely comprehend it.

'I understand,' I tell her, and I mean it. 'And I don't want you to hold back with Lily. She adores you, and it's clear you adore her. That's precious, not problematic.'

'Really?' Melissa looks up at me, hope in her gaze. 'You're

not worried I'm getting too attached too quickly?'

'Life's too short to measure out affection in careful doses,' I say, thinking of Sarah, of how quickly and completely she fell in love with Lily from the moment she knew she was pregnant. 'If there's one thing I've learned, it's that love isn't something to be rationed.'

Melissa's arms tighten around me, her face pressed against my chest. 'I was so afraid to tell you. Afraid you'd think I was using Lily as some kind of... replacement. Or that I was too damaged for you to want to be with.'

'Never,' I say firmly, tilting her face up to meet my gaze. 'You're not damaged, Melissa. You're strong. To survive something like that and still have so much love to give... that's remarkable.'

She kisses me, a kiss full of gratitude and relief and something deeper that makes my heart race. When we break apart, she looks at me with such naked emotion that it takes my breath away.

'I'd never leave you,' I find myself promising, the words emerging before I can consider their weight. 'Not for being depressed, not for grieving, not for anything beyond your control. That's not what partners do.'

'James,' she whispers, her eyes filling with fresh tears. 'You don't know what that means to me.'

We abandon the documentary, making our way upstairs in a tangle of kisses and whispered reassurances. As we pass Lily's room, Melissa pauses, glancing through the partially open door at my sleeping daughter.

'She's so peaceful,' she murmurs. 'So perfect.'

I nod, watching Lily's chest rise and fall, her new haircut fanned across the pillow, making her look somehow older and more vulnerable simultaneously. 'She is.'

'Thank you for sharing her with me,' Melissa says, her voice thick with emotion. 'For sharing your life. I'll try not to overstep, I promise.'

'You're not overstepping,' I assure her, leading her towards my bedroom. 'You're just becoming part of our story.'

Later, as Melissa sleeps curled against me, her breathing deep and even, I find myself staring at the ceiling, turning our conversation over in my mind. Her revelation explains so much about her behavior with Lily, her eagerness to be involved, to create special moments and memories. It transforms what might have seemed like overstepping into something poignant and understandable. I wonder if I should have asked for more details, like the year, the place where she lived then, how she ended up here, if it was somewhere else. Then again, those questions feel intrusive, callous even, in the face of such raw grief. There's time enough for those details later, as our relationship deepens. I think it's enough to know that Melissa has trusted me with her deepest pain, that she has opened herself to the possibility of love again despite the cruel lessons life has taught her. And I've promised not to abandon her, a commitment that feels monumental and right simultaneously.

I drift off to sleep with Melissa's head on my chest, her hand resting over my heart, and the feeling that whatever uncertainties I might have had about our relationship, they pale in comparison to the courage it's taken for both of us to reach this point; to risk loving again after loss has taught us exactly how much we stand to lose.

CHAPTER 8

Rachel

'What about this one?' Greg holds up yet another shirt, an aggressively patterned thing in shades of teal that would look more at home on a Brighton retiree than a thirty something British engineer. 'The sales guy said it's very on trend.'

I push down a laugh, moving deeper into the department store's uncomfortable chair. 'It's very... loud.'

'That's the point,' he says, examining himself in the mirror with concerning enthusiasm. 'I'm tired of boring clothes. Seven weeks in Asia made me realise how conservative my wardrobe is.'

'There's conservative and then there's not looking like a walking optical illusion,' I reply, checking my watch. We've been shopping for over an hour, and all I want is to go home, put on pyjamas, and watch something mind numbing on Netflix. Preferably involving serial killers.

Greg has been back for exactly three days, and while I was initially glad to see him, that feeling is rapidly evaporating under the relentless assault of his newfound energy. He's returned from his business trip with the energy of a Jehovah's Witness, full of stories about street food and cultural experiences and some kind of fucking spiritual awakening he had during a weekend trip to a Thai temple. It would be interesting if it wasn't so exhausting.

'I'm getting it,' he decides, adding the shirt to the already substantial pile of new clothes. 'And maybe these trousers too.'

I nod noncommittally, scrolling through my phone to pass the time. There's a text from James, asking if we're still on for the park tomorrow with Lily. I smile reflexively at the thought of seeing them, then remember I'm supposed to be fully engaged in Greg's Great Wardrobe Transformation.

'Almost done?' I ask hopefully.

'Just a few more things to try,' he says, disappearing back into the changing room.

I sigh and return to my phone, opening Instagram to do my now daily check of Melissa's account. Nothing new since yesterday, just a carefully curated image of her and James at some restaurant, looking like the perfect couple. The sight makes my stomach twist uncomfortably.

'What about dinner tomorrow night?' Greg calls from behind the curtain. 'There's this new fusion place I read about online. Apparently their lemongrass martinis are life changing.'

'Can't tomorrow. I'm seeing James and Lily at the park, remember?'

There's a brief pause. 'Right. I forgot.'

The curtain opens and Greg emerges in yet another shirt, this one marginally less offensive than the last. 'You know, we could always do a double date sometime. Us and James and his new girlfriend. What's her name again?'

'Melissa,' I say, the name tasting sour on my tongue. 'And I don't think that's a good idea.'

'Why not? It would be nice to finally meet this Melissa I hear so much about.' There's an undercurrent to his tone that I choose to ignore.

'Well, they are going through a lot right now, with this new relationship,' I lie. 'I'm not sure he's up for socialising as a couple yet.'

Greg gives me a look that suggests he doesn't believe me,

but he doesn't push it. 'Well, the offer's there if you change your mind. This one's good, right?'

I nod, not trusting myself to give a genuine opinion without snapping. The truth is, the thought of sitting through an entire dinner watching Melissa play the perfect girlfriend while Greg tries to impress everyone with stories of his Asian epiphanies makes me want to scream.

By the time we finally leave the department store, loaded with bags of Greg's 'reinvented image,' it's nearly four and all I want is to go home and chill out.

'How about we try that new cocktail place on High Street?' Greg suggests as we reach the car. 'I read they do these amazing infused gin things with;'

'Actually,' I interrupt, 'could we just go home? I'm pretty tired.'

He looks momentarily disappointed but rallies quickly. 'Sure, we can have a quiet night in. I'll cook! I learned this amazing pad thai recipe in Bangkok.'

'Sounds great,' I lie again, unlocking the car and wondering when exactly my boyfriend turned into an overgrown puppy, endlessly enthusiastic and utterly exhausting.

The drive home is filled with Greg's chatter about everything from Malaysian architecture to the proper way to haggle in night markets. I make appropriate noises of interest while mentally composing my grocery list and wondering if I have enough wine at home to get through the evening.

'...and that's when I realised that we could all learn something from their approach to work life balance,' Greg is saying as we pull into my driveway. 'It's not about how many hours you put in, it's about being fully present in whatever you're doing.'

'Absolutely,' I agree, having lost the thread of conversation somewhere around Singapore's financial district. 'Very insightful.'

Inside, Greg immediately takes over my kitchen, pulling out ingredients and utensils with the confidence of someone who definitely hasn't cooked a proper meal in my house before. I retreat to the living room, moving onto the sofa with a quiet groan of relief.

My phone buzzes with a text from James: 'Melissa's taken Lily for a haircut today. Complete makeover! Very cute but I barely recognised her at first!'

A new burst of unease shoots through me. Melissa taking Lily for haircuts now? Each day she's insinuating herself further into their lives, taking on increasingly maternal roles. James, bless him, seems utterly oblivious to how fast this is all moving.

'What about a double date?' Greg calls from the kitchen, somehow circling back to his earlier suggestion despite the intervening hours and change of location. 'Seriously, Rach, I'd really like to meet your friends.'

I'm about to dismiss the idea again when a thought occurs to me. Maybe a double date wouldn't be such a bad idea after all. It would give me a chance to observe Melissa in a different social context, to see how she interacts with James when other adults are watching. Also, it would give Greg a chance to form his own impressions, hopefully confirming my suspicions that something isn't right about her.

'Actually,' I call back, 'that's not a bad idea. I'll ask James if they're free next weekend.'

Greg appears in the doorway, wooden spoon in hand and a surprised smile on his face. 'Really? Great! I was beginning to think you are keeping me and James' girlfriend apart on purpose.'

'Don't be ridiculous,' I say, a bit too quickly. 'Why would I do that?'

He shrugs. 'No idea. Just a feeling.'

He disappears back into the kitchen, leaving me to contemplate exactly how transparent my feelings might be to someone who's been watching from the outside.

**

'Careful on the big slide!' I call as Lily races ahead of me toward the playground. 'Wait for me before you go up!'

It's a perfect Saturday morning, crisp winter sunshine warming the air just enough to make the park comfortable. Lily is a bundle of energy, having talked non stop in the car about everything from her new school work about planets to the 'special pancakes' Melissa made her for breakfast, shaped like hearts because 'she loves me so much.'

Lily stands at the top of the slide, her overconfidence scaring me a little. 'I'm hot, catch this!' She says as she throws her hat off, leaving it on the cold floor, before shooting down the slide like a bobsled.

I catch up to her at the bottom of the slide, and the sight of her makes me falter mid step. Her hair. What used to be long, dark waves falling past her shoulders has been cut into a neat bob with a fringe, completely transforming her appearance. It's the exact same haircut from Melissa's childhood photo; the one of little Melissa in the pink dress that matches the one she bought for Lily.

'Rachel, look at my princess hair!' Lily twirls, showing off the new style. 'Melissa took me to a fancy salon and the lady gave me chocolate after!'

'It's... very different,' I manage, my heart beating unnaturally fast. 'Did Daddy go with you?'

'Yep! He said I look pretty. Do you think I look pretty?'

I crouch down to her level, forcing a smile. 'You always look pretty, love. Did you choose this haircut yourself?'

Lily shakes her head. 'Melissa showed me in a book. She said it would make me look just like a princess.'

Or just like her, I think grimly. 'Well, it's very nice. Now, how about that slide?'

I watch Lily scramble up the ladder to the top of the slide, my mind racing. This is beyond coincidence now. First the matching dress, now the identical haircut. Melissa is deliberately styling Lily to look like herself as a child. The question is, why? And more importantly, how do I make James see the disturbing pattern forming?

After an hour of playground activities, Lily announces she needs the toilet. I take her hand and we head toward the park facilities, a small brick building near the café.

'Melissa's coming to dinner tonight,' Lily informs me as we walk. 'She's making special pasta that she says I'll love.'

'That's nice,' I say, trying to keep my tone normal. 'You've been spending a lot of time with Melissa lately, haven't you?'

Lily nods enthusiastically. 'She sleeps over lots now. In Daddy's bed, not mine, 'cause mine's too small.'

I bite back a comment about the rapid progression of their relationship. 'And you like having her around?'

'She's fun,' Lily says simply. 'She knows lots of princess stories and she does voices like you. And she said soon I can call her Mummy if I want to.'

I nearly trip over my own feet. 'She said *what*?'

'That I can call her Mummy,' Lily repeats, oblivious to my shock. 'Because she loves me like I was her own little girl.'

We reach the toilets, and I'm grateful for the moment to collect myself while Lily uses the facilities. Melissa telling Lily she can call her 'Mummy' after just over a month of dating James? That crosses so many boundaries I can't even begin to count them. While Lily washes her hands, I glance around the small bathroom, noting the overflowing bin near the sink. Something catches my eye. A small box partially visible among the paper towels. I move closer, pretending to fix my hair in the mirror.

It's a medication box, emptied and discarded. I carefully extract it, turning it over to read the label: Quetiapine, 300mg. The name sounds vaguely familiar, though I can't immediately place what it's prescribed for, but I do recognise the name on the prescription label: Melissa Chambers.

'What's that?' Lily asks, appearing at my elbow.

I quickly pocket the box in my coat pocket, rather than back in the bin where Melissa might have intentionally hidden it. 'Just some rubbish someone left. Are you all done? Let's go try the swings now.'

Back outside, I can't stop thinking about the medication box. Why would Melissa discard her prescription in a public park bathroom? And why does the name of the drug nag at me as something significant?

We spend another hour at the park, Lily chattering away while I push her on the swings, my mind only half present. She talks mostly about Melissa; Melissa's recipes, Melissa's stories, Melissa's plans for a 'special girls' day out' next week. With each new detail, my unease grows.

'Melissa says when I was in her tummy, she used to sing to me every night,' Lily announces as I help her down from the swing. 'She says that's why I'm such a good singer now.'

I freeze, my hands still on Lily's waist. 'When you were in her tummy?'

Lily nods, oblivious to my horror. 'She says I was the most beautiful baby in the whole hospital, even though I was sleeping for a very long time.'

A chill runs through me that has nothing to do with the autumn air. Melissa is telling Lily that she's her biological mother? That she carried her? The delusion is so extreme, so disturbing, that for a moment I can't find words.

'Lily,' I say carefully, kneeling to meet her eyes. 'You know that's not true, right? Melissa didn't have you in her tummy. Your mummy, Sarah, did.'

Lily looks confused. 'But Melissa said–'

'Melissa is confused,' I interrupt gently. 'Your mummy was Sarah, and she loved you very much. Melissa only met you recently, remember?'

Lily's brow furrows in concentration. 'So Melissa wasn't my first mummy?'

'No, love. Sarah was your only mummy before. Melissa is just Daddy's... friend.' I can't bring myself to say 'girlfriend' in this context.

'Oh.' Lily seems to process this, then shrugs with childish

adaptability. 'Can we get ice cream?'

'Of course,' I agree, desperate for a moment to think. 'Let's go to the café.'

As Lily enjoys her ice cream, I quickly google 'Quetiapine' on my phone. The results make my blood run cold. It's an antipsychotic medication, used to treat schizophrenia, bipolar disorder, and major depressive disorder with psychotic features. Melissa is on medication for a condition that can cause delusions and psychosis. And she's telling Lily that she's her biological mother. I need to tell James. Immediately.

As I start to compose a text, I hesitate. James has been dismissive of my concerns about Melissa from the beginning. Would a discarded medication box and Lily's confused recounting of Melissa's statements be enough to convince him? Or would he see it as yet another example of me overreacting, perhaps even sabotaging his relationship out of jealousy, as Melissa has no doubt suggested to him? I bet she's been in his ear about me every day. She is so fucking evil. I need more evidence. And I need someone else to witness Melissa's behaviour, someone James might be more inclined to listen to.

'Lily, I've had an idea,' I say, wiping ice cream from her chin. 'How would you feel if my friend Greg and I came to dinner with you and Daddy and Melissa sometime? Would that be fun?'

'Yes!' Lily bounces in her seat. 'Melissa makes the best pasta ever!'

'Great. I'll talk to Daddy about it, okay?'

By the time I drop Lily back at James's house, I've formulated a plan. Melissa isn't there, thankfully; James mentions she's gone home to 'freshen up' before dinner later.

'Did you notice Lily's new haircut?' he asks, smiling proudly as if he had something to do with the transformation. 'Melissa took her to this fancy salon. Bit different, but it suits her, don't you think?'

'It's certainly a change,' I say neutrally. 'Listen, I've been thinking. Greg's been asking to meet Melissa properly. What about a dinner next weekend? The four of us?'

James looks surprised but pleased. 'That's a great idea. Melissa was just saying she'd like to get to know my friends better. Let me check with her, but I'm sure we'd love to.'

'Perfect. I need to use your bathroom before I go, is that okay?'

Upstairs, I check the bathroom bin, half expecting to find more evidence of Melissa's medication. The bin is empty, but a quick glance in the cabinet reveals a new toothbrush (pink, of course) and various toiletries that definitely don't belong to James or Lily. Melissa is making herself at home in more ways than one.

Back downstairs, I say a quick goodbye to James and Lily, promising to confirm dinner plans once I've checked with Greg.

'Did Lily have fun?' James asks as he walks me to my car.

'Always,' I say truthfully. 'Though she did say something odd. Something about Melissa telling her she was "in her tummy"?'

James frowns slightly, then his expression clears. 'Oh, that. Melissa explained that to me. She was telling Lily a story about pregnancies in general, and Lily got confused. You know how literal she can be.'

'Right,' I say, not believing it for a second. 'That makes sense.'

'Melissa would never try to replace Sarah,' James says, a defensive note entering his voice. 'She knows how important it is for Lily to understand who her real mother was.'

'Of course,' I agree, not wanting to push and make him defensive. 'It was probably just a misunderstanding.'

We part with the usual hugs, and I drive home with my thoughts in turmoil. The evidence is mounting: the matching clothes, the identical haircut, the discarded psychiatric medication, the disturbing claims about being Lily's biological mother. Something is very wrong with Melissa Chambers, and she's sinking her claws deeper into Lily every day.

***

'So let me get this straight,' Greg says later that evening, pausing with a forkful of pad thai halfway to his mouth. 'You think James's new girlfriend is what, exactly? A stalker? A child snatcher? A woman with psychotic delusions who believes Lily is her baby?'

Put like that, it does sound a bit far fetched. 'I don't know what she is, exactly, but the evidence is adding up, Greg. The medication, the stories she's telling Lily, the way she's making Lily look like herself as a child... something isn't right.'

'People with mental health issues date and have relationships all the time,' Greg points out reasonably. 'Taking antipsychotic medication doesn't automatically make someone dangerous.'

'It does when they're telling a five year old that they gave birth to them!' I snap, pushing my barely touched dinner away. 'Can't you see how disturbing this is?'

Greg sets down his fork with a sigh. 'Look, Rachel. I understand you're concerned, but from where I'm sitting, this sounds like... well...'

'Like what?' I challenge.

He hesitates. 'Like you might be a bit too involved in James and Lily's life. Maybe even a bit jealous of this woman taking "your" place.'

'That's not what this is about,' I insist. 'This is about protecting Lily from someone who is clearly unstable and developing an unhealthy fixation on her.'

'Okay,' Greg says, holding up his hands in surrender. 'Then let's do the dinner. I'll meet her, see how she acts, and if I notice anything concerning, I'll back you up when you talk to James. Deal?'

I consider this. Having Greg as an independent witness might be exactly what I need to convince James that my concerns are legitimate, not the product of jealousy or overprotectiveness.

'Deal,' I agree. 'But you have to promise to really pay

attention. Melissa's good at hiding the crazy when she wants to be.'

'I promise,' Greg says solemnly, though there's still a hint of indulgence in his tone that irritates me. 'Detective Greg is on the case.'

I roll my eyes but feel marginally better having a plan in place. 'I'll text James and set it up.'

'Great!' Greg returns to his meal with enthusiasm. 'Now, are you going to eat that? This recipe is seriously life changing.'

I push my plate toward him, my appetite gone. 'All yours.'

While Greg finishes both our dinners, I text James: 'Greg's up for dinner next weekend if you and Melissa are free? Saturday night?'

The reply comes almost immediately: 'Just asked Melissa and she's very keen! Says it's about time she met the famous Greg. Saturday works perfectly. Our place or yours?'

I consider the options. Having dinner at James's house would give me a chance to see how integrated Melissa has become in their home, but hosting at mine would give me more control over the evening.

'Let's do ours,' I decide. 'Greg wants to show off his new cooking skills from Asia.'

'Sounds great,' James replies. 'Melissa says to tell you she's looking forward to getting to know you better in a more relaxed setting. See you then x'

I stare at the message, trying to read between the lines. Is Melissa genuinely looking forward to the evening, or is she just maintaining her 'perfect girlfriend' facade? Either way, the dinner can't come soon enough. With each day that passes, she's establishing herself more firmly in James and Lily's lives, reshaping their reality to fit her delusions.

'All set?' Greg asks, clearing our plates.

'Saturday night at our place,' I confirm. 'You'll need to cook something impressive.'

'Leave it to me,' he says confidently. 'I'll win them over with my culinary genius, and then casually assess Melissa's mental stability between courses. Piece of cake.'

His lighthearted approach irritates me, but I force a smile. 'Just be observant, okay? This is serious.'

'I know, babe,' he says, his expression softening. 'I can tell you're really worried. I promise I'll take it seriously.'

I nod, hoping he means it, because the more I learn about Melissa Chambers, the more convinced I become that she's not just an overeager girlfriend moving too fast. She's potentially dangerous, a woman with untreated, or under treated psychiatric issues who has fixated on Lily in a deeply troubling way. Somehow, I need to make James see it before it's too late.

CHAPTER 9

James

The medication box sits on my bathroom sink like an accusation, its white packaging stark against the dark tiles. I pick it up, turning it over in my hands. Quetiapine, 300mg. Prescribed to Melissa Chambers. I stare at it, trying to recall if Melissa has ever mentioned taking medication. We've discussed many things over the past weeks, growing closer with each conversation, but prescription drugs haven't come up. Especially not something that, according to a quick Google search on my phone, is primarily used to treat conditions like schizophrenia and bipolar disorder.

The sound of the front door closing downstairs interrupts my thoughts. 'James? Lily? I've brought dessert!'

Melissa's voice, cheerful and warm, floats up the stairs. I quickly put the box in the cabinet, unsure whether to mention it or pretend I never saw it. It feels invasive somehow, stumbling across something so personal, yet if Melissa is taking strong psychiatric medication, shouldn't that be something she'd share with someone she's dating?

'Up here,' I call back, deciding honesty is the best approach. 'Just a minute.'

I hear Melissa's footsteps on the stairs, then she appears in the doorway, a bakery box in hand and a smile on her face. 'There you are. Lily said you were up here. I brought those chocolate things she likes.'

'That's nice,' I say, trying to sound normal. 'Um, Melissa, I found something.'

I gesture to the medication box. Her eyes follow my hand, and for a split second something flashes across her face; alarm? Fear? But it's gone so quickly I can't be sure I saw it at all.

'What's that?' she asks, setting the bakery box on the edge of the sink and picking up the medication package. 'Quetiapine? I've never seen this before.'

'It has your name on it,' I point out, keeping my tone gentle, non accusatory. 'The prescription label.'

She brings it closer to her face, squinting slightly. 'So it does. How strange. Where did you find it?'

'It was here on the counter when I came up to use the bathroom,' I explain. 'I thought maybe you'd...' I trail off, unsure how to finish that sentence without sounding like I'm prying.

'Left it here?' Melissa shakes her head, confusion evident on her face. 'I've never taken this medication. And I certainly haven't been carrying empty medication boxes around with me.' She turns it over in her hands, frowning. 'This is very odd.'

'You've never been prescribed it?' I ask, feeling suddenly less certain. The box clearly has her name on it, but her confusion seems genuine.

'Never,' she confirms. 'I don't even know what it's for.'

'According to Google, it's an antipsychotic,' I say carefully. 'Used for schizophrenia, bipolar disorder, things like that.'

Melissa's eyes widen. 'An antipsychotic? James, surely you don't think I'm on antipsychotic medication and hiding it from you?'

There's a hurt in her voice that makes me immediately backpedal. 'No, of course not. It's just... it has your name on it, so I thought I should ask.'

She looks at the box again, her brow furrowed. 'This is so bizarre. Maybe it's some kind of mistake? Or...' She pauses, a new thought seeming to occur to her. 'Was anyone else in the house today?'

'Just Rachel,' I say. 'She brought Lily back from the park earlier.'

'Rachel,' Melissa repeats, her tone shifting to something darker. 'And she was upstairs?'

'She used the bathroom before she left,' I confirm, immediately seeing where Melissa's thoughts are heading. 'But surely she wouldn't...'

'Plant empty medication with my name on it?' Melissa finishes, her voice carefully neutral. 'I don't know. It's just strange that I've never seen this before, and then it appears right after Rachel visits.'

The suggestion hangs in the air between us, uncomfortable and slightly absurd. The idea that Rachel would go to the trouble of creating a fake prescription label with Melissa's name, all to... what? Make her look unstable? It seems far fetched. And yet, the alternative, that Melissa is hiding significant psychiatric issues from me, also feels unlikely given how open she's been about other aspects of her life.

'Maybe it got mixed in with something else,' I suggest, wanting to defuse the tension. 'Or maybe there's another Melissa Chambers in town and there was a mix up at the pharmacy?'

'Maybe,' Melissa agrees, though she doesn't sound convinced. She tosses the box into the bin. 'I don't want to jump to conclusions. It's probably just some strange coincidence.'

I nod, relieved that she's not making a bigger deal of it. 'Right. Should we forget about it and have some of that dessert you brought?'

Melissa's smile returns, though it doesn't quite reach her eyes. 'Absolutely. Lily was very excited when I told her I was bringing chocolate cake.'

As we head downstairs, my phone buzzes in my pocket. A text from Rachel: 'Greg's up for dinner next weekend if you and Melissa are free? Saturday night?'

The timing is almost suspiciously perfect, coming right after this odd incident with the medication. I glance at Melissa, who's already in the kitchen with Lily, unpacking the bakery box with exaggerated enthusiasm that makes my daughter giggle.

Do I believe Rachel would plant fake evidence to make Melissa look bad? No, not really, but her persistent suspicion of Melissa, her reluctance to accept her into our lives, has created an uncomfortable dynamic that seems to be getting worse rather than better. Maybe this dinner is exactly what we need; a chance for everyone to get to know each other better, to clear the air and move past these strange tensions.

'Melissa,' I call, joining them in the kitchen. 'How would you feel about having dinner with Rachel and her boyfriend next weekend?'

'Rachel has a boyfriend?' Melissa asks, looking genuinely surprised. 'She never mentioned him at dinner.'

'Greg,' I confirm. 'He works in engineering, travels a lot. He's been in Asia for the past couple of months, but he's back now.'

'I'd love to meet him,' Melissa says with apparent sincerity. 'It's about time I got to know your friends properly.'

'Great,' I say, relieved at her positive response. 'I'll tell Rachel we're in.'

I text back quickly: 'Just asked Melissa and she's very keen! Says it's about time she met the famous Greg. Saturday works perfectly. Our place or yours?'

As we enjoy the chocolate cake, which is admittedly delicious, I push the medication incident to the back of my mind. Whatever it was; a mistake, a misunderstanding, or something more troubling, it doesn't change the fact that Melissa is here, making my daughter laugh, bringing light and warmth back into our lives in a way I'd thought might never happen again. If Rachel still has concerns about Melissa, well, perhaps this dinner will put them to rest once and for all.

***

Double date night arrives with a mix of anticipation and

apprehension. Melissa has been oddly quiet about the dinner all week, neither expressing enthusiasm nor reluctance, simply accepting it as something we're doing. I wonder if she's nervous about meeting Greg, or perhaps about spending more time with Rachel, given the undercurrents of their previous interactions.

'Does this look alright?' I ask, holding up a blue shirt that's become something of a staple in my limited 'nice dinner' wardrobe.

Melissa looks up from where she's helping Lily with her shoes. 'Perfect. Blue is definitely your colour.'

'Rachel says that too,' Lily pipes up innocently. 'She says it makes your eyes look extra blue.'

A brief flash of something crosses Melissa's face before she smiles. 'Rachel's quite right about that. Your daddy has very nice eyes.'

I change quickly, watching Melissa through the bedroom door as she fusses over Lily's outfit, adjusting the bow in her hair with practiced precision. The two of them have grown so close over the past weeks, developing inside jokes and special rituals that sometimes make me feel like the odd one out. It's heartwarming, this rapid bonding.

'All set?' I ask, joining them downstairs. 'We should probably head out if we want to be on time.'

'Ready!' Lily announces, twirling to show off her outfit; a new dress Melissa bought her last week, paired with shiny shoes and the always present hair bow. 'Do I look pretty?'

'The prettiest,' Melissa assures her, straightening the bow one last time. 'My beautiful angel.'

The drive to Rachel's house is filled with Lily's excited chatter about meeting Greg, who she remembers vaguely from his occasional appearances. Melissa sits quietly in the passenger seat, her hands folded neatly in her lap, her expression unreadable.

'Nervous?' I ask softly, reaching over to squeeze her hand at a red light.

'A little,' she admits. 'I want to make a good impression.

Greg is important to you and Lily, so he's important to me too.'

'He'll love you,' I assure her, touched by her consideration. 'Just be yourself.'

Rachel's house is lit up as we pull into the driveway, warm light spilling from the windows. I can see movement inside; Rachel in the kitchen, Greg presumably nearby. Before I know it, Lily is unbuckling her seatbelt, eager to get inside. 'Come on, Daddy! I want to show Rachel my new dress!'

We approach the front door, Melissa's hand finding mine in a gesture that feels both reassuring and slightly possessive. Rachel answers our knock, wearing a simple dress and a smile that looks only mildly forced.

'You made it,' she says, stepping back to let us in. 'Right on time.'

'We brought wine,' Melissa offers, holding out a bottle of something expensive looking that she insisted on buying despite my protests that it wasn't necessary. 'Red, I hope that's okay?'

'Perfect,' Rachel says, accepting the bottle with a polite smile. 'Greg's just finishing up in the kitchen. He's been cooking all day, very excited to show off what he learned in Asia.'

We follow Rachel through to the living room, where a tall, athletic looking man in an apron appears from the kitchen, wiping his hands on a tea towel.

'You must be James,' he says warmly, extending a hand. 'I've heard so much about you, it's good to finally put a face to the name.'

I shake his hand, immediately liking his straightforward manner. 'Likewise. This is Melissa, and you remember Lily?'

Greg crouches down to Lily's level. 'Of course I do. Though you've grown about a foot since I last saw you. And what a fantastic dress!'

Lily beams, twirling around. 'Melissa bought it for me. And she did my hair too!'

'Melissa has excellent taste,' Greg says diplomatically, rising to shake Melissa's hand. 'It's a pleasure to meet you.

Rachel's told me you're quite the cook yourself.'

'I dabble,' Melissa says modestly. 'Nothing compared to whatever smells so amazing from your kitchen.'

'Malaysian curry,' Greg says proudly. 'Learned it from a street vendor in Kuala Lumpur. Should be ready in about twenty minutes. Can I get everyone a drink in the meantime?'

The initial introductions over successfully, we settle in the living room with drinks; wine for the adults, apple juice for Lily. Greg proves to be an engaging host, full of stories about his travels that manage to be interesting without veering into self important territory. Melissa responds with appropriate questions, seeming genuinely interested in his experiences abroad.

Rachel is quieter, watching the interactions with an intensity that makes me slightly uncomfortable. Her gaze lingers on Melissa, especially when she interacts with Lily, a subtle scrutiny that I hope isn't obvious to anyone else.

'So, Melissa,' Greg says during a lull in conversation, 'James tells me you work in marketing? How are you finding it at his company?'

'It's wonderful,' Melissa says, sipping her wine. 'Great team, interesting projects. And of course, the fringe benefit of meeting James was an unexpected bonus.'

She squeezes my hand, and I smile automatically, though something in her tone strikes me as slightly rehearsed; the practiced lines of someone who's told this story before.

'During a fire alarm, wasn't it?' Greg prompts, clearly having been briefed by Rachel. 'Quite the meet cute.'

'It was fate,' Melissa says with a soft smile. 'Being in exactly the right place at exactly the right time.'

Rachel makes a small noise that might be a suppressed snort, quickly disguised as a cough when I glance her way. 'More wine, anyone?'

Before anyone can answer, a timer dings from the kitchen. Greg jumps up. 'That's dinner! Perfect timing. Everyone to the table?'

Dinner itself is a surprisingly pleasant affair. Greg's curry is delicious, complex flavours that even Lily enjoys after some initial skepticism. Conversation flows relatively smoothly, with Greg carrying much of the social burden, asking questions and sharing anecdotes that keep things moving when awkward silences threaten.

Melissa is at her most charming, complimenting the food effusively, asking Rachel about her work, admiring the house. If she's aware of Rachel's continued scrutiny, she doesn't show it, maintaining an air of relaxed engagement that I find myself envying.

'So, Lily,' Greg says, turning to my daughter who's been impressively well behaved throughout the meal. 'Melissa's been spending a lot of time at your house, I hear. Are you having fun together?'

Lily nods enthusiastically. 'We do princess games and baking and Melissa's going to make my bedroom all pretty.'

'Oh?' Rachel says, her fork pausing halfway to her mouth. 'You're redecorating?'

The question is directed at me, a hint of something in her tone I can't quite identify. I shift uncomfortably in my seat.

'Just talking about it,' I clarify. 'Lily's getting older, time for something a bit more grown up than the nursery decor.'

'I helped paint that room,' Rachel says quietly. 'Sarah and I spent three weekends getting it just right before Lily was born.'

A tense silence falls over the table. Melissa clears her throat delicately.

'I didn't realise you had helped decorate it,' she says to Rachel, her voice carefully neutral. 'That's lovely. But as James says, Lily's growing up. New interests, new needs.'

'And what did you have in mind?' Rachel asks, looking directly at Melissa now. 'For the new decor?'

Melissa's face lights up. 'Oh, I was thinking something classic but with a touch of whimsy. Pale blue walls with silver stars painted on the ceiling. A canopy bed with sheer curtains. Bookshelves shaped like trees. It's similar to what I had as a girl, and I absolutely loved it.'

Rachel's eyes narrow almost imperceptibly. 'Pale blue with silver stars? That's... specific.'

'It's a popular theme,' Melissa says with a small shrug. 'Magical but not too childish. Don't you think it sounds pretty, Lily?'

'Yes!' Lily agrees enthusiastically. 'And Melissa says I can have fairy lights all around the windows!'

'Sounds like you've got it all planned out,' Rachel says, her smile not reaching her eyes. 'I didn't realise you were so invested in interior design, Melissa.'

'Oh, I wouldn't go that far,' Melissa laughs. 'But I do have a good eye for what suits people. Especially people I care about.'

She reaches over to touch Lily's hair affectionately, a gesture that makes Rachel's knuckles whiten around her fork. Greg, apparently sensing the mounting tension, quickly changes the subject.

'James, you still in IT? Must be fascinating with all the changes in technology these days.'

I grasp the conversational lifeline gratefully, launching into a discussion of my work that carries us through the rest of the main course. By the time dessert is served, a delicious looking tropical fruit pavlova that Greg proudly presents, the atmosphere has relaxed somewhat, though an undercurrent of tension remains.

'I need to use the ladies' room,' Melissa announces, setting down her napkin. 'Back in a moment.'

As soon as she's out of earshot, Rachel leans forward, her voice low and urgent. 'James, that bedroom design she described? It's exactly like the one in her childhood photos. The ones on her Instagram. She's recreating her own childhood bedroom for Lily.'

I blink, taken aback by both the accusation and the implication. 'What childhood photos? How would you know what her bedroom looked like?'

Rachel has the grace to look slightly embarrassed. 'I might

have looked into her social media a bit. After finding that medication.'

'Wait, what?' I stare at her, pieces suddenly clicking into place. 'You found that medication box? And left it at my house?'

'I didn't want to upset you in front of Lily,' Rachel says defensively. 'But yes, I found it in the park bathroom. It had Melissa's name on it, James. She's taking heavy duty antipsychotics and not telling you.'

'She says she's never taken those medications,' I counter, anger beginning to simmer beneath my confusion. 'And how exactly do you know they were hers? Maybe there's another Melissa Chambers.'

'In the same park where you happened to be?' Rachel scoffs. 'That's quite a coincidence. And why would she deny it unless she has something to hide?'

'Maybe because it's not true?' I suggest, my voice rising slightly before I remember Lily sitting beside me. I lower my tone. 'Rachel, are you seriously suggesting Melissa is what, mentally ill and lying about it? Based on an empty medication box you found in a public bathroom?'

'Among other things,' Rachel insists. 'The way she's styling Lily to look like herself as a child. The comments she's made to Lily about being her mother. The bedroom design. It all points to an unhealthy fixation, James.'

'What comments about being her mother?' I demand, now genuinely alarmed. 'What are you talking about?'

Rachel glances at Lily, who is happily occupied with her dessert, seemingly oblivious to the tense conversation. 'Lily told me Melissa said she was "in her tummy". That she sang to her every night while pregnant. That's delusional, James.'

I shake my head, remembering Melissa's explanation. 'That was a misunderstanding. Melissa was telling Lily about pregnancies in general, and Lily got confused. You know how literal she can be.'

'And you believe that?' Rachel asks incredulously. 'James, open your eyes. Something is seriously wrong here.'

Greg clears his throat awkwardly. 'Maybe we should change the subject before Melissa returns?'

But I'm too rattled now to let it go. 'You've been against Melissa from the start, Rachel. Always finding reasons to be suspicious, to doubt her intentions. And now you're admitting to stalking her social media, planting evidence in my bathroom, and interrogating my daughter behind my back?'

'I wasn't interrogating her,' Rachel protests. 'And I didn't plant anything. I found that medication box and left it where you would see it because I knew you wouldn't believe me otherwise. I'm trying to protect Lily!'

'From what, exactly?' I demand. 'From someone who loves her and wants to make her feel special? From having a female influence in her life again? Or is it just that you don't want to share her with anyone else?'

The moment the words leave my mouth, I regret them. Rachel recoils as if slapped, her face paling. Even Greg looks uncomfortable, suddenly very interested in adjusting the place settings.

'That's not fair,' Rachel says quietly, her voice tight with hurt. 'You know that's not what this is about.'

'I don't know what it's about anymore,' I admit, the anger draining away as quickly as it came, leaving only confusion and a dull ache in my chest. 'But this has to stop, Rachel. The suspicion, the investigations, all of it. Melissa is part of our lives now. I need you to accept that.'

The sound of footsteps alerts us to Melissa's return. The conversation cuts off abruptly, leaving an awkward silence in its wake. Melissa pauses in the doorway, obviously sensing the tension.

'Is everything okay?' she asks, her gaze moving between Rachel's rigid posture and my flushed face.

'Fine,' I say quickly, forcing a smile. 'Just discussing dessert. It looks amazing, Greg.'

Melissa takes her seat beside me, her hand finding mine under the table. Her touch is pretty reassuring.

The remainder of dessert is slightly awkward, with conversation limping along despite Greg's valiant efforts to keep things light. Rachel barely speaks, focusing on her pavlova as if it contains the secrets of the universe. Melissa maintains her pleasant demeanor, but I can sense her discomfort, a tension in her demeanor that wasn't there before.

After what feels like an eternity, Rachel stands abruptly. 'I should start clearing up. Melissa, would you like to help me in the kitchen?'

The invitation is so unexpected, and delivered in such a forced tone, that everyone stares at Rachel for a moment. Melissa speaks first.

'Of course,' she says, rising as she speaks. 'Happy to help.'

The two women disappear into the kitchen, leaving me with Greg and Lily. Greg gives me an apologetic look.

'Sorry about that. Rachel's been worked up about tonight. I tried to tell her she's overreacting, but you know how she gets when she's concerned about Lily.'

'She's been like this since Melissa and I started dating,' I sigh, keeping my voice low so Lily won't hear. 'I don't understand it. Melissa's been nothing but kind to both of us.'

Greg nods thoughtfully. 'For what it's worth, Melissa seems lovely. Perhaps a bit... intense about Lily, but that's not necessarily a bad thing. Rachel just worries.'

Before I can respond, there's a crash from the kitchen, followed by raised voices. I jump up, but before I can reach the kitchen, Rachel storms back into the dining room, her face flushed with anger.

'I think it's time you all left,' she says tightly. 'This isn't working.'

'Rachel,' Greg begins, standing to put a hand on her arm, but she shakes him off.

'No, Greg. I can't do this. I can't sit here and pretend everything is fine when it's not.'

Melissa appears in the doorway, her expression a carefully controlled mask of calm. 'I think Rachel's right. Perhaps we should call it a night. Lily looks tired anyway.'

Lily, who has been watching this adult drama unfold with wide, confused eyes, looks anything but tired. But I nod, eager to escape the tension that's made the air in the room feel thick and unbreathable.

'Right. We should go.' I turn to Greg, offering an apologetic smile. 'Thank you for dinner. It was delicious.'

'Anytime,' Greg says, looking between Rachel and Melissa with a bemused expression. 'Sorry it's ending on a sour note.'

The goodbyes are perfunctory and awkward. Rachel refuses to look directly at Melissa, focusing instead on giving Lily a quick hug. 'I'll see you soon, love. Be good for your daddy, okay?'

Lily, sensing the adult tension but not understanding it, nods solemnly. 'Okay. Thank you for the pavlova. It was super yummy.'

In the car, Melissa is quiet, staring out the window as we drive away from Rachel's house. Lily, thankfully, falls asleep almost immediately in the back seat, the excitement of the evening and the late hour finally catching up with her.

'Want to tell me what happened in the kitchen?' I ask after a few minutes of silence.

Melissa sighs, still looking out the window. 'Rachel made some... insinuations. About my intentions toward Lily. I tried to be polite, but honestly, James, her suspicion is starting to feel like harassment.'

I feel a little anger at Rachel flaring again. 'What exactly did she say?'

'It doesn't matter,' Melissa says, turning to me with a wan smile. 'She's your friend, and I don't want to cause problems between you. I just wish she could see that all I want is for you and Lily to be happy.'

She reaches over to touch my arm, and I notice her hand is trembling slightly. 'Are you feeling alright?' I ask, suddenly concerned. 'You look pale.'

'Actually, I've got a bit of a headache,' she admits. 'Probably the tension. Would you mind terribly if we didn't stay up late tonight? I think I need to lie down once we get Lily to bed.'

'Of course not,' I assure her, feeling a pang of guilt that she's suffering because of the awkward dinner. 'We'll get you settled as soon as we're home.'

By the time we arrive back at the house, Melissa's headache has worsened. She helps me get a sleepy Lily into pyjamas and bed, but her movements are slow, her smile strained. Once Lily is asleep, Melissa retreats to my bedroom, taking the painkillers I offer with a grateful smile.

'I'm sorry about tonight,' I say, sitting on the edge of the bed as she settles under the covers. 'Rachel was out of line.'

'It's not your fault,' Melissa says, her eyes already closing. 'She cares about you and Lily. I understand that. I just wish she could see that I care too.'

I brush a strand of hair from her forehead, noticing that her skin feels hot to the touch. 'Maybe you're coming down with something? You feel a bit feverish.'

'Just tired,' she assures me. 'I'll be fine after some sleep.'

I leave her to rest, heading downstairs to tidy up the kitchen and have a moment to think. My phone buzzes in my pocket; a text from Rachel.

'I'm sorry about tonight. Shouldn't have ambushed you like that, but I'm worried, James. Really worried. Please be careful.'

I stare at the message, conflicting emotions within me. Part of me is still angry at Rachel's accusations, her apparent determination to find fault with Melissa. However, another part, a quieter part, is unsettled by the medication, by Lily's confused comments about being in Melissa's 'tummy', by the intensity with which Melissa has inserted herself into our lives in such a short time.

'Let's talk tomorrow,' I text back, not ready to either accept her apology or dismiss her concerns entirely. 'Just us. No Melissa, no Greg. Okay?'

'Okay,' comes the immediate response. 'Thank you.'

I put my phone away, rubbing my eyes tiredly. Whatever

is going on, whatever truth lies beneath the surface of this situation, I need to approach it with a clear head. For Lily's sake, if nothing else.

When I finally head up to bed myself, Melissa is deeply asleep, her breathing even and steady. I slip in beside her, careful not to wake her, and stare at the ceiling, my mind still replaying the events of the evening.

I've nearly drifted off when Melissa stirs beside me, mumbling something in her sleep. I turn toward her, making out words through her soft, distressed sounds.

'My baby,' she whispers, her face contorted in what looks like pain. 'Please, my Olivia. Don't take her away again. She's mine. My little girl.'

A chill runs through me as I remember Melissa telling me about her stillborn daughter, the child she lost years ago. Olivia, she'd said. The grief that must still haunt her, surfacing in her dreams.

'Shh,' I whisper, gently stroking her hair. 'It's okay. You're safe.'

'No,' she moans, still deeply asleep. 'She's not dead. She's here. My Lily. My angel. They just changed her name to trick me, but I found her. I found my baby.'

I freeze, my hand still against her head, a cold knot of dread forming. Did I hear her correctly? Did she just say 'my Lily'? That they 'changed her name'?

Melissa turns over, her breathing settling back into the rhythm of deep sleep, apparently undisturbed by the disturbing words she's just spoken. I lie beside her, suddenly wide awake. Could Rachel be right? Is there something more troubling at work here than an eager new girlfriend moving too fast? The medication, the fixation on changing Lily's appearance, the bedroom redesign that mimics Melissa's childhood room, and now these sleep-talking delusions about Lily being her dead baby...

It's too much to be coincidence, but it's also too terrible to fully comprehend.

I lie awake for hours, listening to Melissa's breathing beside me, torn between the urge to wake her and demand explanations and the knowledge that confronting her might be dangerous if Rachel's worst suspicions are true. If Melissa genuinely believes, on some level, that Lily is her deceased daughter...

By the time dawn begins to lighten the sky outside my window, I've made a decision. I need to talk to Rachel, to apologise for dismissing her concerns and to share what I've heard, but I won't tell her about Melissa's sleep talking, not yet. The words were spoken in unconsciousness, and dragging them into the light feels like it would only add fuel to an already volatile situation.

First, I need to understand exactly what's happening. For that, I need more information about Melissa's past, about this stillbirth that clearly still haunts her. And for that, I need time and careful observation, not accusations and confrontations.

Melissa stirs beside me, her eyes fluttering open. For a moment, there's confusion in her gaze, then recognition and a soft smile.

'Morning,' she says, reaching up to touch my face. 'You look like you didn't sleep well.'

'Just thinking,' I say, forcing a smile. 'How's your head?'

'Better,' she says, stretching beneath the covers. 'Sorry about last night. That dinner was a bit of a disaster, wasn't it?'

'Not your fault,' I assure her, watching her face carefully for any sign that she remembers her disturbing sleep talk. There's nothing; just the usual morning drowsiness and affection in her eyes.

'I should get Lily up for breakfast,' I say, slipping out of bed. 'You rest a bit longer if you want.'

As I head to Lily's room, my mind is racing with questions I'm not sure I want the answers to. One thing is clear, though; I need to be more vigilant, more aware of the dynamics developing between Melissa and Lily. If there's even a possibility that Melissa's attachment to my daughter is rooted in delusion rather than genuine affection, I can't afford to ignore the warning signs any longer. For Lily's sake, and perhaps for Melissa's too, I need to find out the truth.

CHAPTER 10

Rachel

I've had a lot of terrible evenings in my time. The night my doctor called about my infertility diagnosis. The night Sarah died. The nights after, when I held James while he sobbed until there was nothing left. But this dinner; this excruciating, failed attempt at normalcy with a woman I'm increasingly convinced is dangerous, ranks right up there with the worst of them.

'She practically admitted it!' I fume, staring out the passenger window as Greg drives us home from James's house. We'd lingered only long enough to help Melissa and James get a sleepy Lily into the car before making our own hasty departure. 'The bedroom design, Greg. It's identical to her childhood room, right down to the fairy lights around the windows.'

Greg sighs, his fingers drumming against the steering wheel. 'Rachel, having similar taste in children's bedroom decor isn't exactly evidence of psychosis.'

'It's not just the bedroom!' I turn to face him, frustration burning in my chest. 'It's everything together. The clothes she buys Lily that match her own childhood photos. The haircut. The medication I found. The way she's been telling Lily she was "in her tummy." The fact that she's known James for barely a month and is already practically living in his house!'

'I understand your concerns,' Greg says in that maddeningly reasonable tone he's adopted since returning from Asia. 'But from what I saw tonight, Melissa seems... I don't know, familiar somehow. Like I've met her before, or someone very like her.'

'Familiar how?' I ask, momentarily diverted from my catalogue of Melissa's red flags.

He shrugs, turning onto my street. 'I can't quite place it. Just something about her mannerisms, maybe? The way she talks about Lily?' He shakes his head. 'It's probably nothing. Just a passing resemblance to someone I've met.'

We pull into my driveway, the headlights briefly illuminating the front of my house before Greg turns off the engine. Neither of us moves to get out. The tension from dinner still hangs between us, a tangible thing filling the car's interior.

'I'm worried about them, Greg,' I say more quietly. 'About James, but especially about Lily. If Melissa genuinely believes on some level that Lily is... I don't know, some kind of replacement for a child she lost or couldn't have, that's not just eccentric. It's potentially dangerous.'

'But you have no actual evidence that she believes that,' Greg points out. 'Just circumstantial things that could have perfectly innocent explanations.'

'Then why did she lie about the medication?' I demand. 'James told me she denied it was hers. Why would she do that unless she's hiding something?'

Before Greg responds, he freezes. 'Hang on. I think I know where I know her from.'

He gets out his phone and scrolls while I wait in silence.

'Got it! Yep! She used to date Scott.'

'Scott? Your workmate?'

'Yeah, I'll give him a call now!'

He dials the number, and I watch his face carefully as the call connects.

'Scott? It's Greg... Yeah, sorry about the late call... Listen, I need to ask you something. That woman you dated a few years back, yeah Melissa, what did she look like?... Yeah, she's blonde, about five six... Wait, really? You're sure?' A pause. 'No, that's... that's quite a coincidence. Listen, would you mind if we stopped by for a few minutes? I know it's late, but... Great, thanks. We'll be there in fifteen.'

He ends the call, turning to me with an expression I can't quite read. 'Rachel, I think you need to hear this. Scott dated a woman named Melissa a few years ago. Blonde, works in marketing. He says the description matches.'

'Your friend Scott dated Melissa?' I repeat, disbelief turning quickly to a surge of validation. 'What are the odds of that?'

'Pretty slim,' Greg admits, starting the car again. 'But he sounded certain when I described her. He wants to talk to us about it. Says there are some things we should know.'

My heart races as Greg backs out of the driveway. Could this be the concrete evidence I've been looking for? Someone who knows Melissa from before, who can confirm that there's something not right about her interest in Lily?

'What else did he say?' I press, unable to contain my impatience. 'Did he say why they broke up?'

'He didn't go into details on the phone,' Greg says, his expression serious now. 'But he sounded... concerned when I mentioned she was dating a friend of ours with a young daughter.'

Scott meets us at his door, a tall man with red hair and the kind of tired expression that comes from working too many hours. I've met him a handful of times at small events; nice enough, divorced, with a son who lives primarily with his ex.

'Sorry about the late night summons,' Greg says. 'But we are just a little worried-'

'How long did you date her?' I interrupt, earning a warning glance from Greg for my lack of social niceties.

Scott doesn't seem bothered by my directness. 'About four months, nearly three years ago. Not a particularly long relationship, but... memorable.'

'In what way?' Greg prompts, as we settle on Scott's rather

uncomfortable sofa.

Scott runs a hand through his thinning hair. 'Melissa was charming, attractive, seemed absolutely perfect at first. Especially with Ben, my son. He was five at the time, had been having a rough time with the divorce. Melissa swooped in and just... dazzled him. Buying him gifts, planning special outings, the works.'

I feel my anxiety rise. 'That sounds familiar.'

'I bet it does,' Scott says grimly. 'It all seemed fantastic at first. Here was this beautiful woman who not only wanted to date me but seemed genuinely invested in my son. I thought I'd hit the jackpot.'

'When did things change?' I ask, already knowing there must have been a turning point.

'About two months in,' Scott says, his face looking distant as if seeing it all play out again. 'She started becoming... possessive of Ben. Wanting to make decisions about his education, his activities, even what clothes he wore. When I pushed back, saying it was too soon for that level of involvement, she'd get tearful, talk about how she just wanted to be a family.'

Greg shifts beside me, his earlier skepticism seemingly fading in the face of Scott's account. 'Did she ever mention having children of her own? Or wanting them?'

Scott nods, his face darkening further. 'That's where it gets complicated. She told me early on that she'd had a stillborn daughter a few years before we met. Olivia. Said it had been devastating, that her partner at the time couldn't handle her grief and left her. It was heartbreaking, honestly. I felt terrible for her.'

'Olivia,' I repeat, the name sending a chill through me. 'And did she ever... did she ever seem to confuse your son with this daughter she lost?'

Scott looks at me sharply. 'How did you know?'

'Just a hunch,' I say, though my heart is pounding so hard I'm sure they can both hear it. 'Please, go on.'

Scott takes a deep breath. 'It started subtly. She'd occasionally call Ben by weird names. Not Olivia, obviously, since he's a boy, but pet names that seemed odd.'

'Like Angel?'

'Yes! That was one. Then one night, I woke up to find her in Ben's room, just watching him sleep. When I asked what she was doing, she said something about making sure "her baby was breathing." It was... unsettling.'

'My angel,' I repeat, my voice barely above a whisper. 'That's what she calls Lily.'

Scott nods, unsurprised. 'It got worse. She'd have these... episodes, I guess you'd call them. Times when she seemed genuinely confused about who Ben was. She'd talk about "when he was in her tummy," tell him stories about "when you were my baby" that couldn't possibly be true. When I confronted her, she'd snap out of it, seem confused about what she'd said. Blamed it on being overtired, or having vivid dreams that felt real.'

'Did you end things then?' Greg asks.

'Not immediately,' Scott admits, looking somewhat ashamed. 'I was... well, I was lonely, and Ben seemed happy. The breaking point came when Ben went to spend a weekend with his mother. Melissa completely fell apart. Sobbing, accusing me of letting "them" take her baby again. She became hysterical, talking about how "they" had stolen Olivia from her and now they were taking Ben too. It was like... like she genuinely believed my son was her child. Her dead child, somehow reborn or replaced.'

I feel physically ill now, my worst fears about Melissa's interest in Lily confirmed. 'What happened?'

'I ended things,' Scott says simply. 'Told her she needed help beyond what I could give her. She didn't take it well. There were tearful phone calls, showing up at my workplace, gifts left for Ben at his school. Eventually, I had to threaten legal action. She disappeared after that. I heard later she'd moved to a different city.'

'And now she's here,' Greg says quietly. 'With James and Lily.'

'If it's the same Melissa,' Scott cautions. 'I'm not a hundred percent certain from your description.'

'It's her,' I say with absolute conviction. 'The medication, the fixation on Lily, the pet names, telling Lily she was "in her tummy," it all fits.'

'What should we do?' Greg asks, looking between Scott and me. 'If she genuinely believes Lily is somehow her lost child...'

'You need to tell your friend the truth,' Scott says firmly. 'I wish someone had warned me about Melissa before things went so far. She needs professional help, not a relationship, and certainly not access to another child she can project her delusions onto.'

I nod, a plan already forming in my mind. 'I'll talk to James tomorrow. Make him listen, even if I have to drag him here to hear it from you directly.'

Scott hesitates. 'Look, I don't want to get involved in any drama. Melissa was... unpredictable when she felt cornered. But I'll confirm what I've told you if your friend asks me directly. He deserves to know what he's dealing with.'

We thank Scott for his time and honesty, and leave with the heaviness of confirmation weighing on us. In the car, I'm quiet for several minutes, processing everything we've learned. The Melissa that Scott described matches exactly with the woman who's insinuated herself into James and Lily's lives. The patterns are identical; the rapid attachment, the inappropriate bonding with the child, the delusions about maternity.

'You have to admit this is serious now,' I say finally as Greg drives us back toward my house. 'This isn't me being jealous or overprotective. Melissa is genuinely unwell, and she's fixating on Lily the same way she did with Scott's son.'

To my surprise, Greg's expression has changed. There's a new skepticism in his eyes that wasn't there at Scott's house.

'I don't know, Rachel,' he says slowly. 'Something feels off about Scott's story.'

'Off?' I repeat incredulously. 'What do you mean, off? It matches everything I've been saying about Melissa!'

'Maybe too perfectly,' Greg says, his brow furrowed. 'Don't you think it's strange that his account aligns so exactly with your suspicions? Almost like he knew what you wanted to hear?'

I stare at him, disbelief turning rapidly to anger. 'Are you serious right now? You think Scott made all that up?'

Greg sighs, pulling into my driveway. 'I'm not saying he made it all up, but Scott has a reputation at work for... embellishing. Exaggerating. Making himself the hero of every story.'

'So what, he invented a psychotic ex girlfriend with delusions about his son?' I demand, my voice rising.

'No, but he might have dramatised certain aspects,' Greg says, turning off the engine. 'The medication could have been for anxiety, like she told him. The "episodes" could have been a stressed woman who got too attached to a child she cared about. Scott's bitter about his divorce, Rachel. He sees betrayal everywhere.'

I can't believe what I'm hearing. 'So now you're defending Melissa? After everything Scott just told us?'

'I'm saying we should be careful about taking Scott's version at face value,' Greg insists as we enter my house. 'From what I saw tonight, she seemed perfectly normal, nice even. Nothing like the unstable woman Scott described.'

'You've met her once!' I exclaim, unable to keep the incredulity from my voice. 'And now you're an expert on her mental health?'

'No, but I know Scott,' Greg counters. 'I've worked with him for years. He has a flair for drama, Rachel. He once told everyone at the office that his ex wife keyed his car when she found out he was dating again. Turned out he'd scraped it himself in a parking garage.'

'This is completely different,' I argue, pacing my living room in agitation. 'We're talking about a woman who's fixated on a child. Who's lied about medication. Who's telling Lily she was "in her tummy."'

'I'm just saying we should consider other explanations,' Greg says, his tone infuriatingly reasonable. 'Maybe Scott misinterpreted things. Maybe Melissa has genuinely changed. Maybe you're seeing patterns that aren't there because you're worried about Lily.'

'I can't believe this,' I say, stopping to face him directly. 'You heard what Scott said. You were there. It's exactly what I've been trying to tell you about Melissa, and now you're dismissing it because what? You met her once and thought she was "nice"?'

Greg's expression hardens slightly. 'I'm dismissing it because I know Scott, and I know how he can twist things. And honestly, Rachel, I think you're so determined to find something wrong with Melissa that you'd believe anything negative about her, no matter the source.'

'That's not fair,' I protest, hurt by the accusation. 'I'm concerned about Lily's safety.'

'Are you?' Greg challenges. 'Or are you just upset that James has found someone? That he doesn't need you to take care of him and Lily anymore?'

The words land like a slap. 'This has nothing to do with James finding someone. This is about Melissa specifically, and the danger she poses to Lily.'

'And I'm saying that danger might be exaggerated,' Greg insists. 'Scott isn't reliable, Rachel. Ask anyone at my office. He tells wild stories, makes himself the hero, demonises anyone who's wronged him. I should have remembered that before I took you there tonight.'

My patience snaps. 'So now you're sorry you introduced me to someone who confirms what I've been saying all along? Someone who might help me protect a child I care about?'

'I'm sorry I introduced you to someone who's feeding your obsession!' Greg exclaims. 'This isn't healthy, Rachel. You're seeing conspiracy where there might just be a normal woman trying to build a relationship with her boyfriend's daughter.'

'Obsession?' I repeat, my voice dangerously quiet. 'You

think being concerned about a child's welfare is an obsession?'

'I think the level of your fixation on Melissa goes beyond normal concern,' Greg says firmly. 'And now you have Scott's wild stories to justify it, which is exactly what you wanted.'

We stare at each other across my living room, the space between us suddenly seeming unfixable.

'I'm going to tell James,' I say finally. 'With or without your support. I'm going to warn him about Melissa.'

'Based on the unreliable account of a known exaggerator?' Greg asks. 'Rachel, think about what you're doing. You could destroy his chance at happiness based on circumstantial evidence and one bitter ex's dramatised account.'

'So what would you have me do?' I demand. 'Ignore everything I've seen? Everything Scott confirmed? Wait until something happens to Lily?'

'I'd have you consider that you might be wrong,' Greg says quietly. 'That Scott might be wrong, or at least not entirely truthful. That Melissa might be exactly what she seems; a woman who loves James and is trying to connect with his daughter.'

I shake my head, a cold certainty settling over me. 'I know what I've seen. I know what I heard tonight. And if you can't support me in trying to protect Lily, then I don't know what you're doing here.'

Greg looks at me for a long moment, something like sadness crossing his face. 'I want to support you, Rachel. But not in this. Not in taking the word of someone like Scott and using it to potentially ruin lives. If you go to James with this, you'd better be absolutely certain you're right.'

'I am certain,' I say firmly. 'And I'm disappointed that you'd take her side over mine.'

'I'm not taking sides,' Greg protests. 'I'm trying to be objective. To see all possibilities.'

'No, you're choosing to believe a woman you've met once over someone you're supposed to care about,' I counter. 'You're dismissing my concerns, just like you have been since you got back from Asia.'

'Because I think your concerns might be disproportionate to the actual situation!' Greg exclaims, frustration evident in his voice. 'Not everything is a crisis, Rachel. Not everyone has hidden motives.'

'This isn't about hidden motives,' I argue. 'This is about specific, concerning behaviors that both I and now Scott have witnessed. The medication. The maternal delusions. The fixation on Lily. The strange pet names.'

'Or it's about a woman with a troubled past who's found happiness and is being judged by her ex's exaggerated account and your predetermined suspicions,' Greg counters.

We're at an impasse, both of us rigid in our positions. The silence stretches between us, heavy with unresolved tension.

'I can't do this anymore,' Greg finally says, his voice soft but decided. 'I can't be with someone who would take Scott's word as gospel truth despite knowing his reputation. Who would potentially harm an innocent woman based on circumstantial evidence and paranoia.'

The words hit me harder than I expected. 'And I can't be with someone who would dismiss valid concerns about a child's safety,' I reply, matching his quiet tone. 'Who would take Melissa's side over mine.'

Greg shakes his head sadly. 'That's the problem, Rachel. You see this as sides. Melissa versus you. Scott versus Melissa. Me versus you. This isn't a battle, it's people's lives. Real consequences for real people.'

'Exactly,' I say firmly. 'Real consequences for Lily if I don't speak up.'

Greg gathers his keys and jacket, pausing at the door. 'I think we need to take a break,' he says. 'Maybe permanently. We're clearly not on the same page about this, and I can't stand by while you potentially destroy lives based on Scott's unreliable testimony.'

The finality in his voice catches me off guard, even though we've been heading toward this moment throughout our argument. 'Fine,' I say, a strange calm settling over me. 'If you trust Melissa over me, then we have nothing more to say to each other.'

'It's not about trust,' Greg insists. 'It's about evidence, objectivity, considering all possibilities. But you've made up your mind, and nothing I say will change it.'

'Because I know what I've seen,' I reply. 'And I know Lily deserves to be protected.'

Greg looks at me sadly. 'I hope you're sure about this, Rachel. I hope you don't end up regretting the damage you might cause.'

'The only thing I'd regret is staying silent when I could have helped,' I say firmly.

He nods once, accepting the divide between us. 'Goodbye, Rachel. I hope for everyone's sake that you're wrong about Melissa.'

'And I hope for Lily's sake that I'm right,' I counter. 'At least then someone will be watching out for her.'

The door closes quietly behind him, leaving me alone with the wreckage of yet another relationship. But unlike the hollow emptiness that usually follows a breakup, I feel a strange, steely resolve forming within me. Greg's betrayal, and that's how it feels, his siding with Melissa over me, has only strengthened my determination. If he can be so easily swayed by one brief meeting with her, dismissing Scott's testimony despite its perfect alignment with my observations, then I truly am Lily's only hope.

I sit on the sofa, exhaustion mingling with newfound purpose. Not only has Melissa inserted herself into James and Lily's lives, but she's now managed to cost me my relationship too. She's taking everything from me, piece by piece. First my role in Lily's life, now Greg. What's next?

My phone sits on the coffee table, James's contact information just a few taps away. I could call him now, tell him everything Scott told us, warn him about Melissa's history of delusional attachment to other men's children. I should call him, really. Every moment Lily spends with Melissa is a risk, but something holds me back. The awareness that, as Greg pointed out, Scott's reliability might be questioned. The knowledge that James has dismissed my concerns repeatedly, and might do so again without more concrete evidence. The fear that if I push too hard, I might push him away entirely, leaving Lily without even my distant protection. No, I need to approach this carefully. I need more than Scott's account, compelling as it is. I need something James can't dismiss or explain away, something that proves beyond doubt that Melissa is not who she claims to be.

Tomorrow, I'll start digging deeper into Melissa's past. The stillbirth she claims to have experienced. The ex-partner who supposedly abandoned her. The farm in Devon where she claims to have grown up. There must be records, people who remember her, evidence that either confirms or contradicts her stories. Then, armed with facts rather than suspicions, I'll confront James again. Make him listen, make him understand the danger Melissa poses to Lily.

I drag myself upstairs to bed, my body shattered but my mind still racing. As I change into pajamas, I catch sight of myself in the mirror and pause, struck by how this situation has consumed me. Yes, Melissa has cost me my relationship with Greg. Yes, she's insinuated herself into James and Lily's lives. But she hasn't won yet. I still have the truth on my side; Scott's account, my own observations, the mounting evidence of her unhealthy fixation on Lily. And I won't stop until I've exposed that truth, no matter what else I might lose in the process.

As I slip between cool sheets, I find myself thinking of Sarah. What would she make of all this? Would she understand my determination to protect her daughter, or would she, like Greg, counsel caution and moderation?

'I'm trying to protect her,' I whisper into the darkness, as if Sarah might somehow hear. 'Your little girl. I promised I would, remember?'

The silence offers no answers, no reassurance. I curl onto my side, unexpected tears sliding down my cheeks as the events of the night catch up with me. Greg, walking out. Melissa, insinuating herself further into James and Lily's lives. Scott's disturbing account of Melissa's delusions. And now, the lonely path ahead, fighting a battle that no one else seems to recognise is even happening. Melissa has taken enough from me. She won't take Lily too. Not while I'm still breathing.

CHAPTER 11

James

I've always considered myself a rational man. Someone who approaches problems methodically, weighs evidence before jumping to conclusions, and generally keeps a level head. Lily calls it being 'boring' sometimes, this tendency to think things through rather than act on impulse. Sarah used to tease me about it too, in that affectionate way that acknowledged it was both my greatest strength and most frustrating quality. Now, as I sit at my kitchen table, watching Melissa help Lily with her breakfast, I feel that carefully constructed rationality crumbling.

'There we go, angel,' Melissa says, cutting Lily's toast into precise triangles. 'Just the way you like it.'

'Thank you,' Lily chirps, reaching for her cup of juice. 'Can we go to the park after school today?'

Melissa looks at me to confirm. I nod, forcing a smile that feels wooden on my face. 'If the weather is alright.'

Three days have passed since the disastrous dinner at Rachel's. Three days since I heard Melissa confuse Lily with her stillborn daughter in her sleep. Three days of careful observation, of subtle questions, of growing unease that I've been trying desperately to dismiss as paranoia. The evidence is mounting, impossible to ignore, sure, but she still isn't doing anything dangerous. So what if there are small inconsistencies in Melissa's stories about her past? But, the medication box with her name on it that she insists isn't hers is hurting me. How can I find out the truth?

'I'd better head off,' Melissa says, looking at her phone. 'Big meeting this morning.' She bends to kiss Lily's forehead, then comes to me, her lips soft against mine. 'See you both later?'

'We'll be here,' I assure her, accepting the kiss automatically while my mind continues its relentless cataloguing of concerns.

After Melissa leaves, I focus on getting Lily ready for school, the familiar routine giving me a nice distraction from my troubled thoughts. It's only when I'm driving back home after dropping her off that I allow myself to fully confront what I've been avoiding... There's something wrong with Melissa's attachment to my daughter. Something that goes beyond the natural affection of a woman dating a single father.

I need facts about Melissa's past; concrete details I can verify. Her stillborn daughter, Olivia. The farm in Devon she claims to have grown up on. The marketing career she's supposedly built. If those check out, perhaps I'm overreacting after all.

I begin with the stillbirth, searching online for birth and death records. Olivia Chambers, born and died approximately three years ago, according to Melissa's account. But after an hour of searching various databases, I find nothing. No birth registration, no death certificate, no hospital records I can access.

Of course, such records aren't always easily available to the public, I remind myself. Also, Melissa might have used the father's surname rather than Chambers. Or perhaps the stillbirth occurred somewhere with different record keeping systems.

I move on to the farm in Devon, searching property records and local news archives for any mention of a Chambers family farm near Exeter. Again, nothing definitive emerges. There are Chambers families in Devon, but none associated with the kind of dairy farm Melissa has described in such detail.

My phone buzzes with a text from Rachel: 'We need to talk. Just us. It's important. I found something in my guest bathroom after Melissa used it. Something disturbing.'

After our argument at dinner, I'd expected to hear from her, but the timing of her message feels almost supernatural, as if she's somehow sensed my increasing doubts about Melissa. Despite our disagreement, despite my frustration with her persistent suspicion of Melissa, I find myself relieved at the prospect of talking to Rachel. She knows me better than almost anyone; might see clarity where I see only confusion.

'Tomorrow? Lunch?' I text back.

'Yes. The café near your office? 1pm?' comes her immediate response.

'I'll be there,' I confirm, already feeling a slight easing of the tension that's been building in my chest.

The front door opens unexpectedly, making me jump. Melissa appears in the doorway to my office, smiling brightly.

'Surprise! My meeting finished early, so I thought I'd come work from here this afternoon.' She notices my startled expression. 'Is that alright? I can go if you'd prefer to be alone.'

'No, no, it's fine,' I assure her, quickly closing the browser tabs with my searches. 'Just wasn't expecting you, that's all.'

She comes to perch on the edge of my desk, her hand resting lightly on my shoulder. 'What are you working on so intently?'

'Just some reports for work,' I lie, hating how naturally it comes. 'Nothing interesting.'

'I was thinking,' Melissa says, apparently accepting my explanation, 'that we could look through more of your family photos later? You promised to show me Lily's baby albums.'

My skin prickles with unease. Rachel had mentioned yesterday how uncomfortable she felt with Melissa's intense interest in Lily's baby photos. 'Sure,' I say, forcing neutrality into my voice. 'They're on the shelf in the living room, if you want to look now. I need to finish this up first.'

'Perfect,' she says, dropping a kiss on top of my head before leaving the office. I hear her moving around in the living room, the sound of books being removed from shelves.

I should join her, I think. Should watch how she reacts to those photos of Lily as a baby, should monitor for any signs of the disturbing fixation Rachel has noted. But I need a moment to collect myself, to decide how to proceed with these growing suspicions.

I close my laptop and head to the living room, where Melissa is sitting cross-legged on the floor, surrounded by photo albums. She looks up as I enter, her face alight with what appears to be genuine delight.

'James, these are wonderful! Look how tiny she was!'

I sit beside her, watching as she carefully turns pages of Lily's first year of life. Sarah's face appears in many of the photos, her smile tired but radiant as she holds our newborn daughter. Melissa doesn't seem troubled by Sarah's presence in the images; on the contrary, she makes appreciative comments about Sarah's natural way with Lily, how happy they look together.

Not the reaction of someone jealous or resentful of Lily's biological mother, I note, feeling a bit of relief. She turns to a particular photo, one taken in the hospital just hours after Lily's birth. Sarah, exhausted but beaming, holding Lily against her chest while I sit beside them on the hospital bed, my arm around them both. Our first family portrait.

'She's so perfect. My little angel.'

A chill runs through me at the possessive pronoun. 'Sarah was so proud,' I say deliberately. 'She used to say Lily was the best thing we ever made together.'

Melissa doesn't seem to register my emphasis on 'we.' 'She's a miracle,' she says softly, still staring at the photo of newborn Lily. 'Sometimes babies come into our lives in unexpected ways, don't they?'

I'm not sure how to interpret that comment. 'I suppose they do,' I say cautiously.

Melissa continues turning pages, commenting on Lily's

first bath, first smile, first Christmas, with an intensity that might be merely enthusiastic or might be something more concerning. I watch her closely, looking for signs that she's seeing Olivia rather than Lily in these images, but her comments remain appropriate, focused on the actual child in the photographs.

When she excuses herself to use the bathroom, I find myself automatically tidying the albums, stacking them neatly, my mind still turning over Melissa's reactions, searching for confirmation or denial of my fears.

As I'm organising the albums, I notice one of Rachel's tote bags tucked under the side table. She must have left it here after her last visit. As I reach to move it aside, something catches my eye. A corner of paper sticking out of an inner pocket. Without thinking, I pull it out.

It's a drawing, clearly done by an adult trying to mimic a child's style: a family portrait labeled in careful handwriting. 'Daddy' (me), 'Mummy' (Melissa), and 'My Angel' (Lily), holding hands beneath a bright yellow sun. But there's a fourth figure in the image, an adult woman with dark hair like Sarah's, standing apart from the happy group. This figure has been violently crossed out, the pencil digging so deeply into the paper that it's torn in places. Above it, written in jagged letters: 'NOT YOUR MUMMY ANYMORE.'

My blood turns to ice in my veins. I stare at the drawing, unable to reconcile the violent emotion it represents with the gentle, loving woman who's been sharing my home, caring for my daughter. Is this how Melissa truly sees Sarah? As competition to be eliminated, crossed out, rejected?

Melissa returns from the bathroom and sees me holding the drawing. The color drains from her face.

'Where did you find that?' she asks, her voice barely above a whisper.

I hold up the paper, my hand steadier than I would have expected. 'In Rachel's bag. Want to explain this, Melissa?'

Her eyes widen in shock, then narrow with what looks like

realisation. 'Rachel's bag? James, that's not mine. I've never seen that before.'

'It shows you, me, and Lily as a happy family, with Sarah crossed out,' I say, my voice hardening. 'It's exactly the kind of concerning behavior Rachel's been warning me about.'

Melissa takes a step toward me, her hand extended. 'James, please listen. I didn't draw that. I would never…' She stops, her eyes filling with sudden understanding. 'Rachel put it there. She's trying to make you think I'm unstable, that I'm fixated on replacing Sarah.'

The accusation against Rachel, my oldest friend, Lily's godmother, the woman who's supported us through everything, strikes me as so outlandish that it only confirms my worst fears about Melissa's mental state.

'So Rachel drew this herself and planted it in her own bag that she left here?' I say, unable to keep the skepticism from my voice. 'That makes no sense, Melissa.'

'I know how it sounds,' she says desperately, 'but think about it. Rachel has been trying to drive a wedge between us from the beginning. She was the one who found that fake medication box, the one who keeps planting doubts about my past-'

'No one's planting anything,' I cut her off, the drawing still in my hand. 'Rachel's concerned, that's all. And frankly, so am I. This?' I hold up the drawing. 'This is disturbing. And your attempt to blame Rachel instead of explaining it is even more concerning.'

'Because there's nothing to explain!' Melissa's voice rises with frustration. 'I didn't draw it! James, please. You know me. You know I would never think of Sarah that way. I've always spoken of her with respect.'

'I think you should go,' I say, the words feeling like stones in my mouth. 'Take some time, get some… help. I can't have this kind of instability around Lily. I'll call you tomorrow.'

Tears fill Melissa's eyes. 'You're choosing to believe a piece of paper over me? Over everything we've built together?'

'I'm choosing to protect my daughter,' I say, though the certainty in my voice masks the doubt beginning to creep in. 'I've seen too many concerning signs to ignore them anymore.'

Melissa stands very still, tears tracking silently down her cheeks. 'Rachel is manipulating you,' she says quietly. 'I don't know why, but she is. And by the time you realise it, it might be too late.'

The crazy statement only cements my decision. 'Please leave, Melissa. I'll pack your things and have them sent to yours.'

She looks at me for a moment, then says, 'I love you, James. And I love Lily. I would never do anything to hurt either of you. I hope someday you'll see that.'

With that, she gathers her coat and bag and walks to the door. She pauses there, looking back at me with an expression of such raw pain that I almost waver. 'Be careful,' she says softly. 'Not everyone who claims to care about you has your best interests at heart.'

With that, she walks out, the door closing behind her with a quiet click. I move to the sofa, the drawing still in my hand, doubt and certainty fighting within me. Rachel has been Lily's godmother since birth, has been my friend for years. Her concern for us is genuine, protective. Not manipulative.

I reach for my phone and text Rachel: 'You might be right about Melissa. I found something disturbing. Still on for lunch tomorrow?'

Her reply comes almost instantly: 'Oh James, I'm so sorry. Yes, definitely still on for lunch. Hope Lily is OK.'

As I sit alone in the suddenly quiet house, waiting for the time to pick up Lily from school, I try to ignore the small voice in the back of my mind that whispers: What if you're wrong? What if Melissa was telling the truth? I've always been a rational man. I make decisions based on evidence, not wild accusations. And all the evidence points to Melissa being unstable, potentially dangerous in her fixation on my daughter. Doesn't it?

I fold the drawing and place it in my desk drawer. I'll show it to Rachel tomorrow. She'll understand what it means, help me make sense of everything that's happened. Help me navigate telling Lily that Melissa won't be in our lives anymore.

Until then, I have to trust that I've done the right thing. That I've protected my daughter from harm. Because that's my job as her father to keep her safe, no matter what. No matter who I have to cut out of our lives to do it.

Even if, somewhere deep down, a tiny doubt refuses to be silenced.

CHAPTER 12

Rachel

The stack of papers on my kitchen table has been growing steadily since dawn. Printouts of Melissa's sparse social media accounts. Screenshots of search results for 'Melissa Chambers' in Bristol. Notes from my conversation with Scott. A rough timeline of Melissa's appearances in James and Lily's lives, with each concerning incident carefully dated and documented. I've been awake since 4:30 a.m., fuelled by a combination of anxiety and determination, assembling what I hope will be an undeniable case against the woman who has wormed herself into my best friend's life. The woman who, I'm increasingly convinced, poses a genuine threat to Lily.

Overnight, I've done more digging into Melissa's background, though there's frustratingly little to find. Her social media accounts only go back to January of this year; her LinkedIn profile shows an impressive career in marketing but with companies that, when I look them up, either don't exist or have no record of a Melissa Chambers working for them. The stillbirth she claims to have experienced three years ago doesn't appear in any public records I can access, though that's not definitive; such records aren't always easily searchable.

What is clear, however, is that Melissa Chambers seems to have materialised out of thin air less than a year ago, with a carefully constructed backstory but little tangible evidence to support it. If it wasn't for Scott, I'd think she was a ghost.

'Please let this be enough,' I say to myself, sorting the papers into a more organised arrangement. 'Please let him listen this time.'

My phone rings, startling me from my thoughts. Scott's name flashes on the screen, unexpected at 7:30 in the morning.

'Scott?' I answer, trying to keep the surprise from my voice. 'Everything alright?'

'Sorry for the early call,' he says, his voice tense. 'I couldn't sleep after your visit last night. There's something else I remembered about Melissa, something important I think you should know before you talk to your friend.'

I reach for a pen, pulling my notepad closer. 'I'm listening.'

'It was toward the end of our relationship,' Scott begins, 'after I'd started to notice her... confusion about Ben. There was an incident at his school.'

My pen hovers over the paper. 'What kind of incident?'

'Melissa picked him up without my knowledge or permission,' Scott says, the memory clearly still disturbing him. 'I was meant to collect him that day, but she went early, told the school there was a "family surprise" planned, and took him to the park.'

I write this down, my hand shaking slightly. 'Did she have permission to pick him up generally?'

'No, that's the thing. She wasn't on the approved list. But she was charming, convincing. Said she was my partner and Ben's stepmum, that I was waiting nearby with a surprise.' Scott pauses. 'When I arrived at the school and Ben wasn't there, I panicked. Called the police, the whole thing.'

'What happened?' I prompt, dreading the answer.

'Found them at the park two hours later. Ben was fine, having ice cream, completely unaware anything was wrong. Melissa seemed genuinely confused by my reaction, kept saying she was "practising" being a proper mum, that she wanted to surprise me with a "family day out." When I told her she'd terrified me, she burst into tears, said I was overreacting, that she'd never hurt "her boy."'

I write down every word. 'And that's when you ended things?'

'The next day,' Scott confirms. 'I couldn't risk it happening again, escalating. The school apologised profusely, tightened their procedures. But Rachel,' his voice drops lower, more urgent, 'the thing that haunts me is how normal Ben thought it all was. How easily she convinced him it was just a fun surprise, nothing to worry about. If I hadn't shown up...'

He doesn't finish the thought, doesn't need to. We both know what he's implying.

'Thank you for telling me,' I say, my resolve hardening. 'This helps.'

'Be careful how you approach your friend,' Scott advises. 'Melissa doesn't respond well to direct confrontation. When I told her I was concerned about her behaviour with Ben, she turned it around, made it seem like I was the one with the problem, like I was trying to keep her from bonding with him because I was still hung up on my ex.'

'Classic manipulation,' I say.

'Exactly. And she was good at it. Very good.' Scott hesitates. 'Look, I don't like getting involved in other people's business, but if your friend's daughter is at risk... well, I wish someone had warned me earlier about Melissa. Maybe things wouldn't have gone so far.'

We end the call with Scott offering to speak directly to James if needed, an offer I tuck away as a last resort. His account of Melissa taking his son from school without permission adds a new, frightening dimension to my concerns. It's no longer just about uncomfortable boundary crossing or troubling fixation; it's about actions that could genuinely endanger Lily.

I add Scott's new information to my growing file, then check the time. Still hours before my lunch with James. Hours to continue building my case, to anticipate Melissa's likely defences, to prepare for what might be my last chance to convince James before something truly terrible happens.

My phone buzzes with a text from James: 'Still on for lunch today?'

'Absolutely,' I respond immediately. 'Looking forward to it.'

I stare at the message from last night about how he's found something about her. Could he be having doubts about Melissa too? Has he noticed something concerning, something that might make him more receptive to what I have to tell him?

'See you at 1,' I text back, trying not to read too much into his words.

The morning passes in a blur of additional research and nervous anticipation. I make more coffee than I should, pacing my kitchen as I rehearse what I'll say to James, how I'll present the evidence without sounding like a jealous friend or an obsessive stalker. I'm sure that's how Melissa will spin it. That's how Scott says she operated when he confronted her; turning his legitimate concerns into evidence of his own issues, his own failings. I need to be prepared for that, need to make my case so clear, so undeniable, that James can't dismiss it regardless of how Melissa might try to manipulate the situation.

By the time I leave for the café near James's office, I've condensed my evidence into a slim folder, containing only the most compelling, concrete concerns. Scott's account of Melissa's unauthorised school pickup. The empty medication box with her name on it. The rapid acceleration of her involvement in Lily's life, from clothes to haircuts to bedroom redesigns. The inconsistencies in her background, the lack of verifiable history before this year. It's still circumstantial, much of it, but taken together it paints a disturbing picture. I only hope James can see it too.

The café is busy when I arrive, the lunch rush in full swing. I spot James already at a table in the corner, nursing a coffee, his expression distracted and tense. My heart lifts at the sight of him, then immediately sinks as I note the dark circles under his eyes, the worried crease between his brows. Whatever's bothering him, it's not minor.

'Hey,' I say, sliding into the seat across from him. 'You look like you could use something stronger than coffee.'

He attempts a smile that doesn't reach his eyes. 'That obvious, huh?'

'Only to someone who knows you well.' I set my folder on the table but don't open it yet. 'Bad day at work?'

James shakes his head, glancing around as if to ensure we're not overheard. 'It's not work. It's... I think you might have been right. About Melissa.'

The words I've been waiting to hear, dreading to hear, hang between us. Relief and alarm war within me, but I keep my expression carefully neutral. 'What's happened?'

He tells me, his voice low and strained, about Melissa's sleep talking, about her confusing Lily with her stillborn daughter Olivia. About the drawing he found in her purse, with Sarah's likeness violently crossed out. About his growing sense that Melissa's attachment to Lily is not entirely healthy or based in reality.

I listen without interrupting, without saying 'I told you so,' though the words press against my teeth, desperate to escape. When he finishes, I reach across the table to squeeze his hand briefly.

'I'm so sorry, James. I know how much you wanted this to work.'

He pulls his hand away, running it through his hair in a gesture of frustration I know well. 'I still don't know if I'm overreacting. She has explanations for everything; the drawing was a therapy exercise, the sleep talking was just a bad dream. Maybe that's all it is. Maybe I'm seeing problems where there aren't any because...' He trails off.

'Because I put the idea in your head?' I finish for him, keeping my voice gentle. 'James, I wouldn't have pushed this if I weren't genuinely concerned. And I have more information now, things you need to know.'

I open the folder, laying out the evidence I've gathered piece by piece, saving Scott's account for last. James listens with growing discomfort, his fingers tapping restlessly against his coffee cup as each new detail emerges.

'So there's no record of a stillbirth?' he asks when I mention my fruitless searches for Olivia Chambers.

'None that I could find,' I confirm. 'Though that doesn't mean it didn't happen. Records aren't always accessible, especially for sensitive cases like stillbirths.'

'But combined with everything else...' He leaves the implication hanging.

'Combined with everything else, it's concerning,' I agree. 'And there's more. Something I learned just this morning.'

I tell him about Scott, about Melissa's previous relationship with another single father, the disturbing parallels to her rapid insertion into James and Lily's lives. When I get to the part about Melissa taking Scott's son from school without permission, James's face drains of colour.

'She took him? Without telling Scott?' he repeats, his voice hollow.

'For two hours,' I confirm grimly. 'Said she was "practising" being a proper mum. That it was supposed to be a nice surprise.'

James stares at his coffee, his expression haunted. 'Lily's school has strict pickup procedures. Melissa's not on the approved list.'

'Not yet,' I say quietly. 'But Scott says she was very convincing. Used her charm, her apparent normalcy, to persuade the school it was fine.'

'Jesus,' James whispers, and in that single word I hear the full weight of his fear, his dawning realisation of the potential danger.

'Scott's willing to talk to you directly,' I offer. 'To confirm everything I've told you.'

James shakes his head, looking suddenly exhausted. 'I believe you. It fits with what I've seen, what I've been feeling but not wanting to acknowledge.'

The admission, so long in coming, brings me no satisfaction, only a leaden sense of dread for what might come next. 'What are you going to do?'

'End it,' he says simply. 'As gently as possible, but firmly. Make it clear that while I care for her, the relationship is moving too quickly, that Lily needs more time to adjust to the idea of someone new in our lives.'

'And if she doesn't accept that?' I press, thinking of Scott's warnings about Melissa's manipulative responses to confrontation.

'She'll have to,' James says, a note of his old confidence returning. 'Lily's my priority. If Melissa can't respect that, can't give us the space we need, then there's no future for us regardless of... other concerns.'

It's diplomatic, measured, entirely James in its rational approach to an emotionally charged situation. But I'm not convinced it adequately addresses the potential danger Melissa might pose.

'James,' I say carefully, 'if Melissa genuinely believes on some level that Lily is her dead child, or some kind of replacement for that child, she might not respond rationally to being separated from her. Scott said when he ended things, Melissa became increasingly desperate, showing up at his workplace, at his son's school.'

'What are you suggesting?' James asks, a defensive edge creeping into his voice. 'That I get a restraining order based on something she said in her sleep and a former boyfriend's account of their breakup?'

'I'm suggesting you be extremely careful,' I clarify. 'That you consider taking precautions; changing your locks, alerting Lily's school to be extra vigilant about pickup procedures, maybe even staying somewhere else for a few days after you end things, just until you're sure Melissa has accepted the breakup.'

James opens his mouth to respond, but is interrupted by his phone buzzing insistently. He glances at the screen, his brow furrowing. 'It's Melissa. That's the third call in the last five minutes.'

'Don't answer,' I say quickly. 'Not until we've finished

talking.'

But the phone continues to buzz, and the worry on James's face deepens. 'What if something's wrong? What if it's about Lily?'

'Lily's at school,' I remind him. 'Safe. Melissa has no reason to be contacting her.'

Even as the words leave my mouth, Scott's account of Melissa taking his son from school echoes ominously in my mind. James must have the same thought, because he answers the call immediately, his voice tense.

'Melissa? What's going on?'

I can't hear her response, but I watch James's face pale, his free hand tightening into a fist on the table. 'What do you mean they called you? You're not on the contact list.'

Another pause, his expression shifting from confusion to alarm. 'Stay there. Don't do anything. I'm on my way.'

He ends the call, already standing, gathering his coat with jerky movements. 'I have to go. Lily's school called Melissa to say Lily's not feeling well, has a fever. But that's impossible; Melissa isn't on the contact list, and Lily was fine this morning.'

'James,' I say, standing as well, alarm coursing through me. 'This is exactly what Scott described. Melissa somehow convincing the school to call her instead of you. It's not a coincidence.'

'I know,' he says grimly, throwing money on the table for our unfinished coffees. 'That's why I need to get there now. Before she does.'

'I'm coming with you,' I insist, gathering my evidence folder with one hand while reaching for my coat with the other.

For once, James doesn't argue, doesn't insist he can handle this alone. 'We'll take my car. It's closer.'

The drive to Lily's school is tense, James pushing the speed limit while I try repeatedly to call the school, to warn them not to release Lily to anyone but James. But the calls go to voicemail, presumably because the office is busy with the lunch hour rush.

'I should have listened to you sooner,' James says abruptly.

'Should have taken your concerns more seriously.'

'Don't do that,' I tell him firmly. 'Not now. Focus on getting to Lily, on making sure she's safe. There will be time for action later.'

He nods as he takes a corner faster than is strictly safe. 'If she's hurt her, Rachel... if she's so much as upset Lily...'

'Lily will be fine,' I assure him, with more confidence than I feel. 'Melissa wants to be her mother, not harm her. And the school would never let her take Lily without proper authorisation.'

Even as I say it, I remember Scott's words: 'She was charming, convincing.' I think of how easily Melissa has manipulated her way into James's life, how thoroughly she's blinded him to her concerning behaviour. Who's to say she couldn't do the same with school administrators?

The school comes into view, a redbrick building with a colourful playground visible behind tall fences. James parks haphazardly, barely waiting for the engine to stop before he's out of the car, striding toward the main entrance with purposeful steps. I follow close behind, my evidence folder clutched tightly, as if it might somehow help in this immediate crisis.

Inside, the school office is quiet, a middle aged receptionist looking up with mild surprise as we burst in.

'James Porter,' James announces without preamble. 'I'm here for my daughter, Lily. I understand she's not feeling well?'

The receptionist frowns, tapping at her computer. 'Lily Porter? I don't have any record of her being unwell today.' She looks up, confused. 'She's in Ms. Parker's class, correct? Year One?'

'Yes,' James confirms, his voice tight with controlled panic. 'Her... my friend Melissa called to say the school had contacted her about Lily having a fever.'

The receptionist's frown deepens. 'Sir, we haven't called anyone about Lily Porter today. And we would only call the contacts listed on her file, which are you and...' she checks the screen again, 'a Rachel Whittaker. There's no Melissa on this list.'

James and I exchange alarmed glances. 'I need to see Lily,' James says, his voice leaving no room for argument. 'Now, please.'

The receptionist must sense the urgency, because she immediately picks up the phone, calling Lily's classroom to request she be sent to the office. The two minutes we wait are among the longest of my life, James pacing the small space like a caged animal, while I stand frozen, scenarios playing out in my head, each more terrifying than the last.

When the office door opens, Lily appears, perfectly healthy, looking confused but pleased to see us. 'Daddy! Rachel! Why are you here? Is school over?'

James crouches down, pulling Lily into a tight hug that clearly surprises her. 'No, pumpkin. I just needed to see you for a minute. Are you feeling okay?'

Lily nods against his shoulder. 'I'm fine. We were just having story time. Is something wrong?'

Over Lily's head, James meets my gaze, the relief in his eyes giving way to a new concern. If Melissa lied about the school calling her, if Lily is perfectly fine and safe, then what was Melissa's purpose in creating this false emergency?

'Nothing's wrong,' James assures Lily, releasing her from the hug but keeping a hand on her shoulder. 'I just missed you, that's all.'

Lily beams, accepting this explanation with the easy trust of childhood. 'I missed you too! Can Rachel come over after school?'

'We'll see,' James hedges, clearly trying to process the implications of Melissa's lie. 'You'd better get back to story time now. I'll pick you up at the usual time, okay?'

After Lily returns to her classroom, escorted by a teaching assistant, James turns to the receptionist. 'Has anyone else inquired about Lily today? Tried to see her or pick her up?'

The receptionist shakes her head. 'No, sir. You're the first visitors we've had for Lily today.'

'If anyone comes asking for her,' James says, his voice

deadly serious, 'anyone at all other than myself or Rachel, do not release her to them. Under any circumstances. Is that clear?'

The receptionist blinks, clearly surprised by his intensity. 'Of course, Mr. Porter. As I said, we only release children to authorised contacts on their file.'

'Even if that person is very convincing,' I add, thinking of Scott's warning. 'Even if they claim to be Mr. Porter's partner or a family friend. Even in an emergency.'

Understanding dawns in the receptionist's eyes. 'Is there a specific concern we should be aware of, regarding Lily's safety?'

James hesitates, clearly uncomfortable with sharing personal matters but equally unwilling to risk Lily's wellbeing. 'Yes,' he says finally. 'My... former partner may attempt to see Lily without permission. She's not dangerous, but she's not authorised to have contact with Lily at this time.'

It's a diplomatic phrasing that doesn't reveal the full extent of our concerns, but seems to convey the seriousness of the situation. The receptionist nods, making a note in the computer system.

'I'll alert Lily's teacher and the head immediately,' she assures us. 'We take these matters very seriously, Mr. Porter. Lily will not be released to anyone but yourself or Ms. Whittaker.'

Outside the school, James leans against the wall, looking suddenly drained. 'Why would Melissa lie about the school calling her? What was she trying to accomplish?'

'Testing the waters, maybe,' I suggest, the possibilities spinning through my mind. 'Seeing if she could convince you that she had legitimate contact with Lily's school. Or creating a situation where she could reasonably be at the school, maybe try to see Lily herself.'

'Jesus,' James mutters, pushing away from the wall. 'I need to find her, confront her about this. If she'd lie about something so easily verifiable...'

'I'll come with you,' I offer immediately.

He shakes his head. 'No, I need to do this alone. And I need you to pick Lily up from school at the regular time, just in case

Melissa tries something else. Will you do that?'

The request, the trust it implies, catches me off guard. 'Of course. But James, are you sure you should confront her alone? After everything we've learned?'

'I'll be fine,' he assures me, though his expression remains troubled. 'I'll meet her in a public place, hear what she has to say. Then I'll end it, make it clear that this relationship isn't working, that I need space.'

It's not ideal, but I understand his reluctance to have me present for what will inevitably be a difficult, emotional conversation. 'Alright. But promise me you'll be careful. Remember what Scott said about how she turns things around, makes it seem like you're the one with the problem.'

'I'll be careful,' he promises, already taking out his phone. 'I'll text you once I've talked to her, let you know how it went.'

'And I'll bring Lily to mine afterward, if that's okay?' I suggest. 'Just for a few hours, until you're sure Melissa has understood the situation and left your house.'

James nods, looking grateful. 'That would be perfect. Thank you, Rachel. For everything.'

We part ways in the school car park, James heading to his car while I walk to mine, still parked at the café several blocks away. As I walk, I can't shake the sense of impending crisis, the feeling that we're still missing something important about Melissa's motivations, her plans. I think of Scott's description of Melissa's escalating behaviour after their breakup; the desperate phone calls, the unwelcome appearances at his workplace and his son's school. Will she react similarly with James? And if so, how far might she go to maintain her connection to Lily, the child she seems to view as a replacement for her lost daughter?

The questions chase themselves around my mind as I walk, each more troubling than the last. By the time I reach my car, I've resolved to call Scott again, to ask for more details about how Melissa responded to their breakup, what specific behaviours James might need to prepare for. One thing is becoming increasingly clear: Melissa Chambers is not just a woman with boundary issues, or even simply a person with untreated mental health concerns. She's someone actively manipulating situations to gain access to a child she has no legitimate claim to, someone willing to lie about serious matters to achieve her goals. Luckily, I have done all I can to let James see the truth.

CHAPTER 13

Melissa

I check my watch again, tapping my foot anxiously against the polished floor of the café. James is twenty minutes late, which isn't like him at all. He's usually punctual to a fault, something I've found endearing about him. But today, his absence feels ominous, especially after the strange tension in his voice when I called about Lily being sick. I didn't understand his reaction, or why they called me, but acting like it is a dangerous situation isn't fair.

I take another sip of my rapidly cooling latte, scanning the entrance for what must be the hundredth time. The barista behind the counter gives me a sympathetic look; the universal recognition of someone being stood up. But James wouldn't do that. Not James, who apologises if he's even two minutes late to anything. My phone sits on the table, screen dark and silent. I've sent three messages since I arrived, each more concerned than the last, with no response. This isn't like him.

I tap my fingers on the table, trying to ignore the knot of anxiety tightening in my chest. I'd planned to tell him today, to finally share the full truth about my past, about the medication I've been taking. But the moment had to be right. Somewhere quiet, just the two of us, with time to explain properly. Now he's not here, and the carefully rehearsed words seem to evaporate from my mind, replaced by a growing dread that something is very wrong.

The bell above the door chimes, and I look up eagerly, relief flooding through me as James finally walks in. But the feeling dissipates as quickly as it came. His face is set in hard lines I've never seen before, his normally warm eyes cold and distant as they find me in the corner.

He doesn't smile as he approaches, doesn't apologise for being late. He simply pulls out the chair opposite me and sits, his posture rigid.

'James?' I reach for his hand across the table, but he subtly shifts it away, out of reach. 'Is everything okay? Is Lily alright?'

'Lily is fine,' he says, his voice flat. 'She was never sick. The school never called you.'

I blink, taken aback by his directness. 'I... they did! Or somebody did...'

'You lied,' he interrupts, the words sharp edged. 'About my daughter. You made me think she was in trouble, that something was wrong with her.'

Ugh. Sounds like Rachel has already got in his head. Why is she so obsessed with me? Maybe she was the one who called...

'Why did you need to see me so urgently?'

I take a deep breath. This isn't how I imagined this conversation going, but I need to tell him now, before things spiral further. I reach for my purse, intending to show him the prescription, the information pamphlet I'd printed out to help explain everything. As I rummage through the familiar contents, a cold feeling spreads through my body. The medication box isn't there. Neither is the pamphlet. I check again, more thoroughly, emptying items onto the table one by one.

'I don't understand,' I say, more to myself than to James. 'It was right here this morning.'

James watches me with that same cold expression. 'What are you looking for?'

'My medication,' I say, abandoning caution. 'I wanted to

explain... about the prescription box you found. It is mine, but I panicked when you confronted me. I've been taking Quetiapine for the past few years, since Olivia died. For the depression, the psychotic episodes I had afterwards.'

His expression changes, but doesn't soften. 'You lied about that too?'

'I was scared,' I admit, still searching futilely through my bag. 'People hear "antipsychotic medication" and immediately think the worst. I didn't want you to see me as damaged, as unstable. I was going to tell you today, properly explain everything.'

'Like you explained about working in marketing, not childcare?' He's not asking a question; he's laying out evidence.

My heart sinks further. 'But you know I work in marketing. You must be mixing me up with a similar name. Why would it matter anyway?'

'Because it's strange, Melissa! Also, I know you engineered that "accidental" meeting with me.'

His words hit me like physical blows. 'Engineered? James, no, it wasn't like that. The fire alarm was genuinely a coincidence.'

'Was it?' His eyes are hard now, skeptical. 'Like the coincidence of wanting to dress Lily exactly like you as a child? Getting her the same haircut? Planning to redecorate her room to match your childhood bedroom?'

A sickening realisation dawns on me. 'You've been talking to Rachel.'

The name hangs between us, charged with all the subtle animosity that has existed between Rachel and me from the start.

'Rachel has concerns,' James says carefully. 'Concerns that I've been too blind to see.'

'Rachel has been trying to sabotage our relationship from the beginning,' I say, hearing the desperation creeping into my voice. 'She's jealous, James. She's been the only woman in yours and Lily's life for so long, she can't stand seeing someone else there.'

'This isn't about Rachel,' he snaps, though something in his eyes wavers. 'This is about you lying to me. About the drawing I found in your notebook, with Sarah's face crossed out.'

'That was Rachel! I told you!' I'm aware of my voice rising, heads turning in the café. I lower it with effort. 'I'd never even seen a photo of Sarah until you showed me your albums.'

'And what about at night?' James leans forward, his voice dropping to a harsh whisper. 'What about when you talk in your sleep, Melissa? When you call Lily "your baby"? When you say "they changed her name to trick you"?'

I feel the blood drain from my face. I've had those dreams before, disturbing dreams where Olivia isn't dead, where she's been taken from me, hidden away. I don't tend to have them, unless I don't take my medication...

'Those are just dreams,' I whisper. 'Terrible dreams, yes, but not reality. I know Lily isn't Olivia. I would never confuse them.'

'Yet you keep calling Lily "my angel", which is what you called Olivia,' James presses. 'You tell Lily stories about when she was "in your tummy".'

'That's not... I was telling her about pregnancies in general,' I protest, but the excuse sounds weak even to my own ears. 'James, please. I've been under stress lately. I think someone's been tampering with my medication. I've been having trouble sleeping, having more dreams, more thoughts that don't make sense. But I would never hurt Lily. Never.'

'I want to believe that,' James says, and for the first time, I see pain cutting through the cold anger. 'But you've lied about so many things, Melissa. How can I trust anything you say?'

'Please,' I reach for his hand again, and this time he doesn't pull away, though he doesn't return the pressure of my fingers. 'Let me show you my medical records. Let me prove that everything I've told you about Olivia, about my treatment afterwards, is true.'

For a moment I think I might have reached him. But then his expression hardens again.

'I spoke to Scott.' He says bluntly.

'Scott? My abusive ex? Are you kidding?'

'He told me about you kidnapping his son.'

'*Kidnapping*? James, he told me to pick him up from school, then when I didn't take him straight home he flipped and beat me at the park, in front of everyone. I'll show you the fucking police report!'

He rolls his eyes. 'It is *always* someone else with you. I think we need to take a step back,' he says, gently extracting his hand from mine. 'This relationship has moved too quickly. For Lily's sake, for everyone's sake, I think we should end things now, before they get more complicated.'

The words hit me like a physical blow. 'End things? James, please, don't do this. I love you. I love Lily. Yes, I've made mistakes, but...'

'It's not just mistakes, Melissa,' he interrupts, standing abruptly. 'It's a pattern of deception. Of unhealthy fixation on my daughter. I can't risk Lily's wellbeing, no matter how much I...' He stops himself, swallows hard. 'I think it would be best if you stayed away from both of us for a while.'

'James, wait,' I stand too, panic rising as he moves to leave. 'There's something else you need to know. About Rachel;'

'Don't,' he cuts me off sharply. 'Don't try to deflect this onto Rachel. She's been there for us since Sarah died. She loves Lily like her own.'

That's exactly what I'm afraid of, I want to say, but the words catch in my throat. Any accusation against Rachel now will only sound like jealousy, like desperation. I want to tell him about when we were at hers, when Rachel told me in the kitchen she would kill me if I tried to take Lily away from her.

'I'll have your things packed up and delivered to yours by the end of the week.' James adds quietly.

With that, he turns and walks away, leaving me standing alone in the middle of the café, surrounded by curious onlookers pretending not to watch the drama unfold.

I sink back into my chair, numb with shock. How has

everything fallen apart so quickly? Just yesterday, we were a family forming, James and Lily and me. Now I'm alone again, cast as the villain in a story I don't fully understand. My hands shake as I gather my things, stuffing them haphazardly back into my purse. As I do, my fingers brush against a small pill bottle in a side pocket I rarely use. I pull it out, confused. It's my Quetiapine, but not in its usual packaging; transferred to a generic bottle with no label. I always keep it in the original box, with the prescription information. Always. Someone *has* moved my medication. Someone has been in my purse. A chill runs through me as unpleasant possibilities align in my mind. The missing prescription box that appeared in James's bathroom. Rachel's increasingly hostile behaviour. The way she looks at Lily, with a possessiveness that mirrors the way she looks at James.

I've been off my proper dosage for days now, I realise with growing alarm. The sleeplessness, the intensifying dreams, the paranoia I've been trying to fight down; all symptoms I recognise from before, when I first began treatment after losing Olivia.

Outside the café, the bright winter day seems mockingly cheerful. I stand on the pavement, uncertain where to go, what to do next. Part of me wants to run after James, to make him listen. But his expression when he left was clear: he's made up his mind.

My phone buzzes in my hand: a text from James. 'Please don't contact Lily or come to the school. I've informed them you're not authorised to see her. I'm sorry it's come to this.'

Something inside me breaks. I lean against the building, fighting back tears. Through the blur, I notice a familiar figure across the street; Rachel, watching me from beside her parked car. When our eyes meet, she doesn't look away or pretend she hasn't been observing. Instead, she holds my gaze, and though I can't be certain from this distance, I could swear she's smiling. How did James not see her? Is she really there?

She climbs into her car and drives away, presumably to pick up Lily from school at this time. To step back into the role of surrogate mother, the role she's never fully relinquished. A terrible clarity begins to form in my mind. What if this isn't about my fixation on Lily at all? What if it's about Rachel's?

I look down at the unmarked pill bottle in my hand. My brain feels foggy, thoughts slipping away before I can fully grasp them. Without my proper medication, the boundary between legitimate concern and paranoid delusion is harder to define. But one thing feels certain: Lily isn't safe with Rachel. I just need to figure out how to prove it before it's too late.

I take a deep breath, trying to steady myself. I need to think clearly. Need to find evidence that Rachel has been manipulating the situation, tampering with my medication, planting things for James to find. I need to protect Lily from whatever game Rachel is playing. First though, I need to get home and take my medication properly. Need to clear my head and make a plan. If I'm right about Rachel; and deep down, I *know* I am; then Lily is in danger from the very person James trusts most to protect her, and he's just given Rachel exactly what she's wanted all along: unrestricted access to his daughter, with me pushed entirely out of the picture.

The thought sends a fresh wave of panic through me, but I force it down. Panic won't help Lily. Clear thinking will. Evidence will. I just need to find it before Rachel realises I'm onto her. I jump in a taxi, my decision made. I'll go home, take my medication, and then begin gathering proof of what Rachel has been doing. And when I have enough, I'll make James listen, make him see the truth about the woman he's entrusted his daughter to. Lily isn't my Olivia; I know that, despite what my dreams might sometimes suggest. She is a child in danger. I won't abandon her, no matter what James believes about me now.

CHAPTER 14

James

The new locks make a satisfying click as I turn the key. Solid. Secure. Different from the old ones Melissa had keys to, and probably made about 5 copies of. I run my finger over the fresh metal, still shiny compared to the old brass of the door handle, and try to ignore the feeling in my stomach. This feels both necessary and somehow surreal; that I'm changing my locks to keep out a woman who, just days ago, I was contemplating a future with.

'All done?' Rachel appears in the hallway behind me, a mug of tea in each hand. She offers one to me with a sympathetic smile. 'How are you holding up?'

'Fine,' I lie, accepting the tea gratefully. It's not fine, of course. Nothing about this situation is fine. 'Thanks for staying to help. I'm not sure I could've managed Lily's questions on my own.'

Rachel squeezes my arm reassuringly. 'That's what I'm here for. Always.'

And she has been. Since my confrontation with Melissa three days ago, Rachel has slipped seamlessly into the gaps that Melissa's abrupt departure left in our lives. Picking Lily up from school. Making dinner. Fielding Lily's increasingly pointed questions about why Melissa isn't coming over anymore. It's a relief how easily she's stepped into the role.

'How was she tonight?' I ask, following Rachel into the living room. 'When you put her to bed?'

Rachel settles onto the sofa, tucking her feet beneath her in that familiar way she has. 'Still confused. She wanted to know if Melissa is angry with her. If that's why she went away.'

I close my eyes briefly, guilt washing over me. 'What did you tell her?'

'The same thing we agreed on. That Melissa needed some time to herself, and that it wasn't Lily's fault.' Rachel pauses, watching me over the rim of her mug. 'It wasn't your fault either, James. You know that, right?'

'Isn't it, though? I let her into our lives, into Lily's life. I didn't see the warning signs until it was almost too late.'

'Melissa is very good at hiding who she really is,' Rachel says firmly. 'She fooled a lot of people, not just you. What matters is that you acted when you realised something was wrong. You protected Lily.'

I nod, not entirely convinced but too exhausted to argue. The past few days have been a blur of difficult conversations, tears (mostly Lily's, though I've shed a few of my own in private), and practical arrangements like changing locks and contact information at Lily's school. Then, there are the messages. Melissa has been relentless since I ended things, cycling between tearful apologies, desperate explanations, and increasingly concerning accusations against Rachel. At first, I responded briefly, trying to be kind but firm. Now I've stopped answering altogether.

'Have you heard from her today?' Rachel asks, as if reading my thoughts.

'Just a couple of texts. More of the same.' I don't elaborate, not wanting to repeat Melissa's wild claims that Rachel is sabotaging her, tampering with her medication, manipulating me. It sounds like the paranoid ramblings of someone becoming unhinged, and saying it aloud feels disrespectful to Rachel, who's been nothing but supportive.

'You should save them all,' Rachel advises. 'In case we need them for... well, in case things escalate.'

The implication hangs in the air between us. In case we need a restraining order. In case Melissa's fixation on Lily turns dangerous. The thought makes my skin crawl.

'I am,' I assure her. 'Though I'm hoping it won't come to that. She seemed to calm down a bit today.'

Rachel looks skeptical but doesn't push it. 'I suppose we should try to be understanding. If what Scott said about her mental health issues is true, then she's probably struggling without proper support.'

I rub my eyes, fatigue settling deep in my bones. 'I just want to move past all this. For Lily's sake. She's been through enough upheaval in her life already.'

'She'll be alright,' Rachel says confidently. 'Children are resilient, and she has us. We'll get her through this together, just like we've gotten through everything else.'

My phone buzzes on the coffee table between us. Melissa's name lights up the screen, along with the preview of yet another text message: 'James, please listen. I've found proof that Rachel...'

I snatch the phone up before Rachel can see the full message, but from her concerned expression, I suspect she caught the gist of it.

'Still trying to turn you against me?' she asks quietly.

I nod, pocketing the phone without reading the rest of the message. 'I'm sorry. This must be uncomfortable for you.'

'Don't apologise,' Rachel says firmly. 'None of this is your fault. Melissa is clearly desperate and looking for someone to blame. It's easier for her to paint me as the villain than to accept that her own behaviour drove you away.'

It makes sense, put like that. Melissa's sudden fixation on Rachel as some kind of mastermind plotting against her feels like classic deflection, an inability to take responsibility for her own actions. Melissa had seemed so genuine in her confusion when I confronted her about the medication, about the school lie. For a moment, I'd almost believed she wasn't crazy. I push the thought away. The evidence against Melissa is substantial, from Scott's disturbing account of her obsession with his son to her own sleep talking confusion of Lily with her stillborn daughter. And now these increasingly erratic messages, the desperate attempts to contact me despite my clear boundaries. It all adds up to someone with serious issues that I can't expose Lily to.

'You should try to get some sleep,' Rachel suggests, breaking the silence that has settled between us. 'You look exhausted.'

'I haven't been sleeping well,' I admit. 'Too much on my mind.'

'Understandable.' She stands, gathering our empty mugs. 'I should head home, let you get some rest. Unless...' she hesitates, 'you'd rather I stayed? On the sofa, I mean. In case Melissa tries something.'

The offer is tempting. The house feels emptier, somehow, since Melissa left. Not that she lived here officially, but her regular presence had filled spaces I hadn't realised were vacant since Sarah died. Now those spaces gape open again, painfully apparent.

'Thanks, but we'll be alright,' I say, though with less conviction than I'd like. 'The new locks are in place, and I've got the school on high alert. She won't get near Lily.'

Rachel nods, though she looks unconvinced. 'Call me if you need anything. Any time, day or night.'

'I will.' I follow her to the door, where she collects her coat and bag. 'And Rachel... thank you. For everything. I don't know what we'd do without you.'

She smiles, something complicated seemingly behind her eyes. 'That's what family does, James. We look out for each other.'

After she leaves, I double-check the locks before heading upstairs. I peek into Lily's room, watching her sleep for a moment, her small chest rising and falling steadily. She looks peaceful now, but bedtime had been difficult again, full of questions I don't have good answers to.

'Why can't Melissa come back?' she'd asked, her lower lip trembling. 'Doesn't she love us anymore?'

How do you explain to a five year old that the woman she'd grown attached to might be dangerous? That her interest in Lily might not have been healthy or normal? You can't, not really. So instead I'd repeated the simplified version Rachel and I had agreed on: that Melissa needed some time to herself, and that sometimes grown ups had to make hard decisions that might be confusing or sad. It felt inadequate, dishonest even, but it seemed kinder than the truth. In my bedroom, I finally pull out my phone to read the rest of Melissa's message:

'James, please listen. I've found proof that Rachel has been tampering with my medication. She's been in my house. I have CCTV footage. She's not who you think she is. Lily isn't safe with her. Please, just meet me so I can show you.'

I stare at the text. Melissa's accusations against Rachel have been escalating, becoming more specific, more elaborate. Now she's claiming to have video evidence? It's disturbing, this apparent determination to drive a wedge between Rachel and me, to cast doubt on the one person who's been a constant support through all of this.

As I'm trying to decide whether to respond or block her number entirely, another text comes through:

'James, I know you don't believe me. But I'm not making this up. I'm scared for Lily. Rachel has been obsessed with her for years. Think about it; how she's always there, how she acts like Lily's mother, how hostile she was to me from the start. Please, just look at the footage. For Lily's sake.'

I set the phone down on my nightstand. Rachel was Sarah's best friend. She loves Lily because of that connection, because she's been part of her life since birth. Her protectiveness is just that; protection, not possession! I think of Rachel downstairs just now, offering to stay the night 'in case Melissa tries something.' Her clear eyed certainty that Melissa is dangerous, that I've had a narrow escape. The way she's seamlessly filled the gaps Melissa left behind. No. I can't allow Melissa to plant these seeds of doubt. Rachel has been nothing but supportive, nothing but loving toward Lily. Her concerns about Melissa have proven well founded. To question her motives now, based on the desperate accusations of a woman who's shown increasingly erratic behaviour, would be both ungrateful and irrational.

I block Melissa's number, a decisive click that feels both necessary and somehow ominous. Then I set my phone aside and get ready for bed, trying to ignore the persistent feeling that something about this situation still doesn't quite add up. I throw a podcast on to sleep to, get into bed, and slowly drift away...

***

CRASH. I wake to the sound of breaking glass. For a moment, I'm disoriented, unsure if the noise was part of my dreams or reality. Then it comes again; a distinctive noise from downstairs, followed by what sounds like footsteps. Someone is in the house. I'm out of bed instantly. Lily. I need to get to Lily. I move swiftly down the darkened hallway to her room, relieved to find her still asleep, undisturbed by the noise. I close her door silently, then grab the cricket bat I keep in the hall cupboard for just such emergencies.

Another sound from below; something being moved or knocked over. I creep down the stairs, bat raised, adrenaline sharpening my senses. The living room is dark but appears undisturbed. The noise seems to be coming from the kitchen. I flip on the light switch, bat at the ready, braced for confrontation.

The kitchen window is broken, a jagged hole punched through the glass just large enough for someone to reach in and unlatch it. Shards glitter on the tile floor. But there's no intruder in sight, just a mess of pulled out drawers and scattered papers. Looks like someone has been searching for something.

I lower the bat slowly, scanning the room for any clue about what happened. Nothing seems to be missing. It's more like someone was looking for something specific and left in a hurry when they couldn't find it. This *has* to be Melissa. Who else would break into our home after everything that's happened?

The kitchen clock reads 3:17 AM, too early to call anyone, too late to go back to sleep. I sweep up the broken glass methodically, board up the window as best I can with cardboard and duct tape, and make myself a strong cup of tea.

By dawn, I've made a decision. I need to call the police. This has gone too far. First, the harassing messages, now a break in. I can't risk Lily's safety any longer, regardless of Melissa's mental state.

I call Rachel as soon as it's a reasonable hour, my voice carefully controlled.

'There's something I need to discuss with you,' I say. 'It's important.'

'Of course,' she responds, sounding concerned. 'Is Lily alright?'

'She's fine,' I assure her, glancing toward the stairs where Lily is still sleeping, blissfully unaware of the nocturnal drama. 'Still asleep. But I'd appreciate if you could come over as soon as possible.'

'I'll be there in twenty minutes,' Rachel promises.

I make breakfast, the routine, mundane task helping to calm my churning thoughts. By the time the doorbell rings, I've decided this is the final straw. We're going to the police today.

But when I open the door, Rachel's expression of concern gives way to something else as she notices the make shift boarded up kitchen window visible behind me; a small look that might be alarm, might be something else entirely.

'James, what happened?' she asks, stepping inside. 'Was there a break in?'

I close the door behind her. 'Someone broke in last night. I think it was Melissa.'

CHAPTER 15

Rachel

I arrive at James's house precisely twenty minutes after his call, as promised. His voice had sounded strange on the phone; tense, controlled, not quite himself. It's been a difficult few days for all of us, but especially for him. Ending things with Melissa, dealing with Lily's confusion and upset, the constant worry that Melissa might try something desperate.

I'm carefully prepared for what I'll see when he opens the door: the window I broke in the middle of the night, the mess I created to make it look like a desperate search. The evidence of a break in convincing enough to finally push James toward the police, toward a permanent solution to the Melissa problem.

'James, what happened?' I ask, stepping inside with practiced concern. 'Was there a break in?'

His expression is dark as he closes the door behind me. 'Someone broke in last night. I think it was Melissa.'

I follow him to the kitchen, surveying the damage I caused just hours earlier. The broken glass, now swept up. The drawers I'd pulled open and rummaged through. The window, now covered with cardboard and tape.

A twinge of guilt hits me as I see the exhaustion in James's face, the worry etched into his features. What I did was wrong, breaking in, staging evidence, manipulating the situation. But

I can't let Melissa worm her way back into their lives. I've seen how she operates, how she draws people in. If she managed to convince James to give her another chance, who knows what she might do to Lily?

'This is too far,' I say, infusing my voice with carefully calibrated outrage. 'First the messages, now this? James, we need to go to the police. Today.'

He nods, looking relieved at my suggestion. 'That's what I was thinking. This can't continue.'

'I'll help you file the report,' I offer. 'Make sure they understand the full pattern here. The harassment, the obsession with Lily, now breaking into your home.'

I pick up my phone, pretending to check a message, then let my expression darken. I turn the screen toward James, showing him the text I'd sent to myself from an untraceable number hours earlier:

'You won't win, Rachel. I know what you're doing. I'll make James see the truth about you before you can hurt Lily.'

He reads it, his face hardening. 'She's threatening you now too?'

'It's not the first message,' I admit, taking my phone back. 'I've been getting them since yesterday, but I didn't want to worry you with it. You have enough to deal with.'

'We're definitely going to the police,' James says firmly. 'Today. This is escalating, and I don't want to wait until she does something worse.'

I nod in agreement, relief flooding through me even as shame prickles at the edge of my consciousness. This was necessary. Unethical and criminal, yes, but necessary to protect them from Melissa's manipulations. I've gone too far to turn back now, crossed too many lines.

'We should go as soon as possible,' I say. 'But what about Lily? Should she come with us to the station, hear all of this?'

As James discusses arrangements for Lily, I push away the guilt. The staged break in was the final piece needed to ensure Melissa would be seen as dangerous, unstable, someone to be kept away permanently. The nail in the coffin of any chance she might have had of explaining herself to James. If breaking a window and creating a false narrative was what it took to keep Lily safe, to preserve the family we've built together... well, some prices are worth paying for the people you love.

CHAPTER 16

James

It's been three days since we filed the police report. Three days of checking locks twice, of jumping at unexpected sounds, of watching Lily with a vigilance that borders on paranoia. Three days of no contact from Melissa, which should be a relief but instead has left me with a gnawing worry that I can't quite shake.

'You're doing the right thing,' Rachel assured me this morning over coffee, her hand warm on mine. 'Melissa needs professional help, not a relationship. Not access to Lily.'

I nodded, grateful for her steady presence, her unwavering support. Without Rachel, I'd be drowning in doubt. She's picked up all the pieces that Melissa's abrupt departure left scattered; helping with Lily's confused questions, taking over school runs when work keeps me late, bringing dinner when I'm too exhausted to cook.

'I know, I just hope she's alright.'

'That's because you're a good person,' Rachel said, squeezing my hand. 'But you've done all you can. The rest is up to her.'

Now, as I walk through the school gates, Lily's bright drawings from yesterday tucked under my arm to return to her, I try to focus on the positive. She's been more settled these past few days, asking fewer questions about Melissa, sleeping better. Children adapt, as Rachel keeps reminding me. They're resilient in ways that still surprise me.

The playground is busy with parents collecting their children, but the familiar crowd outside the after school club room is noticeably absent. Strange. I check my watch; I'm not early, if anything I'm running a few minutes late.

Mrs. Chen, who runs the club, is tidying up when I enter the room. She looks up in surprise.

'Mr Porter? Did you forget something?'

A cold feeling spreads through my chest. 'I'm here to collect Lily.'

Her expression shifts to confusion. 'But Lily was collected earlier.'

The coldness turns to ice. 'What? By whom?'

'A blonde lady,' Mrs. Chen says, her own expression now showing concern. 'She had the password and everything. Said there was a change of plans today.'

'The password?' My voice sounds distant, strange to my own ears.

'Yes, the emergency collection password. She knew it was "dinosaur".' Mrs. Chen is now looking properly alarmed. 'She said she was a family friend; that you was caught up with something, and she was sent to collect Lily instead.'

'Did she give a name?' I ask, already knowing the answer.

'Rachel, I think. She showed ID. Said she'd collected Lily before.'

The room seems to tilt around me. I grab the doorframe for support.

'Mr Porter? Is everything alright?'

'Call the police,' I manage to say. 'Now. It wasn't Rachel who collected Lily. She shouldn't even know the password.'

As Mrs. Chen rushes to the phone, I pull out my mobile with shaking hands, calling Rachel.

'Hey,' she answers cheerfully. 'I was just about to call you. I've got that chicken Lily likes for dinner.'

'Lily's gone,' I cut her off, my voice breaking. 'Melissa took her from school. She knew the emergency password.'

A sharp intake of breath. 'What? How? That password was only known to you, me, and the school.'

'I don't know,' I say, panic rising with each passing second. 'Rachel, she has Lily. She has my daughter.'

'I'm coming,' Rachel says immediately. 'Where are you?'

'Still at school. They're calling the police.'

'I'll be there in ten minutes.' Her voice catches, 'we'll find her. I promise.'

I end the call, my mind spinning with terrible possibilities. How did Melissa know the password? Where has she taken Lily? What if we can't find them? What if Rachel was right, and Melissa truly is dangerous?

The school secretary appears, her face panicking. 'Mr Porter, the police are on their way. They've asked us to check the CCTV footage immediately.'

I nod, following her in a daze as my daughter's face fills my mind; her trusting smile, her easy acceptance of Melissa into our lives.

'Please be safe,' I whisper, though there's no one to hear my desperate prayer. 'Please be safe, Lily. I'm coming to find you.'

CHAPTER 17

Melissa

My hands won't stop shaking. It's been days since I've taken my proper medication. I've searched every drawer, every cupboard, every pocket, but the pills are gone. Not misplaced; gone. Taken. I know who did it. I know what she's doing. Rachel.

The name burns in my mind like acid. *Rachel* who has always been there. *Rachel* who has been watching James and Lily for years. *Rachel* who couldn't stand seeing someone else take the place she believes is rightfully hers.

I pace the small confines of my house, photographs and notes spread across every surface. Evidence I tried to show James, evidence he refused to see. A man blinded by years of trust, unable to recognise the monster hiding behind a friend's face.

'Think, Melissa,' I say to myself, pressing my palms against my temples to quiet the static that's been building there since my medication disappeared. 'Think clearly.'

My reflection in the hallway mirror catches my attention. I look terrible; hair unwashed, dark circles under my eyes, skin pale and clammy. I look unstable. I look exactly how Rachel wants James to see me.

'She's turned him against you,' I tell my reflection. 'She's making sure he won't listen.'

Maybe he's already lost to me. The thought stings, brings tears to my eyes that I angrily wipe away. James trusted Rachel's word over mine, believed her lies, her manipulations. He changed the locks, blocked my number, reported me to the police for trying to warn him. But Lily... Lily is different. Sweet, innocent Lily who smiled at me like I mattered, who held my hand without hesitation, who called me her angel when I tucked her in at night. Lily who is now alone with Rachel, unprotected, vulnerable.

'She's not safe,' I whisper, the realisation crystallising with terrible clarity. 'Rachel won't stop until she has everything; James, Lily, the perfect little family she's always wanted.'

My phone buzzes with a news alert. Child abducted in Bristol, authorities appealing for witnesses. Not Lily, some other child, but it's enough to send my thoughts spiralling in new, frightening directions.

What if Rachel decides James isn't enough? What if she decides to take Lily away, somewhere they can be together without James's interference? The thoughts come faster now, more urgent, more convincing. Rachel has always been obsessed with Lily, has always acted more like a mother than a friend. What's to stop her from taking that final, terrible step? I grab my car keys, a half formed plan taking shape. School pick up is in an hour. Rachel sometimes collects Lily on Thursdays; I remember this from conversations with James, from the detailed schedules Rachel insisted on maintaining. My hands are steadier now, my purpose clear. I may have lost James, but I won't lose Lily. I won't let Rachel hurt her.

In the bathroom, I quickly wash my face, apply some make-up to hide the evidence of sleepless nights. My blonde hair is a disaster, but a quick brushing and a ponytail make it presentable enough. I change into something Rachel might wear; conservative, practical, nothing like my usual style.

'You're just keeping her safe,' I tell my reflection. 'Until you can prove what Rachel is doing. Until someone believes you.'

The drive to Lily's school is a blur of rehearsed lines and racing thoughts. I know the emergency password; 'dinosaur'. Overheard it once when James was on the phone with the school. I know the collection procedures, the names of Lily's teachers, all the little details gleaned from weeks of being part of their lives.

I park down the road, checking my appearance one final time. The ID in my bag isn't quite right, but school administrators are busy, distracted. They see what they expect to see.

'You're Rachel Whittaker,' I practice aloud. 'James is caught up. Emergency change of plans.'

The school playground is crowded with parents when I arrive, but I move with purpose, with the confidence of someone who belongs there. The office staff barely glance at the ID I flash, too caught up by end of day chaos to look closely.

'Rachel Whittaker,' I say, my voice steady. 'I'm here for Lily Porter. James asked me to collect her; he's caught up with something.'

'Of course, Ms. Whittaker,' the woman says, checking her computer. 'I'll just need the password.'

'Dinosaur,' I say without hesitation, the word bitter on my tongue.

She nods, picking up the phone to call Lily's classroom. Minutes later, Lily appears, her face lighting up when she sees me.

'Lissa!' she exclaims, rushing forward.

I crouch down, putting a finger to my lips. 'Hi, angel. We're playing a little game today, okay? I'm pretending to be Rachel.'

Lily's eyes widen with delight at the idea of a secret game. Children love secrets, love being part of adult conspiracies. 'Why?'

'It's a surprise for your daddy,' I improvise. 'But we have to keep it very quiet until we're ready to surprise him, okay?'

She nods solemnly, always eager to be involved in surprises for James. The school administrator smiles indulgently, seeing nothing but a child's excitement and a trusted family friend.

'We're going straight to after school club, right?' the woman asks.

'Actually, change of plans today,' I say smoothly. 'James asked me to take Lily for a special outing. She won't be attending club.'

The woman makes a note on her clipboard. 'No problem. Have a lovely afternoon, Lily.'

Hand in hand, we walk out of the school, Lily chattering about her day, oblivious to the racing of my heart, to the enormity of what I'm doing. I help her into the back seat of my car, buckling her in carefully, the routine domestic act at odds with the turmoil in my mind.

'Where are we going?' Lily asks as I start the engine. 'Is it part of the surprise?'

'Yes, angel,' I say, meeting her eyes in the rearview mirror. 'We're going somewhere safe. Somewhere Rachel won't find us.'

'But I thought you were pretending to be Rachel,' Lily says, confusion clouding her face.

'That was just for the school,' I explain, pulling away from the curb. 'But now it's just us, and we can be honest. The truth is, I needed to get you away from Rachel. She's not... she's not who your daddy thinks she is.'

'What do you mean?' Lily's voice has lost some of its excitement now, uncertainty creeping in.

'It's complicated, angel,' I say, trying to sound reassuring. 'I promise I'll explain everything soon. Right now, we're going on an adventure. Just you and me.'

In the mirror, I see Lily settle back against her seat, temporarily satisfied with this explanation. Children are trusting, adaptable. She still sees me as a safe person, someone her father invited into their lives, someone who read her bedtime stories and made heart shaped pancakes.

I turn onto the motorway, heading west. My grandmother's old cottage in Wales. Empty for years, isolated, but still in the family. No one will think to look for us there, not immediately. Enough time to gather more evidence, to find a way to make James understand the danger Rachel poses.

'Just until they believe me,' I say to myself, too quietly for Lily to hear. 'Just until they see the truth.'

If a small voice in the back of my mind whispers that this is wrong, that taking a child from her school under false pretenses crosses a line I can never uncross, I silence it with the certainty that I'm doing this for Lily. To protect her from the woman who has been manipulating her father for years, positioning herself to take the place of the mother she lost.

I look again at Lily in the rearview mirror. She's looking out the window now, watching the city give way to countryside, unaware that she's just become part of a desperate gamble. Unaware that her father will soon be frantic with worry, that police will be searching, that everything has changed.

'It's going to be okay, angel,' I promise her, and myself. 'Everything will make sense soon.'

As we drive farther from the city, from James, from everything familiar, I feel a bit of doubt creeping in. Without my medication, can I trust my own perceptions? The certainty that felt so unshakable in my house now seems more fragile with each passing mile. No. I force the doubt away. I've seen the evidence with my own eyes. The photographs Rachel kept hidden, the obsessive surveillance of James and Lily, the scratched out images of Sarah. Rachel is the one who isn't well. Rachel is the danger, and until someone believes me, I'll do whatever it takes to keep Lily safe.

CHAPTER 18

James

My heart is hammering so hard against my ribcage I can barely hear the police officer speaking. Words filter through the panic in fragments: amber alert, description, last seen wearing. Lily's school photo is being passed between officers, her little smile beaming out from her most recent school picture day, oblivious to the terror swirling around her image now.

'Mr Porter?' The detective's voice finally breaks through. 'We need to focus on where Ms Chambers might have taken your daughter. Any locations with particular significance?'

I run my fingers through my hair, trying to think clearly through the fog of panic. 'Her house, maybe? Though she must know that's the first place we'd look.'

'We've already dispatched officers there,' the detective assures me. 'No sign of them yet, but we'll keep watch. Think of anywhere else; places she mentioned from her past, somewhere she took Lily that they enjoyed together.'

Rachel paces beside me, her face tight with controlled fear. She arrived at the school minutes after I called her, and hasn't left my side since.

'The farm park,' Rachel suggests, stopping her pacing. 'Remember? She took you both there on your first proper outing with Lily. She seemed to have a strong attachment to that day.'

'Willow Farm Park,' I confirm, the memory surfacing. 'Lily loved it there. Melissa said she grew up on a farm, that it reminded her of her childhood.'

The detective nods, making notes. 'Good. We'll send a unit. Anything else?'

'I can't think…' My voice breaks as a wave of helplessness crashes over me. My daughter is missing, taken by a woman who I thought I loved, and I have no idea where they might be.

'Yes, near Exeter.' Though I realise, with a sickening thought, that I don't know exactly where. Melissa had talked about her childhood farm in general terms, but never specified its location. Another detail I'd failed to question.

'I'd like to check her house myself,' Rachel says decisively. 'There might be something the officers missed, some clue in her personal belongings that would make sense to us but not to them.'

The detective begins to object, but Rachel cuts him off.

'I know her. I've seen how her mind works. And I know what matters to Lily. Please, we need to try everything.'

After a moment's consideration, the detective reluctantly agrees. 'We can have an officer escort you, Ms Whittaker. But you can't touch anything that might be evidence.'

'Understood,' Rachel agrees.

'I want to check the farm park,' I say. 'It's only twenty minutes away. If there's even a chance they're there…'

The detective looks like he wants to argue, to tell me to leave this to the professionals, but something in my expression must dissuade him.

'Call immediately if you see any sign of them,' he instructs. 'Do not approach Miss Chambers yourself. We have reason to believe she may be unmedicated and potentially unstable. We've put an alert out for her vehicle and have officers checking all major roads out of the area.'

I nod mechanically, already reaching for my car keys. Twenty minutes until the farm park. Twenty minutes of helpless waiting, of imagining worst case scenarios, of questioning every interaction I ever had with Melissa.

'I'll let you know if I find anything at her house,' Rachel promises, squeezing my arm. 'We'll find her, James. I swear.'

The drive to Willow Farm Park is a blur of speed limits pushed to their maximum and desperate prayers to a God I don't really believe in. The car park is half empty when I arrive, the place winding down for the day. I scan the vehicles frantically, looking for Melissa's silver Volkswagen, but don't see it among the scattered cars.

The teenage attendant at the entrance looks alarmed when I rush up, wild eyed and breathless.

'Sir? Are you alright?'

'My daughter,' I gasp. 'Five years old, dark hair in a school uniform. Has anyone seen her? She might be with a blonde woman, early thirties?'

The attendant's expression shifts from alarm to concern. 'I don't think so, not today. Let me ask my manager.'

Minutes tick by with excruciating slowness as the attendant speaks in hushed tones to an older woman who's emerged from the gift shop. They both glance at me with poorly disguised worry.

'Sir,' the manager approaches cautiously. 'We haven't had any children in school uniform today, and we've been fairly quiet. Is everything alright? Should we call someone?'

'The police are already involved,' I say, heart sinking. 'My daughter's been taken from her school. I thought they might have come here.'

The manager's face pales. 'I'm so sorry. We'll keep an eye out. Do you have a photo we could reference?'

I pull out my phone, showing them the lock screen; Lily on her last birthday, beaming at the camera with chocolate cake smeared across her cheek. The manager studies it carefully, but shakes her head.

'I haven't seen her, I'm afraid. But we'll alert all staff immediately.'

My phone buzzes in my hand, and I snatch it up, hoping for news from the police. It's Rachel.

'James, I'm at Melissa's. The police broke in, but there's no sign of them. But I've found something you need to see.'

'What is it?' I ask, stepping away from the concerned park staff.

'Photos, dozens of them. Surveillance photos of you and Lily going back months. And pictures of Sarah, from your albums, I think, with her face scratched out.'

It takes all my strength not to throw up. 'Like the ones she tried to convince me you had taken.'

'Exactly like those,' Rachel confirms, her voice grim.

'Is there anything there that might tell us where she's gone?' I aak, running back to my car, the farm park clearly a dead end.

'I'm looking. There's so much here, James. It's... disturbing. She's been planning this for a long time.'

A terrible thought occurs to me. 'The diary. Is there a notebook, a journal? She always kept one in her bag.'

I hear rustling through the phone, as if Rachel is searching through papers. 'Yes, I see it. Hang on...'

More rustling, then a sharp intake of breath. 'James, there's an address here. Some place in Wales. A cottage that belonged to her grandmother.'

'Wales?' I repeat, starting the car. 'That's hours away. She could be halfway there already.'

'I'm giving the address to the police now,' Rachel says. 'They're calling Welsh authorities to check the property. Don't even think about driving there yourself, James. It's too far, and the police will get there faster.'

She's right, though every instinct in my body screams to drive west, to find this cottage myself, to tear apart the countryside until I find my daughter.

'I can't just sit here doing nothing,' I say, jumping into my car.

'Come to Melissa's,' Rachel suggests. 'There's more here to

go through, things that might help us understand where else she might take Lily if the cottage is a dead end.'

It's logical, practical advice, exactly what I need when my own judgment is clouded by fear. 'I'm on my way.'

As I drive back toward the city, toward Melissa's, my phone rings again. Unknown number. I answer immediately, hope surging.

'Hello? Lily?'

'Mr Porter?' An unfamiliar male voice. 'This is Sergeant Whitfield with Avon and Somerset Police. We've located Ms Chambers' vehicle.'

My heart leaps. 'Where? Is Lily with her? Is she alright?'

'The car was found abandoned at Severn View Services, sir. There's no sign of Ms Chambers or your daughter, but we believe they may have switched vehicles.'

'Switched vehicles?' I repeat numbly. 'How?'

'CCTV shows Ms Chambers and a child matching Lily's description getting into a dark coloured Range Rover. We're working to identify the registration now.'

'A Range Rover?' I struggle to process this new information. 'Melissa doesn't know anyone with a Range Rover. At least, she never mentioned...'

I trail off as a memory surfaces: Melissa, that first night at the restaurant, mentioning a cousin with a holiday home in the Cotswolds. A detail so insignificant I'd forgotten it until this moment.

'Sergeant, she might be heading for the Cotswolds. She has family there.'

'Do you have an address? A name?'

'No,' I admit, frustration boiling over. 'She just mentioned a cousin once. I don't even know if it's true; so much of what she told me turned out to be lies.'

'We'll add it to the search parameters,' the sergeant assures me. 'And Mr Porter? We will find your daughter. Every officer in the southwest is looking for her.'

I end the call as I pull up outside Melissa's house. Rachel

meets me at the door, her face drawn with worry.

'They found her car,' I tell her before she can speak. 'Abandoned at a service station. They think she's switched to a Range Rover, possibly heading for the Cotswolds.'

Rachel's eyes widen. 'The Cotswolds? Did she mention having connections there?'

'A cousin, apparently. Though god knows if that's true either.'

I walk inside, and I'm immediately struck by the chaos of Melissa's. Papers are strewn everywhere, photographs pinned to walls, strings connecting some in a tangled web that makes no immediate sense.

'The police think she's having some kind of psychotic episode,' Rachel explains, gesturing to the disturbing display. 'This is like something from a crime thriller; surveillance, conspiracies, paranoid connections.'

I move closer to the wall, examining the photos. Many are of me and Lily in various locations; the park, outside Lily's school, even through the windows of our home. All taken from a distance, secretly. But, what truly chills me are the photographs of Sarah. Not recent ones, obviously, but pictures that must have been taken from our family albums during Melissa's visits to our home. In each one, Sarah's face has been methodically scratched out, gouged away with something sharp.

'She must have been unwell for a long time,' Rachel says quietly, standing beside me. 'The police found her medication in the bathroom. Antipsychotics, just like we thought. But she hasn't been taking them. The prescription was filled weeks ago, but the pills are almost all still there.'

I turn away from the wall, unable to bear the sight of Sarah's desecrated image. 'Did they find anything else about the cottage in Wales? Or this cousin in the Cotswolds?'

Rachel shakes her head. 'Nothing specific about the cousin. The cottage is being checked now. It's near a place called Tregaron, apparently.'

My phone rings again; the detective this time. I answer

immediately, putting it on speaker so Rachel can hear.

'Mr Porter, we've had confirmation from Welsh police. The cottage near Tregaron appears empty, no sign of disturbance or recent occupation.'

My momentary hope deflates. 'What about the Range Rover? Any trace of that?'

'We're still working on identifying it from the CCTV. The images aren't clear enough to make out the registration.'

'So we have nothing,' I say, the pain about to overwhelm me.

'Not nothing, sir. We know they're in a dark Range Rover, likely heading west or northwest. All police forces have been alerted, and we're monitoring major roads and tolls.'

After the call ends, I sit on Melissa's sofa, head in my hands. Hours since Lily disappeared from school. Hours she's been with a woman who, judging by the evidence surrounding me, is deeply unwell and fixated on my daughter in a way I failed to recognise until it was too late.

'We should check her computer,' Rachel suggests, moving to the small desk in the corner. 'There might be search history, emails, something to indicate where she's gone.'

The laptop is password protected, but the detective had mentioned they were bringing in a specialist to access it. For now, all we can do is continue to search the house for any overlooked clues. As Rachel methodically checks drawers and cupboards, I find myself drawn back to the wall of photographs. There's something almost ritualistic about the way Melissa has arranged them, grouped them into categories that make sense only to her.

One section seems focused on Lily's school; photos taken from a distance, schedules, even what appears to be a printed copy of the school's security protocols. Had she been planning this for weeks? Months? While I invited her into our home, into our lives?

'James, look at this,' Rachel calls, holding up a stack of papers from Melissa's desk. 'It's a printout of cottage rentals in the Lake District. Several are circled.'

I join her, examining the papers. 'These are recent searches, dated just days ago.'

'After you ended things with her,' Rachel points out. 'She might have abandoned the Wales cottage idea, knowing we'd find it in her journal.'

I pull out my phone, calling the detective again to relay this new information. He promises to extend the search northward, to alert Cumbria police to check the marked properties.

'Do any of them look familiar?' Rachel asks after I end the call. 'Did she ever mention the Lake District to you?'

I start to shake my head, then pause as a memory surfaces. 'Not specifically, but... she did talk about wanting to take Lily somewhere with mountains and lakes. Somewhere "away from city influences." I thought she just meant for a holiday.'

'Or somewhere isolated to hide a child,' Rachel says grimly. 'James, I hate to say this, but the more I see here, the more convinced I am that Melissa has been planning to take Lily for a long time. This isn't just an impulsive act by someone off their medication. This is calculated.'

The thought sits in my stomach. Melissa's apparent warmth, her interest in Lily, her rapid integration into our lives; had it all been a prelude to this moment? Had I invited a predator into our home?

'I can't just wait here,' I say suddenly, standing up. 'I need to do something, go somewhere.'

'The police are handling this,' Rachel reminds me gently. 'The best thing we can do is stay where they can reach us quickly with updates.'

'I know, but; ' My phone interrupts me mid-sentence, an unfamiliar number flashing on screen. 'Hello?'

'Daddy?'

The small, frightened voice sends a jolt of electricity through my entire body. 'Lily? Lily, is that you?'

'Daddy, I want to come home.' Her voice is tearful, uncertain. 'Melissa says we're on an adventure, but I don't like it anymore. I want you.'

'Lily, love, where are you?' I ask, frantically gesturing to Rachel, who's already dialling the police on her own phone. 'Can you see anything around you? Are you in a house? A car?'

'A house. It's dark outside now. There are lots of trees.'

I try to keep my voice calm, though my heart is racing. 'That's good, Lily. You're doing brilliantly. Is Melissa there with you now?'

'She's in the other room. She said I could call you to say I'm okay, but not to tell you where we are because Rachel might find out.'

Rachel, still on her own call with the police, raises her eyebrows at this.

'Lily, can you tell me anything else about where you are? Did you see any signs when you were driving? Or names of towns?'

'I don't remember,' she says, her voice wobbling. 'It was a long drive. We stopped at a big place with lots of food and toilets. Then we got in a different car with Melissa's friend. He wasn't very nice.'

'A friend? A man?'

'Yes. He had a scratchy face. Melissa said he's her cousin, but I don't think she likes him very much. They were arguing.'

A male accomplice. This changes everything. 'Lily, is this man still with you?'

'No, he left after he brought us to the house. Melissa said he's coming back tomorrow.'

Thank god for small mercies. 'Lily, this is very important. I need you to look for something that might tell me where you are. Can you see any papers with an address? Or look out a window and tell me what you see?'

'I tried to look out the window, but it's all black outside. Just trees. Lissa keeps talking to herself.'

My blood runs cold. 'Lily, I want you to listen to me very carefully. I'm coming to find you. The police are helping me. But until we get there, I need you to be very brave and do exactly what Melissa tells you, okay? Don't make her upset or angry. Can you do that for me?'

'Yes,' she whispers. 'I'm scared, Daddy.'

'I know, pumpkin. But you're the bravest girl I know, and I'm going to find you very soon. I promise.' I try to keep the fear from my voice, to project a confidence I don't feel. 'Is there anything else you can tell me about where you are?'

'There's a big lake. I saw it before it got dark. Melissa said we might go in a boat tomorrow.'

A lake. The Lake District theory seems increasingly likely. 'That's very helpful, Lily. Now-'

'I have to go,' she interrupts suddenly, her voice dropping even lower. 'Melissa's coming back. I love you, Daddy.'

'I love you too, Lily. So much. Be brave.'

The line goes dead. I stare at the phone in my hand, torn between elation at hearing my daughter's voice and renewed terror at what she's revealed.

Rachel ends her call with the police. 'They were tracking the location. It's bouncing off a tower in the Lake District, but they need more time to narrow it down. Did she tell you anything useful?'

'There's a man involved,' I say, still processing this new information. 'A cousin of Melissa's, apparently. And they're near a lake, in a house surrounded by trees.'

'That narrows it down to about half the Lake District,' Rachel says, frustration evident in her voice. 'But it's something. And they know she's alive and physically well.'

'She said Melissa's been talking to herself. I think you're right about her having some kind of psychotic break.'

Rachel's expression darkens. 'The detective said they've been in touch with Melissa's psychiatrist. Apparently she has a history of psychosis following her stillbirth. Without her medication, she's at high risk for delusions, especially ones related to her lost child.'

I grab my coat, unable to remain still any longer. 'I'm going to the police station. They'll have updates there first, and if they locate her, I want to be ready to go immediately.'

Rachel doesn't try to stop me this time. 'I'm coming with you. We'll leave a note for the computer specialist in case they arrive while we're gone.'

As we drive to the station, my mind replays Lily's frightened voice, her description of Melissa's deteriorating mental state. My daughter, my precious, innocent daughter, trapped with a woman losing her grip on reality.

'Please let them find her,' I whisper, not realising I've spoken aloud until Rachel reaches over to squeeze my hand.

'They will,' she says with fierce certainty. 'And when they do, Melissa will never be able to hurt either of you again. I promise.'

But as reassuring as Rachel's words are intended to be, they can't dispel the image of Lily, alone and scared in a dark house by a lake, with a woman who might be capable of hurting her.

CHAPTER 19

Melissa

The small country churchyard is deserted when I pull up, gravel crunching beneath the Range Rover's tyres. Morning mist still clings to the headstones, giving the place an ethereal quality that feels appropriate. Sacred, somehow. The perfect place for a reunion that's been years in the making.

'Where are we?' Lily asks from the back seat, her voice small and wary. She's been quieter since the phone call to James earlier, watching me with careful eyes that remind me too much of her father's scrutiny.

'Somewhere special,' I tell her, turning off the engine. 'Somewhere I need to show you.'

I check my appearance in the rearview mirror, barely recognising the woman who stares back. My blonde hair hangs limp and unwashed, dark circles shadow my eyes, and there's a feverish quality to my gaze that even I can see isn't quite right.

'I don't want to get out,' Lily says, shrinking back against her seat when I open the rear door. 'It's scary here.'

'It's not scary,' I assure her, though I understand her hesitation. Churchyards can be intimidating for children. 'It's peaceful. There's someone here I want you to meet.'

'Who?' Lily asks, her small face creased with confusion.

I hesitate, unsure how to explain in a way her five year old mind will understand. 'Someone very special to me. Someone I lost a long time ago.'

Lily's eyes dart to the weathered headstones visible through the car window. 'A ghost?'

Despite everything, I smile. 'No, angel. Not a ghost. Just... a memory. It won't take long, I promise.'

I reach for her hand, but she pulls back, shaking her head firmly. 'I want to stay in the car.'

A bit of frustration sparks through me. We don't have time for this resistance. My cousin will be looking for us by now, angry that I've taken his Range Rover without permission, furious that I've involved him in something he doesn't understand. And the police will be closing in, guided by James and Rachel, the woman who's orchestrated my downfall with such meticulous precision.

'Lily, please. This is important,' I say, unable to keep the edge from my voice.

Her lower lip trembles. 'You promised we'd go home today. You said after our adventure, we'd go see Daddy.'

Did I say that? I can't remember. The past few hours blur together in a haze of adrenaline and muddled thinking. Perhaps I did promise, in a moment of weakness, hoping to stop her tears when she wouldn't sleep.

'We will,' I say, trying to sound reassuring. 'But first, I need to do this. You can wait here if you're scared.'

Relief floods her face. 'I'll wait. I promise I won't touch anything.'

I hesitate, torn between insisting she come with me and acknowledging that perhaps this moment should be private anyway. A final goodbye that belongs to me alone.

'Alright,' I concede. 'Lock the doors after I close them. Don't open them for anyone but me.'

Lily nods, reaching to press the lock button as soon as I close the car door. I watch her through the window for a moment, her little face looking sad.

The path to the graves is overgrown, last autumn's leaves still decaying between the headstones. This isn't a well tended churchyard with fresh flowers and manicured lawns. It's older, forgotten, the perfect resting place for a child whose existence has been systematically erased.

I know exactly where I'm going, though I've only been here once before. The small headstone in the far corner, beneath the sprawling oak tree. Simple, unadorned, with an inscription that contains the sum total of a life that never truly began:

*Olivia Chambers
Born Sleeping
June 17, 2020
Forever Loved*

I sink to my knees before it, the damp earth immediately soaking through my jeans. The cold is clarifying, anchoring me to this moment, to this reality that no one; not James, not Rachel, not even my own cousin; believes exists.

'I found her, Olivia,' I whisper, reaching out to trace the engraved letters of her name. 'Your... I don't know what to call her. Your echo, perhaps. The child who carries your spirit.'

The words sound delusional even to my own ears, a symptom of the psychosis my doctors warned would return if I stopped my medication, but I didn't stop by choice. The pills were taken, hidden, *replaced*; another of Rachel's careful manipulations, ensuring I would spiral, become exactly what she needed me to be: unstable, dangerous, someone to fear rather than believe.

'She's so much like you would have been,' I continue, tears beginning to track down my cheeks. 'Smart and funny and kind. She has your smile; the one I used to dream about when you were growing inside me.'

I look back at the car, where Lily sits watching me with large, solemn eyes. She can't hear me from this distance, can't know that I'm talking to the daughter I lost, the daughter I sometimes, in my most confused moments, believe she might be.

'I know she's not you,' I admit quietly, turning back to the headstone. 'I know that, Olivia. Even without the medication, even with the confusion, I know Lily is James and Sarah's daughter. But there's something about her... a connection I can't explain.'

A sob breaks free from my chest, the first of many as the dam finally breaks. Three days of fearful flight, of desperate plans and fragmented thinking, all culminating in this moment of terrible clarity. I've destroyed everything. My relationship with James. My career. My freedom. All in the name of protecting a child from a danger that exists only in my increasingly unreliable perception.

'I'm so sorry,' I weep, pressing my forehead against the cold stone. 'I'm sorry I couldn't protect you. I'm sorry I couldn't be the mother you deserved. I'm sorry I've let this... this sickness twist your memory into something so broken. Goodbye, my angel,' I whisper.

CHAPTER 20

Rachel

The tension in my body makes every muscle ache. I don't care. Physical discomfort is nothing compared to the rage and fear coursing through my veins like ice water. It's been five hours, five hours since Melissa took Lily from her school; five hours of James's anguish, of police searches, of the horrifying knowledge that Lily is in the hands of someone deeply unstable.

I push the car faster along the winding country roads, the GPS directing me to the small churchyard I discovered mentioned in Melissa's journal. A place I almost overlooked; a single line referencing 'visiting Olivia' with an address scribbled in the margin. The police are on their way, but I couldn't wait. Not when Lily's safety hangs in the balance. Not when every second that passes is another second she's with a woman who believes she's her dead child.

Rain spatters against the windscreen, matching my dark mood as I rehearse what I'll do when I find Melissa. The rational part of me knows I should wait for the police, but that voice is drowned out by a more primitive instinct: protect Lily at all costs. The child I've loved since before she was born, the child I promised Sarah I would always look after, the child who should have been mine.

I slow down as I approach the churchyard, pulling off the main road onto a narrow gravel track. Through the rain streaked windscreen, I can make out a dark vehicle parked near the entrance; a *Range Rover*. Melissa's cousin's car. My heart pounds against my ribs as I turn off the engine, scanning the area for any sign of movement.

Then, I see her. Melissa, alone on a bench beneath a big oak tree, her head in her hands, shoulders shaking with what appears to be sobs. But no Lily. No sign of the little girl anywhere. Why is Melissa crying? Where is Lily?

I fumble for my phone, my hands shaking as I dial James's number.

'Rachel?' His voice is strained, desperate. 'Any news?'

'I'm at the churchyard,' I whisper, though there's no chance of Melissa hearing me from this distance. 'I can see Melissa, but Lily's not with her. Melissa's crying, James. I'm scared she's…'

'Don't,' he cuts me off, unable to even hear the possibility voiced. 'The police are twenty minutes out. Wait for them, Rachel. Please.'

'I can't,' I say, my decision already made. 'If something's happened to Lily, we need to know now. Every minute counts.'

'Rachel-'

'I'll call you back,' I promise, ending the call before he can argue further.

I step out of the car, the cold rain immediately soaking through my light jacket. I don't bother trying to stay dry. Stealth seems pointless, the gravel path will announce my approach regardless. Instead, I move with purpose, with the singular focus of someone who has nothing left to lose.

Melissa doesn't notice me until I'm almost upon her. When she finally looks up, her face is a blend of grief and exhaustion, her normally perfect hair hanging in strands around her pale face. For a moment, just a moment, she looks genuinely ill, genuinely broken. Then her eyes widen in recognition and fear.

'Where is she?' I demand, my voice low and dangerous even to my own ears.

Melissa scrambles to her feet, backing away from me. 'Rachel? How did you-'

'WHERE IS LILY?' I advance on her, closing the distance between us. 'What have you done with her?'

Something changes in Melissa's eyes; confusion, then a dawning comprehension that chills me to my core. 'You think I've hurt her?' Her laugh is hollow, unhinged. 'Of course you do. That's been your plan all along, hasn't it? Make me look unstable, dangerous. Turn James against me.'

'You took a child that isn't yours,' I spit. 'You've been fixating on her for months, trying to replace your dead daughter. And now she's nowhere to be seen and you're crying in a graveyard. What am I supposed to think?'

Melissa's eyes dart toward the parking area, then back to me. 'She's safe. She's in the car. She didn't want to come to the grave with me.'

Relief floods through me, quickly followed by skepticism. 'Prove it.'

'Look for yourself,' Melissa gestures toward the Range Rover. 'She wouldn't get out. She's scared of cemeteries.'

I turn slightly, trying to see the car while keeping Melissa in my peripheral vision. From this angle, I can just make out a small shape in the back seat; possibly Lily, though it's hard to be certain through the darkness.

'Why did you bring her here?' I ask, not relaxing my stance. 'To what, introduce her to your dead child? Make her understand why you've kidnapped her?'

Melissa flinches as if I've slapped her. 'I wanted to say goodbye,' she whispers. 'To Olivia. To the delusion that Lily could somehow... replace her.' She shakes her head, droplets of rain flying from her hair. 'I know how it sounds. I know I'm not well. Without my medication, everything's gotten mixed up, confused.'

'Your medication?' I repeat, injecting as much innocent confusion into my voice as possible. 'The medication you claim I tampered with?'

'I know you did,' Melissa's voice hardens. 'Just like I know you've been obsessed with James and Lily for years. I found the photographs, Rachel. The surveillance. Your shrine to a family that isn't yours.'

Anger surges through me, hot and familiar. 'You broke into my house? Planted false evidence? And you expect James to believe your delusions over me?'

'Not planted,' Melissa insists, a desperate edge to her voice. 'Found. Hidden in your bedroom. Photos of James and Sarah going back years. Photos of you with Lily, with Sarah scratched out. You've been planning to replace her from the beginning.'

I take another step toward her, rage building like a physical force inside me. 'You really are insane. You've constructed this entire fantasy to justify your obsession with my goddaughter.'

'Your goddaughter?' Melissa laughs again, the sound brittle and sharp. 'Is that what you tell yourself? That's not how you see her, Rachel. I've watched you with her. The possessiveness. The way you try to be her mother. The way you've systematically sabotaged every relationship James has attempted since Sarah died.'

Her words hit too close to home. 'You don't know anything about me. About my relationship with James or Lily.'

'I know Sarah was your best friend,' Melissa says, her voice quieter now. 'I know you were there when Lily was born. When Sarah died. I know you stepped in, became the mother figure Lily needed. And somewhere along the way, that role became your identity. So much so that you couldn't bear the thought of someone replacing you.'

Something inside me snaps. The careful control I've maintained for years fractures, sending shards of rage and buried grief exploding outward. I lunge forward, my hands finding Melissa's shoulders, shoving her backward with a force that surprises us both.

She stumbles, losing her footing on the wet grass, and falls hard. Before she can recover, I'm on her, my fist connecting with her jaw in a burst of pain that radiates up my arm. I barely feel it through the adrenaline.

'You took her!' I scream, punctuating each word with another blow. 'You manipulated your way into their lives! You tried to replace me!'

Melissa raises her arms to protect her face, but makes no real effort to fight back. 'Rachel, stop! Lily can see, she's watching!'

The mention of Lily cuts through my rage like a knife. I freeze, my fist raised for another blow, and turn toward the car. There, pressed against the back window, is Lily's terrified face, her eyes wide with horror as she watches me attack the woman who kidnapped her.

I scramble off Melissa, suddenly aware of what I'm doing, of how this must look to a child already traumatised by the events of the past two days. I back away, breathing hard, as Melissa pushes herself up to a sitting position. Blood trickles from her split lip, and the beginnings of bruises darken her pale skin.

'I'm going to get Lily,' I say, my voice shaking with adrenaline and lingering rage. 'And then the police can deal with you.'

'She won't go with you,' Melissa says quietly, making no move to stop me. 'Not after what she just saw.'

I ignore her, turning away and walking swiftly toward the Range Rover. Behind me, I hear Melissa struggling to her feet but don't look back. My focus now is entirely on Lily, on getting her safely away from this place, from Melissa's disturbing fixation.

As I approach the car, I can see Lily more clearly. She has tears streaming down her face as she watches me through the window. When I try the door, I find it locked.

'Lily,' I call, keeping my voice gentle despite the storm of emotions still raging inside me. 'It's Rachel. I've come to take you home to Daddy. Please unlock the door, love.'

She hesitates, glancing past me to where Melissa stands some distance away, watching but not interfering. Then, with obvious reluctance, Lily reaches out and presses the unlock button.

I open the door and crouch beside her, fighting the urge to grab her and run. She looks physically unharmed but emotionally exhausted; dark circles under her eyes, her school uniform rumpled from the journey.

'Are you hurt?' I ask, scanning her for any sign of injury. 'Did Melissa hurt you?'

Lily shakes her head. 'She said we were on an adventure. But I want to go home.' Her lower lip trembles. 'Why did you hit Melissa? You made her bleed.'

The question catches me off guard. How do I explain my actions to a five year old? How do I make her understand that Melissa is dangerous, disturbed, without terrifying her further?

'Melissa did a very bad thing,' I say carefully. 'She took you from school without Daddy's permission. Everyone's been so worried about you. The police are looking for you, and Daddy's been so scared.'

Lily's eyes fill with fresh tears. 'Melissa said we had to hide from you. She said you were trying to take me away from Daddy.'

My heart clenches at the manipulation Melissa has subjected this child to. 'That's not true, love. I would never take you from Daddy. I've been helping him search for you.'

I look back at Melissa, who stands in the rain watching us, making no attempt to interfere or flee. There's something defeated in her posture, something almost resigned. Part of me wants to go back and finish what I started, to make her pay for the fear and anguish she's caused, but Lily's welfare comes first. I take out my phone and dial 999, relief washing through me when the operator answers immediately.

'I need police,' I say, keeping my voice steady. 'I've found Lily Porter, the missing girl. We're at St. Michael's churchyard near Kendal. The woman who took her is here too.' I pause, looking at Melissa's battered face, the evidence of my own violence. 'She's injured. I... she resisted when I tried to get Lily.'

It's not the full truth, but it's close enough. The operator assures me police are minutes away, instructs me to stay on the line and keep both Lily and Melissa in sight if possible. I agree, though I have no intention of letting Lily anywhere near Melissa again.

'Come on, love,' I say, holding out my hand to Lily. 'Let's wait in my car. It's warmer, and we can call Daddy to let him know you're safe.'

She hesitates, looking past me to Melissa once more. 'Is Melissa going to jail?'

The question is so innocent, so childlike in its directness that it momentarily takes my breath away. 'That's for the police to decide,' I say carefully. 'But what she did was very wrong, and there are consequences for that.'

Lily slides out of the car, taking my offered hand with a trust that makes my throat tight. As we walk toward my car, she looks back at Melissa one last time.

'Bye, Melissa,' she calls, her small voice carrying in the stillness of the churchyard.

Melissa raises a hand in a small wave, her bloodied face a mask of grief and resignation. 'Goodbye, Lily,' she calls back. 'I'm sorry.'

I usher Lily into my car, buckling her into the back seat before sliding behind the wheel. The rain has eased somewhat, but the sky remains dark and threatening, matching the turbulence of my own emotions. I call James, my hands shaking so badly I can barely dial.

'Rachel?' His voice is tense, hopeful.

'I have her,' I say, tears of relief finally breaking free. 'She's safe, James. She's right here with me.'

His sob of relief is so raw, so genuine that it brings fresh tears to my eyes. 'Put her on. Please. I need to hear her voice.'

I pass the phone to Lily, watching in the rearview mirror as her face transforms at the sound of her father's voice. 'Daddy! Rachel came and found me! We're waiting for the police and then we're coming home.'

As Lily chatters to James, telling him about the 'adventure' Melissa took her on, I keep my eyes on the cemetery, where

Melissa sits once more on the bench, head in her hands. She makes no attempt to approach us or to flee. It's as if all the fight has gone out of her, leaving behind only the broken shell of a woman who lost touch with reality.

When Lily finishes speaking to James, I take the phone back, reassuring him that we'll be home soon, that the police are on their way, that everything is going to be alright now. As I end the call, I hear sirens in the distance, growing closer.

I turn to look at Lily, this child who has somehow become the centre of my world. 'It's over now,' I tell her, reaching back to squeeze her small hand. 'You're safe. And I promise you, I will never let anyone take you away again. Never.'

She squeezes back, her trust in me unshaken despite witnessing my violence. 'I knew you'd find me,' she says with the simple faith of childhood. 'Daddy always says you keep us safe.'

The words fill me with a fierce joy that I try to temper with the knowledge that I've crossed a line today; attacked a mentally ill woman, lied to the police. But looking at Lily's face, at her absolute trust in me, I can't bring myself to regret any of it. For her, I would do it all again in a heartbeat.

As the police cars pull into the churchyard, lights flashing against the darkening sky, I make a silent promise to myself, to Sarah, to Lily: Nothing and no one will ever come between us again. I'll make sure of it.

No matter what it takes.

CHAPTER 21

James

I'm the worst dad ever. How could I have let her in my life like this? What is wrong with me. I spot them the moment they turn into the hospital car park; Lily's unmistakable shape in the back seat of Rachel's car, Rachel's tense profile behind the wheel. It's been hour after hour of imagining every worst case scenario, of blaming myself for bringing Melissa into our lives in the first place. And now, finally, Lily is here, safe, coming back to me.

I'm running before I can think, leaving behind the police officers who've been stationed with me since Rachel's call, my entire focus narrowed to the small figure emerging from the car. Lily looks up, spots me, and breaks free from Rachel's hand, racing toward me with a cry that tears straight through my heart.

'Daddy!'

I drop to my knees on the wet ground, uncaring of the rain or the cold or anything except the solid warmth of my daughter launching herself into my arms. I clutch her to my chest, breathing in the familiar scent of her hair, feeling her small body trembling against mine.

'I've got you,' I whisper, my voice breaking as tears blur my vision. 'I've got you, pumpkin. You're safe now.'

Lily clings to me, her arms wrapped so tightly around my neck it's almost painful. I don't care. I'd happily let her cut off my circulation entirely if it meant never losing her again.

'Lissa said we were on an adventure,' she cries against my shoulder. 'But I didn't like it. I wanted to come home.'

Even hearing Melissa's name sends a spike of rage through me, so intense it's almost dizzying. Later. I'll deal with that later. Right now, my daughter needs me to be strong, to be a source of comfort and security after the trauma she's endured.

'You're home now,' I assure her, pulling back just enough to see her face, to reassure myself that she's really here, really safe. 'No one is ever going to take you away again. I *promise*.'

Rachel approaches hesitantly, giving us space for our reunion. When I look up at her, the emotions on her face are complex; relief, exhaustion, something else I can't quite name. I suddenly remember her call, the sounds of a confrontation with Melissa, and notice for the first time the cuts on her knuckles.

'Thank you,' I say, the words entirely inadequate for what she's done. 'Rachel, I don't know how to…'

'Don't,' she interrupts gently. 'You don't need to thank me. Not for this. Not ever for this.'

I stand, lifting Lily with me, unwilling to break physical contact with her even for a moment. She settles against my hip, her head on my shoulder, happy to be carried despite being well past the age where she usually allows it.

'The doctors want to examine her,' Rachel explains quietly. 'Just to be sure she's alright. The police will want to talk to her too, but they've agreed to keep it brief for now.'

I nod, dreading the process but understanding its necessity. 'Where's Melissa?'

Rachel's expression hardens slightly. 'Being treated in A&E, under police guard. She didn't… when I found them, she attacked me.'

There's something in her tone that makes me wonder exactly what happened at that churchyard, but those questions can wait. For now, all that matters is getting Lily through the necessary examinations so we can take her home, where she belongs.

Inside the hospital, we're immediately ushered into a private examination room in the children's ward. A kind faced doctor introduces herself as Dr. Patel and explains that she needs to give Lily a quick check up. I refuse to leave the room, sitting beside Lily on the examination table, holding her hand throughout.

The physical examination reveals no injuries, no signs of mistreatment. Lily is tired, slightly dehydrated, but otherwise physically unharmed. It's the psychological impact that concerns me most; the trauma of being taken from her school, kept away from home by someone she trusted.

'She seems remarkably resilient,' the doctor tells me quietly as Lily sits with Rachel, drawing on a pad provided by a nurse. 'However, I'd strongly recommend speaking with a child psychologist in the coming days. An experience like this can have delayed effects, especially in young children.'

I nod, watching Lily with Rachel. They've always had a special bond, a connection that predates Lily's birth. Seeing them together now, Rachel's gentle encouragement as Lily draws, her protective posture, the obvious love between them, fills me with a complicated gratitude. Without Rachel, who knows if we'd have found Lily at all?

'Mr. Porter?' A police officer appears at the doorway. 'Could we have a moment?'

I glance at Lily, reluctant to leave her side even briefly.

'I'll stay with her,' Rachel assures me. 'We're good here, aren't we, Lily bean?'

Lily nods, absorbed in her drawing. 'I'm making a picture of you saving me,' she tells Rachel, and I can see Rachel's face change to pure delight.

In the corridor, the officer updates me on Melissa's situation. She's being treated for facial injuries ('sustained during the confrontation with Ms. Whittaker,' the officer says delicately), but once medically cleared, she'll be formally charged with child abduction and possibly additional offences pending further investigation.

'We found concerning material at her house,' the officer explains. 'Evidence of long term surveillance, fixation on your daughter. The psychiatric assessment is ongoing, but preliminary findings suggest she was experiencing a psychotic episode at the time of the abduction, likely related to her diagnosed condition.'

I listen numbly, trying to reconcile this clinical description of a dangerous, mentally ill woman with the Melissa I thought I knew; the warm, loving woman who made heart-shaped pancakes for Lily, who read bedtime stories, who seemed so perfectly normal. How could I have missed the signs? How could I have invited such danger into our lives?

'Will she go to prison?' I ask, the question feeling surreal on my tongue.

'That's for the courts to decide,' the officer says carefully. 'Given her mental health status, it's possible she'll be remanded to a secure psychiatric facility instead. Either way, Mr. Porter, I can assure you she won't be a threat to your family again.'

I nod, processing this information with a detachment that feels necessary to maintain my composure. Later, when Lily is safely home, when I can be sure she's sleeping peacefully in her own bed, then I'll allow myself to feel the full weight of what's happened; the anger, the guilt, the devastating knowledge that my own judgement put my daughter in danger.

When I return to the examination room, Lily is showing Rachel her completed drawing; stick figures standing by what appears to be a car, one significantly smaller than the other. Rachel looks up as I enter, a question in her eyes that I answer with a short nod. She understands; Melissa won't be a problem anymore.

'Can we go home now, Daddy?' Lily asks, the simple question bringing a fresh wave of emotion.

'Yes, pumpkin,' I manage, lifting her into my arms once more. 'Let's go home.'

The drive feels both endless and too short, a liminal space between the nightmare of the past three days and the reality of what comes next. Lily falls asleep in her car seat almost immediately, the exhaustion of her ordeal finally catching up with her. In the rearview mirror, her face in sleep looks younger, more vulnerable, reminding me painfully of how close I came to losing her.

Rachel drives in silence, her own exhaustion evident in the slump of her shoulders, the tension around her eyes. I want to ask her more about what happened at the churchyard, about the confrontation with Melissa, but not now. Not with Lily, even sleeping, so close.

At home, I carry Lily straight upstairs to her bedroom, grief and relief warring within me as I lay her gently on her bed. Rachel follows, hovering in the doorway as I remove Lily's shoes and tuck her beneath her familiar duvet with its pattern of stars and moons. She doesn't wake, too deeply asleep to register the transition, though her hand automatically reaches for Daddy Bunny when I place the well loved toy beside her.

I stand there for a long moment, simply watching her breathe, the steady rise and fall of her chest, a miracle I'll never take for granted again. When I finally turn away, Rachel is still in the doorway, her own eyes fixed on Lily's sleeping form with an intensity that speaks volumes.

Downstairs, in the quiet of the kitchen, I finally ask the question that's been burning in my mind. 'What happened at the churchyard, Rachel? The real story, not the dodgy version you gave the police.'

Rachel slumps into a chair, the exhaustion of the past days finally catching up with her. 'I found them by Olivia's grave; Melissa's stillborn daughter. Lily was in the car, safe. Melissa was...' she hesitates, choosing her words carefully, 'not well. Rambling about saying goodbye, about accepting that Lily wasn't her child. When I confronted her, she started making accusations.'

'About you,' I guess, remembering Melissa's increasingly

paranoid texts.

Rachel nods. 'She'd convinced herself I was manipulating everything. That I'd somehow engineered your breakup, tampered with her medication, all to keep my place in Lily's life.' She shakes her head, a bitter laugh escaping her. 'As if I'd need to resort to that. As if my relationship with Lily isn't real, isn't based on years of love and care. When I called her out for being crazy, she lost it and attacked me.'

'You fought her?' I say quietly, eyeing her bruised knuckles.

'Yes.' She meets my gaze unflinchingly. 'She lunged at me and fell down, so I hit her. More than once. I don't think Lily saw it happen... but, it is still not my finest moment...'

I should be disturbed by this admission, by the evidence of violence from someone I've always known to be gentle, controlled. Instead, I feel a shameful kinship; because given the opportunity, I might have done worse to the woman who took my daughter.

'I guess I am kind of grateful it was you, because I would have done a hell of a lot worse.' I say after a moment.

Relief flashes in Rachel's eyes, quickly hidden. 'Thank you. I'm not proud of fighting her, especially in front of Lily, but what was I supposed to do? I'd do it again if it meant bringing her home safely.'

'I know you would.' I reach across the table to squeeze her hand, careful of the bruised knuckles. 'You've always protected her. Both of us. I don't know what we'd do without you, Rachel.'

'You're never going to have to find out,' she says softly. 'I'm not going anywhere, James. Not ever.'

The certainty in her voice is both reassuring and, in some indefinable way, slightly weird, but I'm too exhausted, too emotionally raw to overthink that feeling now. Rachel has been my rock for years, has just saved my daughter from unimaginable trauma. If her devotion to us seems intense, it's only because her love for Lily has always been so profound.

'Stay tonight?' I ask impulsively. 'I'd feel better having you here, in case Lily wakes up upset.'

'Of course,' Rachel agrees immediately. 'I'll take the sofa. Just let me know if either of you need anything.'

Later, after Rachel has settled on the sofa with blankets and a pillow, I check on Lily one more time before heading to my own room. She's still sleeping peacefully, one arm flung above her head in that characteristic pose I've watched since she was a baby.

The enormity of what's happened, what *could* have happened, hits me with such force that I have to grip the doorframe to stay upright. My daughter was taken by someone I invited into our lives, someone I began to love. Someone who, in her sickness, saw Lily not as herself but as a replacement for a child she had lost.

The guilt is crushing, suffocating. What kind of father am I, to have missed the signs, to have allowed such danger close to my daughter? The logical part of my brain tries to argue that Melissa hid her illness well, that no one could have known she would spiral so dramatically, but the father in me, the protector, rejects these excuses. I should have known. Should have seen. I sink to the floor beside Lily's bed, unable to leave her, watching the gentle movement of her breathing in the dim glow of her nightlight. My beautiful, resilient daughter, who survived an ordeal no child should ever face. Who trusted that I would find her, that she would come home. Who still believed in the safety of the world because I had always promised to protect her. A promise I failed to keep.

'I'm so sorry,' I whisper, though she can't hear me. 'I'm so sorry, Lily. I'll never let anyone hurt you again. Never.'

In that moment, I make a silent vow: to be more careful, more vigilant. To trust my instincts, and Rachel's, when it comes to who we allow into our lives. To rebuild the sanctuary of home that Melissa's actions have violated.

I fall asleep there on Lily's floor, unwilling to leave her even for the short distance to my own bed. And if my dreams are haunted by what might have been, by all the terrible endings this story could have had, I'm saved from the worst of them by the sound of Lily's steady breathing beside me, reminding me with each rise and fall that she's home, she's safe, she's here. For tonight, for this moment, that has to be enough.

CHAPTER 22

Rachel

Three months. Three months since that rainy day at the churchyard. Three months since I brought Lily home, since everything changed between James and me. Three months of carefully rebuilding a sense of safety and normalcy, of helping Lily process her 'adventure' with Melissa through play therapy and endless patient conversations. Three months of gradually, cautiously allowing myself to believe that this new reality might actually be permanent.

'More pancakes?' James asks, sliding another perfectly golden circle onto my plate before I can answer. He's wearing the ridiculous 'Kiss the Cook' apron Lily and I gave him for Christmas, his hair still messy from sleep, smiling at me with a casual intimacy that still makes my heart skip.

'I'm going to explode,' I protest, though I pick up my fork anyway. Sunday morning breakfasts have become something of a ritual for us. For our family, I correct myself, still savouring the sound of that word.

'Daddy makes the best pancakes,' Lily declares from across the table, her face smeared with syrup despite the napkin tucked into her collar. At six now, she's bounced back from her ordeal with the resilience that still amazes me about children. The nightmares have largely subsided, and she only occasionally asks questions about Melissa.

'And Rachel makes the best hot chocolate,' James adds, winking at me over Lily's head. 'We're a good team.'

We are. It still feels surreal sometimes, how quickly everything has fallen into place since that terrible day. How naturally we've become what we were always meant to be; a family, complete and whole. The transition from best friend to partner happened with surprisingly little fanfare. One night, about three weeks after Lily's return, James had simply taken my hand across the dinner table and said, 'I think we both know this is where we've been heading, don't we?'

I had nodded, too full of emotion to speak, because yes, this is where we'd been heading all along. I finally have a family, something the doctor told me I would never have. I finally have a daughter.

'I was thinking we could go to the garden centre today,' James says, pulling me back to the present. 'Start planning the spring planting. What do you think, Lily bean?'

'Can I get my own plants?' Lily asks, bouncing slightly in her seat. 'Cari at school has a fairy garden with tiny plants that look like trees.'

'I don't see why not,' James agrees easily. He looks to me. 'Rachel? Garden centre mission?'

'Sounds lovely,' I say, and mean it. These ordinary weekend activities; shopping, gardening, the comfortable domesticity of it all, still feel like gifts I can't quite believe I'm allowed to have.

We finish breakfast, and I help Lily wash the sticky syrup from her hands and face while James clears the dishes. This easy choreography of family life, the small routines we've established, feels both new and familiar, as if we've been doing this forever.

'I'll go grab my jacket,' Lily announces, dashing upstairs with the boundless energy of childhood.

James slides his arms around my waist from behind, pressing a kiss to the side of my neck. 'Morning,' he murmurs, though we've been awake for hours.

I lean back against him, allowing myself to savour the solid warmth of him. 'Morning yourself.'

'You seemed far away at breakfast. Everything okay?'

I turn in his arms, studying his face; the kind eyes, the worry lines that have begun to smooth out in recent months. 'Everything's perfect,' I assure him. 'Just... still getting used to it, I suppose.'

He smiles, understanding in his expression. 'Me too, sometimes, but it feels right, doesn't it? Like this is how things were always supposed to be.'

'Yes,' I agree, resting my head against his chest, listening to the steady beat of his heart. 'It does.'

And it does, mostly. Except for the thoughts I can't quite banish, the ones that creep in at odd moments, usually when I'm lying awake while James sleeps beside me. Thoughts of Melissa. Of her horrible face. Of her evil demeanour. Of her lies she might still try to convince James of.

'I'm ready!' Lily announces, thundering back down the stairs in her puffy blue jacket and ladybird wellies, though the day is sunny and dry.

James releases me with a quick kiss. 'I'll get the car keys.'

As they move toward the door, I take a moment to survey the kitchen; our kitchen now, officially, since I gave up my house last month. My cookbooks on the shelf beside James's. My favourite mug in the drying rack. My herbs growing on the windowsill. Evidence of my presence, my belonging, everywhere I look. Everything I've wanted for so long. Everything I've worked for, waited for, positioned myself perfectly to achieve.

'Rachel, come on!' Lily calls impatiently from the doorway.

I follow them out to the car, settling into the passenger seat while James helps Lily buckle up. The familiar domesticity of it all still brings a rush of satisfaction so intense it's almost dizzying.

As we drive toward the garden centre, my thoughts drift back to Melissa, as they so often do these days. Melissa, who almost ruined everything with her unstable fixation on Lily. Melissa, who saw the same potential in Lily's bright smile, in James's kind eyes, that I had seen years before. Melissa, who came so close to taking it all away from me just as it was finally within reach.

She's in a secure psychiatric unit now, awaiting trial. The thought should bring comfort, closure, but instead it tugs at me, a loose thread I can't help pulling. In my darkest moments, I wonder if Melissa and I aren't more alike than I care to admit. Both of us drawn to a family that wasn't ours, both determined to make a place for ourselves within it. The difference, I tell myself firmly, is that my love for Lily and James has always been real, has been built on years of genuine connection. Melissa's was a delusion, a sick fantasy projected onto a child who happened to fit the image of the daughter she lost.

'You're quiet today,' James observes as we pull into the garden centre car park. 'Sure everything's alright?'

I push away the troubling thoughts, focusing on his concerned face, on Lily's excited chattering in the backseat. 'Just thinking about which plants might work best in the back border,' I lie smoothly. 'The soil's quite clay heavy there.'

He accepts this without question, another small deception to add to the one or two that form the foundation of the life we're building together. Not malicious lies, I tell myself. Just necessary omissions. Like not mentioning how I've tracked Melissa's case details through a contact at the prosecutor's office. Or how I sometimes drive past the psychiatric facility where she's being held, wondering what she's thinking, what she remembers, what she knows.

The garden centre is busy with weekend shoppers, families like ours planning spring projects. We wander through aisles of seedlings and shrubs, Lily darting ahead to exclaim over particularly colourful flowers, James pushing a trolley that gradually fills with plants and compost and tools.

'What do you think about renovating the shed this summer?' James asks, examining a display of exterior paint.

'Turn it into a bit of a summer house? Somewhere to sit when the weather's nice but not quite warm enough for the garden proper.'

'That sounds lovely,' I agree, imagining summer evenings, the three of us sharing meals at a small table, watching the sunset over the garden we've created together.

'Daddy, look!' Lily calls from a few aisles over. 'They have the tiny trees for fairy gardens!'

James grins at me. 'Duty calls. Coming?'

'You go. I'll look at these herb plants. See if there's anything interesting to add to the windowsill collection.'

He squeezes my hand before heading toward Lily's excited voice, leaving me alone among the neat rows of aromatic plants.

I can't deal with this. I need to see her. I need to look her in the eyes and tell her to her face. I wish I killed her that night. I wish she was locked away forever. Tomorrow, I visit her. I've decided. Tomorrow, is the end.

CHAPTER 23

Melissa

The windows in the dayroom face east, which means mornings are always flooded with light. It's one of the small pleasures I've come to appreciate during my time at The Green Psychiatric Facility; watching the sunrise paint the institutional walls with a gentle warmth they lack the rest of the day.

'Good morning, Melissa. Sleep well?' Dr. Winters settles into the chair opposite me, her familiar notebook balanced on her knee.

'Better,' I admit. 'The new dosage seems to be helping.'

She makes a note, nodding with evident satisfaction. 'That's excellent. And the dreams?'

'Less frequent. Still there, but... they don't feel as real anymore.' I wrap my hands around my mug of tea, drawing comfort from its warmth. 'I can tell the difference now, when I wake up. Between what happened and what my mind created.'

'That's significant progress.' Dr. Winters has been my psychiatrist for three months now, ever since I was transferred here from the secure unit. She's younger than I expected, with a directness I've come to value. No platitudes, no false reassurances. Just careful, methodical work to help me untangle the mess in my mind.

We talk for the full session; about my medication, about the grief group I've started attending, about the paintings I've been working on in art therapy. Olivia features in many of them, not as a ghost or an accusation, but as a brief, bright moment in my life that I'm finally learning to honour without letting it consume me.

'I've had a visitor request form submitted,' Dr. Winters mentions as our session winds down. 'I wanted to discuss it with you before approving.'

My heart gives a strange little lurch. 'James?'

She shakes her head gently. 'No. Rachel Whittaker.'

The name lands like a stone in still water, sending ripples of confusion through me. 'Rachel? Why would she want to see me?'

'She didn't specify. I can decline the request if you'd prefer.'

I consider this, turning the possibility over in my mind. Rachel, who found Lily at the churchyard. Rachel, who I'd convinced myself was manipulating everything, poisoning James against me. Rachel, whose face was the last thing I saw before they took me away. The old anger flares up briefly, then subsides; dampened by medication and months of therapy, by the slow, painful process of separating paranoid delusions from reality.

'No,' I decide finally. 'I think... I think I'd like to see her.'

Dr. Winters studies me carefully. 'May I ask why?'

I look out at the morning light, gathering my thoughts. 'Closure, maybe. And I owe her an apology, for the things I believed about her. The accusations.' I meet Dr. Winters' gaze. 'It's part of making amends, isn't it? Acknowledging the harm I caused, even if I wasn't fully aware of it at the time.'

'It can be, yes.' Dr. Winters makes another note. 'If you're certain, I'll approve the visit. However, Melissa...' her voice takes on a cautionary tone, 'remember your coping strategies if the conversation becomes distressing. You've made remarkable progress, but seeing someone connected to such a traumatic event could be triggering.'

'I understand.' And I do. Three months of intensive therapy has given me tools I never had before; ways to recognise when my thoughts are spiralling, techniques to ground myself in reality when the boundaries begin to blur.

'Thursday afternoon, then,' Dr. Winters says, closing her notebook. 'I'll be on site if you need me afterwards.'

The days until Thursday pass in the structured routine that has become my life. Medication in the morning. Group therapy. Art sessions. The grief support group where I'm finally able to talk about Olivia without dissolving into the dangerous fantasy that she's somehow still here, still findable. Meals at regular times. Evening medication. Sleep.

There's comfort in the predictability, in knowing exactly what comes next. No decisions more significant than which paint colour to use, which book to check out from the small patient library. It's a stark contrast to my life before; the demanding marketing job, the social obligations, the constant pressure to appear perfect and put together while crumbling inside.

By Thursday morning, I feel surprisingly calm about Rachel's visit. I dress with care in the few clothes I have here; clean jeans, a soft blue sweater that was a favourite before. Before everything. Before Lily and James, before the descent into paranoia and delusion, before the churchyard and the arrest and the headlines.

'Melissa?' Nurse Heaton appears at my door. 'Your visitor has arrived. She's waiting in the family room.'

I take a deep breath, centering myself. 'Thank you. I'm ready.'

The family room is designed to feel less institutional than the rest of the facility, with comfortable furniture and warm colours. Rachel stands as I enter, and I'm struck by how unchanged she appears; the same neat clothes, the same carefully styled hair, the same watchful eyes.

'Hello, Melissa.' Her voice is neutral, giving nothing away.

'Rachel.' I sit across from her, hands folded in my lap to

hide their slight trembling. 'Thank you for coming. It was... unexpected.'

She studies me for a long moment. 'You look better. More yourself.'

'The medication helps,' I say, unsure where to begin. 'And the therapy.'

Rachel nods, settling back into her chair. 'I imagine it would.'

An uncomfortable silence stretches between us, filled with unspoken accusations, unanswered questions. I decide to start with what matters most.

'I want to apologise,' I say, meeting her gaze directly. 'For the things I believed about you. The accusations I made. I wasn't well, but that doesn't excuse the pain I caused you and James and especially Lily.'

Something flashes across Rachel's face; surprise, perhaps, or something else I can't quite identify. 'You're apologising to me?'

'Yes.' I take a steadying breath. 'I convinced myself you were manipulating everything, tampering with my medication, trying to keep me away from James and Lily. I know now that was the psychosis talking, not reality.'

Rachel tilts her head slightly, a small smile playing at the corners of her mouth. 'That's an interesting interpretation.'

'I'm not asking for forgiveness,' I continue, unsettled by her reaction but pressing on. 'What I did, taking Lily, frightening her, putting everyone through that ordeal, it's unforgivable. I know that. I just wanted you to know that I understand now, how unwell I was. That I'm getting help.'

'And what if,' Rachel says, leaning forward slightly, her voice dropping to a near whisper, 'what if you weren't entirely wrong?'

I stare at her, uncertain I've heard correctly. 'What?'

'About me. About what I did.' The smile grows, spreading across her face in a way that makes my skin prickle with unease. 'You weren't entirely wrong, Melissa.'

My heart begins to race, the familiar sensation of anxiety rising. I try to remember Dr. Winters' exercises; breathe deeply, stay grounded, challenge intrusive thoughts.

'I don't understand what you're saying,' I manage.

Rachel glances toward the door to ensure we're not overheard, then returns her gaze to me, something almost gleeful in her expression now.

'I did tamper with your medication,' she says matter of factly. 'Found your prescription when you left your bag unattended that day at James's house. The day you went to the bathroom and I "accidentally" spilled your bag. Easy enough to replace the pills with something similar looking but ineffective.'

The room seems to tilt around me. This can't be happening. This has to be another delusion, another break from reality.

'Remember when someone tried to pick Lily up from school?' Rachel continues, clearly enjoying my stunned silence. 'I was the one sent someone else to try picking her up while you and James were at work. Just to plant seeds in his mind that you was mad.'

'No,' I whisper, shaking my head. 'You're lying. This isn't... this can't be real.'

'Oh, but it is.' Rachel looks almost serene, her hands relaxed in her lap like we're discussing nothing more consequential than the weather. 'The evidence in your house? I planted most of it. The surveillance photos, the ones of Sarah with her face scratched out. I've always been good with Photoshop, you know.'

The monitors on my wrists, required for all patients in the transitional ward, must be registering my skyrocketing heart rate by now. I try the grounding techniques, desperately attempting to separate reality from delusion. Is this real? Is Rachel really saying these things, or am I hallucinating?

'Why?' I manage to ask, my voice barely audible. 'Why would you do that?'

Rachel's smile fades, replaced by something harder, colder. 'Because he was mine. They were mine. Long before you showed up with your beautiful hair and your charming smile and your sudden interest in a child that wasn't yours.'

'But you helped find her. You brought Lily home.'

'Of course I did,' Rachel scoffs. 'What choice did I have? Once you actually took her, which, I admit, I didn't think you'd go quite that far, I had to be the one to bring her back. Had to be the hero.' She leans back, satisfaction evident in her posture. 'And it worked perfectly. James finally saw what had been right in front of him all these years. Me. Us. The family we were always meant to be.'

My head spins, nausea rising in my throat. 'This isn't real,' I mutter, more to myself than to her. 'This is another episode. I'm hallucinating.'

Rachel reaches across the space between us, grasping my wrist with surprising strength, her fingers digging into my flesh. 'Feel that? I'm real, Melissa. This conversation is real. And there's not a damn thing you can do about it because…' her eyes look meaningfully to the monitors on my wrists, to my patient ID bracelet, 'who would believe you? The woman who abducted a child because she thought she was her dead daughter? The woman on psychiatric meds. Who would believe the fruit loop?'

I jerk my arm away, stumbling to my feet. 'Dr. Winters, the staff, they know I'm better now. They'll listen.'

'Will they?' Rachel stands as well, perfectly composed while I feel myself unraveling. 'Or will they see a patient having another psychotic episode? Claiming wild conspiracy theories, becoming agitated, requiring sedation?'

As if on cue, Nurse Heaton appears in the doorway, concern evident on her face. 'Melissa? Your monitors are showing elevated heart rate and blood pressure. Is everything alright?'

I open my mouth to tell her everything Rachel has just confessed, but the words stick in my throat as I see the look in Rachel's eyes; the absolute certainty that she's already won.

'Melissa's getting a bit upset,' Rachel tells the nurse, her voice dripping with manufactured concern. 'I think seeing me might have been too triggering after all. I was just trying to make peace, to tell her that James and Lily are doing well, but…'

She trails off with a helpless gesture.

'I understand,' Nurse Heaton says sympathetically, approaching me with the careful movements they use for agitated patients. 'Melissa, why don't we get you back to your room? Perhaps this visit should wrap up.'

'She's lying,' I say, my voice rising despite my efforts to stay calm. 'Everything she just told me. She admitted to tampering with my medication, to setting me up, to orchestrating the whole thing!'

The nurse's expression shifts subtly, and I recognise it immediately. The look they get when they think a patient is becoming unstable.

'Melissa,' she says gently, 'remember your breathing exercises. Let's focus on calming down.'

'I'm telling the truth!' I insist, even as I feel the situation slipping beyond my control. 'Ask her! Make her tell you what she just told me!'

Rachel shakes her head sadly. 'I knew this might happen. Dr. Winters warned me it could be distressing for her to see me, but I thought... I hoped we could have some closure.' She turns to the nurse. 'I should go. I don't want to make things worse.'

'No!' I lunge forward, but Nurse Heaton blocks my path, her hand already reaching for the emergency call button on her belt. 'You can't let her leave! She's the one who's been lying, not me!'

More staff appear in the doorway, summoned by the alert. I recognise the warning signs; the careful way they position themselves around me, the calm but firm voices, the hand moving toward the medication trolley.

'Melissa, I need you to take some deep breaths with me,' Dr. Winters says, appearing from nowhere, her presence usually reassuring but now part of the closing trap. 'You're having a stress response right now.'

'Listen to me,' I plead, desperate to be heard before the medication takes me under. 'She confessed. She planned it all. She wanted James and Lily for herself, she's been manipulating everything from the beginning!'

I see the syringe, the needle, feel the gentle but firm hands on my arms. Beyond them, Rachel stands in the doorway, watching with what appears to anyone else as concern but what I now recognise as satisfaction.

'I'm telling the truth,' I say again, my voice breaking as the sedative begins to flow into my veins. 'Please, you have to believe me.'

The last thing I see before the medication pulls me under is Rachel's face, a small, private smile playing at her lips as she turns to leave, victory complete. In that moment, as darkness closes in, I understand that this is my reality now. To know the truth and be forever unable to speak it. To be written off as delusional, even when I'm seeing clearly for the first time. Mainly because I'm on medication.

'Goodbye, Melissa,' Rachel calls softly from the doorway, a final twist of the knife. 'Take care of yourself.'

As consciousness slips away, I wonder if this is how it will always be; Rachel walking free, building her perfect family on a foundation of lies, while I remain locked away with a truth no one will ever believe.

EPILOGUE

James

Six months pass quickly when you're rebuilding a life. Six months of therapy for Lily, of careful conversations about trust and safety, of watching the shadows gradually fade from her eyes. Six months of settling into a new normal with Rachel, of family dinners and weekend outings and the gentle rhythm of shared domesticity. They say kids bounce. Six months of praying that is true.

'Race you to the swings!' Lily calls, already sprinting across the park, her ponytail bouncing with each step. Six months, and she's almost fully herself again; the bright, fearless girl she was before Melissa entered our lives.

'No fair, you got a head start!' I laugh, jogging after her at a deliberately slow pace. These Saturday morning park visits have become a tradition, our time together while Rachel catches up on work or shopping.

Today she's sorting through the last of her belongings at her old house, the final step in officially combining our lives. Three months of living together has confirmed what we perhaps always knew; that Rachel fits seamlessly into our world, that the three of us work as a family unit in a way that feels both new and somehow predestined.

'Daddy, push me higher!' Lily demands, already settled

on her favourite swing. I oblige, carefully gauging the height, always conscious of safety while trying not to be overprotective. The therapist says that's the balance to aim for; vigilance without anxiety, caution without fear.

My phone buzzes in my pocket. Rachel.

'James, could you stop by my house on your way home? The removal men left a few boxes in the hallway cupboard, but they're too heavy for me to manage alone.'

'Of course. We'll head over in about half an hour?'

'Perfect. The door's unlocked; I'm just popping to the corner shop for some bin bags. The boxes are in the hall cupboard, top shelf.'

I pocket my phone and return to push duty, marveling as always at Lily's remarkable resilience. The child psychologist tells us this is normal, that children process trauma differently from adults. That with proper support, they can emerge stronger, more adaptable.

Melissa's name is never mentioned now. The trial was swift and conclusive, her guilty plea with diminished responsibility meaning Lily didn't have to testify. I sometimes feel a pang of something. Not quite regret, not quite sympathy, when I think of Melissa. The genuine warmth I'd occasionally glimpsed beneath the instability. The woman she might have been without the illness that distorted her perception so completely. Those moments pass quickly. We've moved on. We're happy.

An hour later, we pull into the driveway of Rachel's soon-to-be-former house. The 'SOLD' sign on the front lawn still gives me a small thrill; another symbol of our commitment to this new life together.

'Can I help carry boxes?' Lily asks, already unbuckling her seatbelt.

'We'll see how heavy they are, Rachel said they might be too much even for me.'

The front door is unlocked as promised, and we step into the nearly empty hallway. It's strange seeing the house like this; bare walls where Rachel's artwork used to hang, empty shelves where her books once lived. All of it now integrated into our home, making our space richer, more complete.

'Rachel?' I call, but there's no answer. She must still be at the shops.

The hall cupboard is tucked beneath the stairs, one of those awkward spaces that seem designed to hide forgotten items. I can see why the removal men missed it, you'd have to know to look. The stepladder is still here from the move, and I drag it over to reach the high shelf.

'Lily, why don't you go check if Rachel left any of your books in the living room?' I suggest, wanting her safely out of the way while I maneuver heavy boxes.

The first box is indeed heavy, filled with what feels like books from the weight of it. I ease it down carefully, my back protesting slightly. The second box is lighter but awkward, and as I slide it toward me, it catches on something at the back of the shelf.

The box tilts, and before I can steady it, the unsealed flaps fall open. Several items tumble out, landing at my feet with soft impacts that seem unnaturally loud in the empty house.

I climb down to collect them: a small notebook bound with an elastic band, some loose papers, what looks like a prescription box. Standard detritus of moving, the sort of odds and ends that get hastily shoved into containers during the chaos of packing; but as I bend to gather them, something stops me dead.

The prescription label, partially visible beneath the notebook's elastic band. The name printed in clinical black text: Melissa Chambers.

For a moment, I simply stare. There has to be an explanation. Perhaps it's something work related? But even as I think it, I know it doesn't make sense... and why would she have Melissa's prescription?

My hands shake slightly as I remove the elastic band. The notebook falls open, and a strip of photographs slides out, serving as an improvised bookmark. School photos of Lily. Not the standard copies sent home to parents, but the slightly off center versions usually kept in school files. The kind only someone with access to school records would have.

My mouth goes dry. I flip through the notebook, each page making less and less sense. The early entries are mundane: shopping lists, work reminders, normal life annotations, but as I continue reading, the content shifts.

James drops Lily at school 8:15 most mornings. Takes lunch break 12:30-1:30 Tuesdays and Thursdays.

M. keeps spare key under the third flowerpot. Alarm code likely birthdate or anniversary.

M. *Melissa*.

I sink onto the stepladder, the notebook trembling in my hands. The handwriting is definitely Rachel's. I know her well enough for that.

With growing horror, I reach for the box I lowered first, pushing aside the newspaper padding. Underneath, a stack of photographs. Black and white prints, clearly taken with a telephoto lens. Melissa entering her house. Melissa in her garden. Melissa at the grocery store. And worse? Photos of me. Of Lily. Images taken from across streets, through car windows, from hidden vantage points. Some date stamped from over two years ago, long before Melissa ever appeared in our lives. Why?

My breath comes in short gasps. This isn't possible. Rachel couldn't have… she wouldn't have… but the evidence keeps mounting. At the bottom of the box, beneath layers of photographs, I find something that makes my vision tunnel: a small collection of family photos I thought were lost. Pictures of Sarah, Lily, and me from holidays, birthdays, quiet moments at home. Photos I remember being mysteriously missing from our albums. In every single one, Sarah's face has been methodically scratched out with a pen, her features obliterated by angry black scribbles. Just like the ones Melissa dropped…

'Daddy?' Lily's voice from the living room sounds impossibly far away. 'I found my fairy book!'

I can't answer. Can't breathe properly. The pieces are falling into place with horrible clarity, and I don't want to see the picture they're forming.

Melissa's insistence on her innocence, even after the guilty plea. Her bewildered protests that she'd never taken those photos of Lily, never broken into our house. The way the evidence appeared so conveniently, so perfectly timed to Rachel's growing presence in our lives.

Rachel had been the one to find the pills, to find Lily, to comfort me through the shock of discovering that our 'safe space' had been violated.

At the very bottom, a single sheet of paper that makes my heart stop entirely: a detailed psychological profile of Melissa Chambers, including her medical history, her vulnerabilities, her prescription medications and dosages. Information that would have taken months of careful observation to compile. Information that someone could use to manipulate her. To push her towards increasingly erratic behavior. To ensure she'd be perfectly crazy when the time came.

The sound of a car in the driveway makes me freeze. Through the frosted glass of the front door, I can see Rachel's silhouette approaching, shopping bags in hand. I shove everything back into the box with shaking hands, my mind racing. How long has she been planning this?

'James?' Rachel's voice calls as the front door opens. 'How are you getting on with those boxes?'

'Fine,' I manage, surprised my voice sounds almost normal. 'Just finishing up.'

Except nothing is fine. Nothing has been fine for months, maybe years. The woman I love, the woman I've welcomed into my home, into my daughter's life, is...

I don't even have words for what she is.

'Daddy!' Lily appears in the hallway, holding her book. 'Rachel! Look what I found!'

'That's wonderful, sweetheart,' Rachel says, and her voice is exactly the same as always; warm, loving, completely genuine. She sets down her shopping bags and ruffles Lily's hair with the same gentle affection she's shown for months.

I watch this interaction from beside the cupboard, the box of evidence at my feet, and feel reality tilting on its axis. This is the woman who makes Lily laugh, who comforts her after nightmares, who's helped rebuild her sense of security after trauma.

This is also the woman who orchestrated that trauma in the first place.

'Everything all right?' Rachel asks, and I realise I've been staring. Her eyes are concerned, searching my face with the same intuitive care she's always shown. 'You look pale.'

'Just tired. These are heavier than they look.'

She smiles, and it's the same smile that's made me feel safe and loved for months. 'Well, let's get them loaded and get home. I was thinking of making that pasta dish Lily likes for dinner.'

Home. The word that used to comfort me now fills me with dread. She has keys. She's been sleeping in my bed, eating at my table, tucking my daughter into bed at night.

'That sounds perfect,' I hear myself say, hefting the box that contains the evidence of Rachel's deception. 'Let's go home.'

As we load the boxes into my car, Lily chatters happily about her recovered book. Rachel's hand finds mine with familiar warmth, I'm not thinking about dinner or home or any semblance of normalcy.

I'm thinking about how to keep my daughter safe from the woman who's been living in our house for three months. The woman who destroyed an innocent person's life to clear her own path to us. The woman who's been playing a role so perfectly that I fell in love with a complete fiction.

I'm thinking about how someone capable of this level of calculation and manipulation isn't finished with us yet. This was never about rescuing us from Melissa's obsession.

This is the obsession. And I have no idea what to do.

Thanks for reading! For updates, follow me on @alexgwauthor on the socials.

Out Now On Amazon

Shadows Of The Green

One phone call. A desperate mother. A friend gone missing.

Jay thought he'd escaped The Green, the rough estate that shaped his childhood. Now, trapped in a dead end marriage and a life he barely recognises, he's dragged back when his old friend, George, disappears. But finding George means confronting the past they both thought they escaped... and the secrets they left buried there.

With nothing but a few cryptic leads and a gut feeling something is wrong, Jay is forced to reunite with his old crew: Az, the cold and calculating gym obsessed enforcer, and Will, the reckless addict whose mouth is as dangerous as his habits. Together, they follow the shadows of their past, deep into a world of debts unpaid, violence unresolved, and the ghosts they tried to leave behind.

For fans of Shuggie Bain and Trainspotting, Shadows of the Green is a raw, unflinching exploration of Male Friendship, unspoken pain, and the courage it takes to break generational cycles.

Printed in Dunstable, United Kingdom